DEATH IN THE NIGHT

Rance heard someone run by the room, and he yelled: "Guss! What's the matter?"

The man did not stop. He passed to the front of the house. The building was a hollow square built around a patio, a hall separating the rooms from the patio. Rance's room was at the rear, at the end of the hall from the German's. He began to kick at the lock, but the oaken planks were as solid as stone.

There was another shot. It had the force and hollow thunder of a cannon blast, and immediately afterward a man screamed. Rance turned to the window and climbed out that way. He heard horses crossing the front yard. With his gun cocked, he slipped along the wall to the front.

Three horses were running past the corral toward the trail, but the saddle of the lead horse was empty, and there was a sodden-looking form thrown across the swell of the first rider's saddle. The horse, frightened by the burden and the odor of death, was throwing its head and trying to buck-jump, but the horseman kept a tight rein and spurred savagely.

FRANK BONHAM

THE CAÑON OF MAVERICK BRANDS

LEISURE BOOKS NEW YORK CITY

A LEISURE BOOK®

February 2001

Published by special arrangement with Golden West
Literary Agency.

Dorchester Publishing Co., Inc.
276 Fifth Avenue
New York, NY 10001

ISBN 0-8439-4835-3

The name "Leisure Books" and the stylized "L" with design are
trademarks of Dorchester Publishing Co., Inc.

Printed in the United States of America.

TABLE OF CONTENTS

THE MUSTANGER

Frank Bonham had the good fortune, when he embarked upon his professional career as an author of Western stories, to have Captain Joseph T. Shaw as his agent. Once one of the most illustrious editors of *Black Mask* magazine in which he showcased Dashiell Hammett and Raymond Chandler as well as Todhunter Ballard, Shaw wanted Bonham to stress character in his stories and certainly did not object to Bonham's tendency to include a mystery element in many of his Western stories. Although Bonham soon graduated from contributing stories regularly to pulp magazines such as *Dime Western* and *Lariat Story Magazine* to writing for *Blue Book* and *The Saturday Evening Post*, Mike Tilden, editor of *Dime Western*, told Captain Shaw that he would be most pleased to publish anything whatever Bonham cared to submit. "The Mustanger" first appeared in the July, 1951 issue of *Dime Western*.

I

Balanced on a rail of the loading chute, Ross Chance watched the yellow buggy rattle across the tracks. It swung past the station and rambled on toward the cattle pens. It was a rented buggy from the livery stable, but he recognized the rigid, red-faced man driving it. The buggy stopped at a pen farther up the tracks, where two cowboys were cutting cattle for shipment, and Lamar Shelton spoke briefly with them.

Chance was looking at the girl beside Shelton. He thought her face was turned toward him, and on sudden impulse he signaled slightly with the cattle prod he held. A moment later the girl faintly fluttered her fingers at him. Chance smiled to himself and glanced down at the cattle lunging up the chute.

A railroad man atop the cattle car shouted: "Lock 'er up!" and the door was slid shut and padlocked. Chance became aware that the man, straddling the chute bars across from him, was watching. His name was Gunlock, a rancher from the same area as Lamar Shelton. He kept his brown face sober, but there was a glint of amusement in his eyes.

"One thing Shelton didn't hire you for, Chance," he said, "is to wave handkerchiefs with his wife. Know what I mean?"

"I can figure it out," Chance said.

They dropped to the ground for a smoke while the next car was moved up. Gunlock was taking two cars of herd cattle up the valley. He ducked under the chute, and they walked to a canvas waterbag hanging from a corral post. The Shelton buggy was rolling toward them. A hot wind swept the gritty dust before it.

Gunlock drank from the alkali-crusted spout, and both men watched the girl on the buggy seat.

"He's a little techy about Laurel," Gunlock said. "Sometimes I think he's jealous. I don't know why. He's only thirty years older than her."

Smiling, he handed the waterbag to Chance. Chance drank. He was a hard-shouldered man not much over average height, but with strong wrists and the whittled hips of a horseman. He wore a faded blue shirt and denim trousers, and his blond hair was roached like the mane of a mule. He had big, practical hands and an assured jaw. But he had the gentle blue eyes of a man who might have an impractical idea now and then, such as waving at an employer's wife.

Gunlock glanced past him and frowned. "Them damned fools are going to get my cows on the prod yet," he said.

As they passed, Ross Chance said the thing he had been thinking for three days but had never expected to say. "I wonder why a woman like Missus Shelton would marry a man like him?"

Gunlock's gaze was slow and amused and yet somehow critical. "That's something that puzzles me, too," he remarked. "A year ago she was a sheriff's daughter, doing her own washing and setting her own bread. She had half the bucks in town after her. Some of them were making up to forty dollars a month. Then she ups and marries a man who's only got a hundred thousand acres of range and twenty-five men on his payroll. . . . I guess I never will figure it out," he sighed. He walked off.

Because it was exactly what Chance figured, he was disappointed. He had hoped for some novel explanation.

Shelton halted the yellow turnout, jumped down, and walked up the line to where Gunlock was now talking with some others. Holding the waterbag in his hands, Chance watched Laurel Shelton. After a moment she took up a parasol and stepped from the buggy. He caught a glimpse of lace petticoats and saw the sweet curve of her bosom as she smoothed her gown. She opened the parasol, laid it back over her shoulder, and walked straight toward him.

He had a queer, breathless instant. He didn't know what he was going to say. But it didn't matter. She was before him, saying softly: "I'd love a drink of water. It *is* warm, isn't it?"

"Some would call it hot," Chance assured her. He looked down at the bag. "There's a-plenty, Missus Shelton, but everybody's been drinking out of this."

She tilted her chin. "Are you trying to keep it all for yourself?"

Chance drew the cork carefully and handed her the water-bag. He watched her tilt it. Her throat was dusky and soft, and the movement of it was obscurely stimulating. She was a dark, vivid woman with a slow way of speech and a conscious grace. She wore a striped blouse with starched shoulders, a wide white belt, and a dotted blue-and-white skirt. Her skin was exceptionally smooth, with olive tones, and her eyes were a dark green. Her hair was black.

She lowered the bag. Her moist lips glistened. "Thank you," she said. She glanced at the train. "You've almost finished, I see."

"We'll leave at sundown. Be in Horsehead Crossing by tomorrow afternoon, they tell me. How long will it take you on the coach?"

"I'll get there sometime tonight. The train's made up now." Laurel Shelton looked at the deep pack of clouds massing over the mountains north of town. "You're going to be rained on."

"Was a trainload of stock ever moved that it didn't rain?"

"You talk as though you'd done this before."

"Not for pay. Only for myself."

She regarded him curiously. "If you're a rancher, why take a hard job like this?"

"I'm a mustanger, ma'am. This is betwixt seasons work. Take a herd up, bring another back." He had agreed to help water and feed Lamar Shelton's stock on the trip up the valley.

She looked toward her husband, who was moving along the pens toward them with his foreman, and Chance's glance unconsciously dropped to the deep cleft of her bosom. When he glanced up, she was looking at him. Something close to anger sparkled in the green eyes.

"What were you and Mister Gunlock saying about me?" she asked. It caught him with his hand upraised to replace the waterbag. He made an obvious hesitation. He was scrambling

10

for a plausible lie. Then he heard her saying: "You mustn't believe everything you hear, you know. Small towns have to make the most out of gossip."

"It wasn't gossip," he said finally. "Don't blame Gunlock, anyway. I asked about you, and he said you were a sheriff's daughter. That was about it."

She shook her head. "That's a lie. But I didn't give you much time, did I? Probably it's just as well. But I'm not a sheriff's daughter, exactly. I was, for a long time. Then I was a convict's daughter for three months. And now I'm nobody's daughter . . . I'm Lamar Shelton's wife."

He said: "I . . . I see," feeling put in his place, feeling bitterly angry with himself — yet sorry that the relationship had gone from one of friendship to stiffness.

The cattle car was in place. A trainman was opening the gate. The girl's face didn't show resentment. It was tranquil again.

"A mustanger," she said. "We seem to be having a migration of them. Another mustanger came in a few months ago. He's been working the ranches for wild horses. He's on ours now."

"What's his name? Maybe I know him."

"Bladen Ramsey," she said. "They call him Blade."

For an instant everything slowed down. It was expected, yet unexpected. Chance stirred, smiling. "He sounds like a fast operator. Tell your husband to look out for him."

"My husband looks out for himself. And so do I, as Mister Gunlock was probably saying."

He felt his face heating. There was nothing to say to it. He raised the blue bandanna about his neck and wiped his forehead. He gazed distantly down the line of cattle pens. His hands were hot and red and heavy.

"You haven't told me whether you know Blade," she reminded him.

11

"I've heard of him," he said, holding his face expressionless. "I think he was in Nevada about the time I was."

"Did you get your rings at the same place? He wears one like yours." She glanced at his hand, resting on a chute bar.

Chance said: "He does?"

"Yes," she smiled. "It's Mexican, isn't it? I've seen them across the river. But the face on his is a man's, where yours is a woman's. I suppose that's the difference in taste between a man's man and a lady's man."

You can't be too careful, thought Chance tardily. *You set out on a hunt like this, a wild horse hunt with your trap set for man-size quarry, and then you left a smell on the gate to scare the man off.*

He looked at the black onyx cameo inset in silver. "Nobody's ever called me a lady's man before, Missus Shelton. But thanks."

"Don't be silly," she said. "The man's man is the one who really likes the ladies. So he wears a lady on his finger, like you. The lady's man, like Blade, always seems to me to be in love with himself. So naturally he wears a profile of himself on his finger."

They heard her husband approaching. She gave him a look of reproof but with sympathy moving in it. It was a thoroughly confusing expression.

"Good luck, anyway. I hope you like our country and stay a while. It's not a bad climate. Seldom too cold, never too warm."

Shelton had a lofty and truculent manner that had annoyed Chance when he had asked for the job yesterday. Necessity was the monitor that kept him civil before the rancher's carping eye. Coming up now, Shelton looked at the two of them until the moment was awkward. Then he said: "I don't want to break this up, Laurel. But your train leaves in five minutes. They might not hold it . . . even for you."

12

"That's all right," the woman said. "Mister Chance has promised to throw himself in front of it in case it tries to get away." She spun the parasol and looked at her husband, and in the look Chance knew all he needed to know about the married life of the Sheltons. Laurel Shelton hated her husband.

The rancher's chill dislike was in his stare at Chance. "I'd stop it another way, if I were you. You've got one crippled leg already. A man with a gimp is lucky to get work of any kind in this country. That leg of yours won't give out on the way?" he asked.

Chance's bald dislike traveled over him. He disliked Shelton's brick-red face and his light-gray brows and hair. He didn't like the stubborn bronco look of his mouth.

"It got me this far," he said. "I cracked an ankle breaking a horse last spring. It's still stiff. I'll get your cows there."

"I'll be along to make sure of it." Shelton tilted his head. "Get back to your work."

"Yes, sir," Chance said. He raised his hand to tip his hat, but he was looking at Mrs. Shelton when he did it. "A nice trip, ma'am. I hope you beat the rain."

"Thank you. I hope it isn't too wet for you," she told him.

She smiled. The sage-green eyes said good bye. They said she wasn't angry about anything. And they pinned it down for him suddenly as to the kind of woman she was. Laurel Shelton was the kind of woman who made you feel guilty in front of her husband. . . .

▌▌

Toward sundown the clouds massed deeper and blacker over the gaunt hills and mesas. Thunder crashed over El Paso, and just before the cattle train pulled out large, warm drops of rain began to fall. Ross Chance crouched on the catwalk to take the jolting start.

The train smoked northward along the Rio Grande in a broad valley of mesquite, salt cedar, and truck crops. Lamplighted windows glowed in the little Mexican villages. His eyes yearning, Chance watched them pass. A mustanger lived without roof and beds. He worked hard in tough country where the wild horses ran, saving and dreaming and thinking about the ranch he was going to buy. It would have a sound roof, windows that could be shut against sandstorms and snow. It would contain a stove, a bed, table, a woman. The woman would be entirely unlike the kind of women a man knew when he came to town for a week at a time. She would be neat and attractive, and she would not have lived so close to mechanical pianos that she rang of untuned strings when she talked. Her cooking would be magnificent. She would be practical, but despite this she would be a loving woman whose arms would be soft and white in the darkness.

Not too long ago he had had a toehold on these things. One more season. . . . The big corral in the Colorado aspens had been filled with wild horses, and the good ones, the broncos worth breaking, were being groomed for the market. But one of them had fallen on him, and, when it came time to move them, he was still in a hotel bed in a mountain village with his ankle in a cast.

His partner — a marvelous horseman, if a little wild — had told him not to worry, and he'd gone off with their capital and a town floozy and all of the horses. Evidently he'd got lost. He'd never come back. . . .

The cattle cars stank of manure and wet hides. Ross thought of the warm comradeship of tobacco smoke in the caboose. He limped back along the wet catwalk.

The caboose was empty except for the big, dark-skinned rancher named George Gunlock. Chance threw his soaked Stetson on a bunk and pushed a piece of wood into the stove. Gunlock, in shirtsleeves and vest, sat at a small table bolted to the floor, rolling dice. A cigar fumed in his mouth.

"It's a game of skill, friend, not a game of chance. Watch the little cubes closely and place your bet."

"Suppose I watch the little crapshooter closely?" Chance smiled.

Chuckling, Gunlock leaned back, "Where's the big 'un?"

"Shelton? Up where it's warm, I reckon. In the engine."

"Where you from, Chance?" Gunlock asked.

"Lots of places."

"Reach under the mattress on that bunk," the rancher said. "There's a bottle."

Chance grubbed it out but shook his head when Gunlock pulled the cork. "Not on wet catwalks."

"Drunk is the only way to navigate them. You go with the jolts."

"Sometimes you jolt when they don't."

The big cattleman laughed and drank. He wore a mustache as wide as his upper lip. He was likable. In a slightly dissipated way he was good-looking. His eyes were dark and quick and his grin amiable. But what Laurel Shelton had said had opened a breach between them.

15

The train jolted to a stop. Through streaked windows Chance saw the lights of a shack set back from the tracks.

"Wood stop," Gunlock yawned.

They heard boots atop the car ahead of them.

"Well, it was nice while it lasted," Chance said. "I'll go put some cows back on their feet and try it again."

He was going out the door onto the rear platform when George Gunlock said: "I'll go along."

Reaching the ground, Chance heard Shelton's voice in the caboose. "Chance! Wait a minute."

The rancher came onto the platform, thick-set, glowering, his face glistening. "Where the hell have you been? There's a cow down in the third car ahead."

"There wasn't two minutes ago. I just finished the tour."

"I'm talking about now, not two minutes ago. George, how long has he been in the crumby?"

"The man said two minutes." Gunlock shrugged.

Shelton's rancor embittered his voice. "Railroad bums and cow-country cripples. By God, there isn't an honest-to-God man among them!"

Something like heat came up into Chance's chest, something like heat but more like hate. He said mildly: "You go to hell." He limped up the gravel toward the cattle cars. He thought: *The things a man will take when he hasn't got train fare!*

Shelton didn't follow. When they reached the car, Shelton's foreman, Guinn Campbell, was already working to raise the downed cow. He was cursing cattle and rain in a nasal voice. He looked too young and touchy to ramrod a big outfit.

"Chance, git around the other side," he ordered. "This brute's about done. Take your prod and mash her in the bag. Only way to move her."

He was a wiry man with thin blond brows and a mouth like a black bass. A sodden cigarette was going to ruin in his lips.

Over a striped jersey he wore a denim brushpopper, black with rain.

The cow was badly injured by the time they had her on her feet. The hoof of another animal had cut an eyeball. In the light of a brakeman's lantern Campbell inspected her through the bars.

"Damn, she won't drop nothing but off-breeds now! Her right hind leg's broke. Where the hell were you while this was going on?"

"I was holding a bull on my lap. He was lonesome for his mammy."

Campbell's lips pulled back on his teeth. "Listen, cowboy. If we want funny men, we'll hire a minstrel show . . . not gimps. I asked where you were while this cow was getting kicked to hell and gone."

Chance took Campbell's shirt front in his grasp and rammed him against the car. "I'm going to give you a recipe for making gimps, Campbell. You take an ornery bronc' and set a man on him. Then you turn around and set the bronc' on the man. Then you got a gimp."

The ramrod's hand defiantly went up to grip Ross's wrist.

"Another way," Chance said, "is to turn a man loose with an outsize mouth and let him use it. Sooner or later, you've got another gimp. *¿Comprende?*"

Campbell blew drops of rain from his lip. "Yeah. I *comprende.* I *comprende* that I'm going to catch hell from the boss when he sees this cow, too."

"Tell him to see me. I'll take the hell direct, but I won't take it from you."

Campbell grumbled. "All right. Hurry up and look over the rest of the cars. We don't have all night."

Gunlock's cars, filled with herd cows he was taking north to his own ranch, were ahead of Shelton's. He walked with the

17

mustanger as Chance inspected the rest of the cattle. Suddenly he chuckled. "You don't take much, do you?"

"Not on some subjects."

Gunlock chewed his cigar and presently said: "Neither does Shelton, by the way. His worst subject is his wife."

"Is that advice?"

"Call it advice. When she's around . . . keep busy. You didn't look very busy today."

"I wasn't very busy. So why not talk, if she wanted?"

Gunlock frowned and spoke carefully. "The thing of it is, she's apt to want to talk with too many fellows, Ross. Shelton's no Romeo. Maybe she thought she could get Romeo and Shylock under the same hat. If she did, she's wrong."

"You don't have to explain it," Chance said curtly. "If Shelton wants to heat up over nothing, that's his business. But I don't take it from him. She's his wife and his problem, not mine."

"That's a good way to leave it," Gunlock remarked. His eyes brooded on the steamy redness beneath the engine. "I courted Laurel for a couple of years myself. How far did I get? Well, she's Missus Lamar Shelton now, and she's got four Mexican women to help her around the house, and the damned house itself is the biggest thing in *this* county. But I guess what goes on in the house isn't what she bargained for. She spends a lot of time in town."

"What's this about her father being a convict?" Chance inquired, another of those questions he knew he had no business asking.

"Who told you that? Shelton?"

"No. She did."

Gunlock grunted. "Getting right cozy with her, eh? Well, there was a rash of cow rustling. Shelton was being hit worst. Marshal Smith . . . that was her father . . . just sat and didn't do anything. Finally he was voted out. Then one day a cattle association posse caught a couple of boys, throwing a long loop on Shelton's range. Guess who had a running iron in his boot? Laurel's old man." He shrugged, as if it were a man's own business whose cattle he stole. "Tough on the girl, of course. The old man died a few months after he went up." He turned, briskly slapping his hands together. "Better get back and have that smoke, Chance."

Chance stared after him. He was tense. Gunlock's casual recital had left him shaken. His hands ached, and he looked down and saw the cold knots of his fists, gleaming whitely. He unclenched them. Slowly he turned and walked back down the tracks. What he needed, he decided, was to be around town a while. To see a lot of women and get his balance again. It was no tragedy that a girl was beautiful and married to a man too old and rich for her. It seemed tragic to Chance only because he had become interested in her before he knew what was happening.

With a wet bleat of the whistle the cattle train broke out of the stop. Chance stood on the gravel until the lights of the caboose joggled near him. Then he put up a hand and caught the grab-iron. He slung aboard and went into the caboose. The air was stale and overheated. Lamar Shelton and George Gunlock were playing poker. Guinn Campbell, who knew which side his bread was buttered on, was atop the cars somewhere, cold, wet, but hanging onto his job.

Dropping his hat near the stove, Ross lay on a bunk. Shelton gave him a tart stare across his cards. "We're in the wrong line, George," he said to the other rancher. "Some fellows can make more money lying down than I can standing up."

"Well, lay down, then," Chance yawned.

Gunlock laughed.

Shelton's face acquired the complexion of a side of beef. After a moment he said: "Want to set in?"

"I wouldn't be wet-nursing cattle if I had the price of a poker game."

"I'll loan you a dollar. Maybe you can win back what you owe me."

Looking at him, Chance saw the hard glint of irony in his smile. "You mean I'm paying to do this?"

"You're paying for the cow you let me lose. If you'd been on the job, we'd have had the cow on her feet before she broke a leg. I paid sixty dollars for that cow. Deducting what I owe you, you're still into me for fifty."

Chance sat up and swung his feet to the floor. In the rocking flare of the lamp he was an unshaven, stony-eyed man with his fingers gripping his knees. "How drunk can you get, Shelton?"

Shelton leaned out of his chair, holding onto the table with one hand. There was a bottle on the table. Chance saw that he was actually drunk, although he had not thought so.

"When you're working for me," he said, "keep your damned mouth shut. You'll shell out fifty dollars at the end of the run, or I'll have you jailed."

Gunlock, watching them, riffled the greasy deck of cards. There was the crisp sound of the cards, the muted clamor of the caboose, and no other sound until Ross laughed.

"That's one fifty you're going to have a hell of a time collecting."

"All right. This is one ride you're going to finish on foot." The rancher swayed toward the back of the car. Chance watched him take a red lantern from a locker.

"If that's to signal with," he said, "put it back."

Raising the chimney, Shelton struck a match. "Pack your things. You're getting off."

With the match flaring, Shelton lost his balance and stumbled back against a bunk. He came up again, angered that his drunkenness was revealed, and laid the flame against the oily black wick. The flame rose. He snapped the chimney down and strode to the platform. Chance started toward him to seize the lantern and hurl it into the wet darkness. Then he thought better of it, turned, and walked back into the car. His mouth was gray with fury.

Chance heard Gunlock snap: "Look out!"

As Chance turned, crowding against the wall with his shoulder upraised protectively, the rancher was lunging in. His hand was raised, and he held a Colt by the frame. The blued steel slashed down.

Chance said something bitterly under his breath and went in beneath the gun. He came up against the big, soft body and was amazed at the way his fist sank into Shelton's belly. The man's pain came out in a shout as his hand struck an overhead beam. The gun clattered down. George Gunlock stepped away and stood by the door as they collided with the table.

"Easy boys!" he said. "For God's sake!"

Panting, the rancher tried to grapple. Chance threw him off like a shouldered wheat bag. He watched him fall with a jolt in the trash of cigarettes and sandwich crusts. He would have left the fight stop there. He despised this man, but he didn't hate him. Shelton was groping for the gun. Chance kicked it down the aisle. He stood spraddle-legged as Shelton got to his hands and knees, to his knees, then to his feet.

Out of his mottled, stricken face, Shelton whispered, "Damn chippy-chasing cripple!" As he staggered back, Ross walked to meet him, his teeth set. Shelton's swing was a huge roundhouse effort that mussed the mustanger's hair. Chance's fist landed in the middle of Shelton's face. It sounded like a man's hands clapping together.

They were standing near the door when Ross hit Shelton.

The blow blinded Shelton. He reeled back, and all at once Chance lunged for him. He shouted at Gunlock: "Grab the fool!"

Shelton was reeling backward onto the platform.

Gunlock's hand missed him. At that instant the rancher stumbled. Twisting, he seemed to grasp at the wet, black railing. His hand dropped onto it, but he was too deep in stupor to hold it. He appeared for a moment to be sitting on the railing casually, like a man having a cigar with a friend.

The sickness of horror in him, Chance saw this and knew Shelton was falling. Suddenly he was aware of the hollow, rattling roar of a bridge under them. He was looking at Shelton and seeing in the background the dark sheen of the river.

Then Shelton was gone.

The car resounded with the roar of the trestle. Then it was quieter again. The train had crossed the river. In the clattering emptiness Gunlock and Chance stared at each other. Chance rushed onto the platform. Barbs of rain darted through the green and red steam of the caboose lamps. Gripping the railing, he stared down the tracks. The trestle was lost in the night and mist.

While Chance still stood there, he heard a man coming down the cupola ladder. Shelton's foreman, Campbell, dropped onto the floor. Ross stared at him with a flinching of his whole being. Campbell looked around, puzzled.

"Where's Mister Shelton?"

Gunlock didn't move. His tall, square-set frame was relaxed against the wall by the door. His cigarette burned rapidly in the draft.

"Climb up and signal them to stop," he said. "Shelton's fell off."

"He's . . . ? My God!" Campbell exclaimed. "Is this a joke?"

"It ain't to Shelton. Chance, fetch that red lantern."

The horror in Campbell's face was diluted by suspicion. He looked at the mustanger. "Chance!" he said. "Did they . . . ?"

"Get a lantern!" Gunlock snapped.

Chance carried the lantern to the ramrod, who took it with a slow stare.

Gunlock threw his cigarette down and gave Campbell a shove. "He's laying out there on the trestle, and you stand, gawking! Stop the train, will you?"

Campbell ran back to the ladder and hastily mounted it. The small door banged after him.

Gunlock turned and looked down the tracks for a moment. He swung back. The mustanger was now standing by the table. Gunlock nodded at the bottle and said: "There's some liquor left."

Chance dully picked it up and started to drink. Then he wiped the neck with his bandanna. As he drank, he thought of the look Campbell had given him. He recalled the way he'd roughed him at the wood stop.

After that Gunlock drank, sat on a bunk, and looked at Chance. Ross's face was blank and miserable.

"Maybe you ought to tell me a little bit about yourself," Gunlock said. "It might help me to know what to say when they ask me what happened."

"You saw what happened," Chance snapped. "He tried to slug me. I hit him and. . . ."

"And killed him," Gunlock said with a faint smile.

"No! He tripped. You saw that. You were standing right there. You saw. . . ." His mouth went dry. He stood, pointing at the floor. His face stiffened, and he looked at the floor and then at the rancher. "In fact, he tripped over your foot. There wasn't anything else for him to trip on."

"There was his spurs." Gunlock shrugged.

"He wasn't wearing spurs."

"Wasn't he?" Gunlock's eyes were dark brown, hard and steady under his heavy brows. His mouth, that smiled so easily, was tight. He got up off the bunk. At that moment brakes were applied and the train began to slow. "I thought he was," he said. "I thought it was accidental. . . ." He paused. "All right, you handle it. I'll back you up."

Chance knew he had missed a cue. He sat down and stared at the open door. The clicking of the trucks was slowing. "That's all I'm asking," he said. "What else can I do?"

Gunlock thoughtfully bit off the tip of a cigar. "I was thinking of what you said to me when I asked if you wanted a drink. 'Not on wet catwalks.' He could have been up on the catwalk, couldn't he?"

The cold, the wet, seemed to have settled in Chance's body. He wished they would thaw, that he could warm to some straight thinking. Sitting dully, he said: "Why lie about it? He slugged me, and I hit him. He tripped and fell over the railing."

"Not exactly murder, you mean?" said Gunlock. "Just second cousin to it. Manslaughter. I get you. I reckon," he added, "you might get off with six or seven years, was you lucky. Well, here they come."

The train's momentum died in a harsh scraping of metal. The lamp pitched with gurglings of coal oil. Cattle bawled lustily. Atop the car ahead men were walking with swift, careful tread toward the caboose.

"You'd back me up?" Chance asked.

"Why not?"

"Why?" Chance insisted.

Gunlock's hairy hand pushed the cork into the whiskey bottle. "Because I hate to see a good man suffer for a bad. Shelton was no damned good. A scrounger. A double-dealer. A drunk. Why make it hard on yourself?"

Suddenly the train lurched again. The car shuddered. The couplings gave and lost slack, took hold again, and the train began to back.

With hard shock a thought bolted through Chance. *What if he isn't dead? Then I'm in it!*

Above them the small door opened to a hiss of rain. A man's boot groped for the top rung. "If he ain't dead," Gunlock said softly, "then it ain't murder."

Lanterns gave a thin light as they backed toward the river. Everyone had gathered in the caboose except the engineer. There were four cowboys with various bunches of cattle, the fireman, a brakeman, a switchman, Campbell, Gunlock, and Ross.

"It was on the bridge," Gunlock said, staring across the brake wheel into the darkness. Wet brush rustled at each side of the train. "Right in the middle."

"What happened?" Campbell asked.

Chance felt his eyes on him. "We were playing poker," he said. "He decided to see how that cow was doing. I told him to let me, but. . . . You know how he'd take any suggestion of mine. He was so drunk he could hardly get up the ladder. A minute later we heard him fall off the roof."

A man exclaimed: "There's the river!"

They backed slowly onto the bridge. Chance stood with the rest of them on the platform. His lame ankle throbbed. There was silence, except for the slow click of the trucks. He heard Campbell say: "He told me he was going to catch a couple of hours' sleep. Funny he went out again."

A red fire barrel slid past on its small platform on the trestle. Between the ties the river could be seen in darkly slotted gleams twenty feet below. Then the water was gone. They were on the graveled roadbed again.

The switchman signaled. The train stopped. They jumped out and some of them looked on the bank, and two men started back along the ties at either side of the train. The brakeman ran back and set a flare. Ten minutes later they came back.

"Not a sign," said the brakeman. "Well, boys, this is going to sound rough, but we got trains coming behind us. Rain is no time to set down and hunt bodies."

"I reckon not," said George Gunlock. "Campbell, you can send a wire to Missus Shelton from Mejia. The railroad people will send back to hunt his body. That's all anybody can do."

Campbell's face was slick with rain, his blond brows laden with drops, his mouth tight as a scar. Without a word he climbed the platform steps and went into the caboose.

The cattle train rumbled back across the river.

III

During the night they ran out of the wet weather. At noon of the following day they entered a small cattle town in a pocket of gaunt hills. The look of fall was on the land. On the roofs of adobe farmhouses red chilis were laid to dry. Withered leaves swirled out of the chinaberry trees, sheltering the village. The pens at the railroad station thronged with cattle, ready for shipment.

Chance helped unload the cattle. He worked with Gunlock and Campbell, and they were all silent, waiting for Mrs. Shelton to appear.

Gunlock's brother rode in, a strange man of forty with lank features and dark, staring eyes. His name was Webb. When he put out his hand to Ross, Chance saw that three fingers were missing. It was an odd handshake, and the man himself gave Chance a left-handed feeling. While Webb Gunlock was inspecting the herd cows his brother had brought, George Gunlock talked quietly to Chance.

"Don't sell Webb short. He's the best judge of livestock this country's got. Just keep him off religion and he's as steady as either of us."

"Why religion?" Chance asked.

"Notice his hand? He hit a revival preacher one time when he called him a sinner for having liquor on his breath. Then he got to worrying over whether he'd hit God. One night he went out to chop stove wood. . . ."

"Cut it out," Chance said with a grimace.

Gunlock chuckled. "Fact!"

Ross looked up the street. The station was at the foot of the main street, the broad, uneven road lying between one-story adobe buildings and chinaberries with whitewashed trunks. At the far end was a plaza with a bandstand. A couple of oxcarts were on the street, a dozen horsemen, a few turnouts, and Gunlock nodded at one of these and said: "There's Laurel."

Chance didn't look. He steadied his fingers by the rolling of a cigarette. It had gone further than he had believed it could in three days. She was just a woman — married, at that. One out of two people was a woman. What made it seem so special that she was a woman and Ross was a man? It was the kind of woman she was, he knew. It was her gracefulness, her way of laughing with her eyes, her prettiness, and her figure. It was the fact that, if she had been unmarried, he would have let himself fall in love with her that first hour. Because he couldn't, he had been inwardly upset ever since.

He thought: *I'm getting as loco as Webb Gunlock.*

George Gunlock spoke narrowly. "You never did tell me much about yourself, Chance. What are you up here for?

Where do you come from?"

"You know the answer to the first question. The second's none of your business."

"Men like you don't take a three-day job for ten bucks."

Chance lighted the cigarette he had rolled and smoked it. He took the cigarette out of his lips, looked at it, and put it back.

Gunlock said softly: "All right, be shut-mouthed. I like them shut-mouthed. In fact, I'll give you a job, breaking horses for me, if you want to stay around a while."

"You don't need a horsebreaker."

"Not steady, no. But I could give you work for a month or two."

The buggy was pulling into the station. On the seat were Laurel Shelton, a man with a marshal's shield, and a lean elderly woman. Panic exploded in Chance's head. He turned his gaze away and heard himself saying: "I . . . ask me later. I don't know. Let's get through with this before we tackle anything else."

The marshal seemed more like a preacher than a peace officer, Chance thought. He was stringy and had a cement-colored face completely without warmth. He came around to confront the men.

"Now, what is all this?" he asked.

"Did you get our wire?" Gunlock asked. "That was all there was to tell. This is Ross Chance. He helped with the cattle. Marshal Coles, Chance."

Coles looked at Chance. He was a man of sixty who wore a dirty collar-band shirt and a dusty coat and trousers. He put several piñon nuts in his mouth, and his front teeth worked ceaselessly on the thin shells.

"Did you see it happen?" he asked Chance.

Laurel was standing beside him. Her face grave, she watched

the mustanger. There was a faint rose color in her cheeks — rouge, Chance supposed — and that would be enough to damn a woman in a town the size of Horsehead Crossing. When he answered the marshal's question, he was looking at the girl.

"No, I didn't see it. He'd gone up to look at some cattle. We heard him stumble, and a minute later he fell."

"How could you hear him stumble with all the rattle and bang of a caboose?" Coles spat piñon shells.

"That was one more bang than we were used to."

"Was he drunk?"

It was the middle-aged woman at the marshal's left. Looking at her, Chance's smile came. The woman's cheeks ran more to powder than to blood. He thought of the meager body inside the shell of black alpaca and whaleboned undergarments.

Laurel's head turned. "What an unkind thing to say, Missus Coles. Of the man who put your husband in office. Was he drunk!"

"Was he?" insisted the marshal's wife.

"He. . . ." Chance hesitated. "He was able to walk on a dry floor. Maybe not on a wet catwalk."

Mrs. Coles's lips hugged a thin smile to themselves.

"Was any kind of search made for him?" Coles demanded.

"Not by us," Gunlock said. "Train couldn't wait. Haven't they found him yet?"

Laurel shook her head. "We haven't heard a thing."

Ross moistened his lips. "Missus Shelton, I . . . I'm right sorry."

She looked at him gravely. "Thank you. We . . . we're all terribly upset."

From Mrs. Coles came a slight grunt. "I'd say you didn't have a worry in the world, girl."

The girl's dark head turned. "What do you mean by that?"

Mrs. Coles looked across the tracks and didn't answer.

Laurel would have pressed her question, but just then the door of the station opened, and they heard the chirping of a telegraph key. Everyone's head turned. A man wearing an eyeshade and black sleeve protectors was in the doorway.

"Missus Shelton, can I talk to you a minute?"

Laurel Shelton nodded. She told Campbell, who had walked up, to get the cattle on the road to the ranch as soon as he could and then went into the station.

After getting his things out of the caboose — a couple of packages, a straw suitcase, and a carbine wrapped in newspapers — Ross stood by the tracks, looking up the street into town. He liked the look of it. A placid feel to it, not unprosperous, not noisy with quick money, yet solid.

Then he saw Campbell, talking with the marshal. The marshal was staring across the crowded pens at Ross. Chance's heart jolted.

After a moment he left the tracks and stepped up on the splintered planks, surrounding the station. Gunlock was with his cattle now, but Campbell and the marshal were still talking. Chance was almost past them when Coles said: "Chance."

He looked back — a frowning man, his flat Stetson on the side of his head, who favored his left leg a bit as he stood. "What is it?"

"Missus Coles would like to talk with you," Coles said. He spat a piñon shell. "Over yonder."

The agitation in Chance's stomach stilled for a moment. The woman had moved to the thin broken shade of a leafless poplar. He regarded her, puzzled. "OK." Presenting himself, he set his parcels down, resting the gun against a tree. "Yes, ma'am?" he said.

On Mrs. Coles's cheek was a thin flush, but the skin of her face looked cold and loose. "Are you going to keep on working for her?" she asked tensely.

30

"I don't know. She didn't ask me. Why not?"

Mrs. Coles said deliberately: "She's going to go absolutely wild. Ab-so-lute-ly wild!"

"How's that?"

"You don't know about her?"

"She seems nice," Chance hazarded.

"Yes! That's what's trapped so many of them. You didn't know her father died in prison?"

"Is it any of my business, if he did?"

Her eyes held his face. "You'll think so, if you go out there to work. Her father was marshal before my husband. The decent element put him out of office. After that he went wild . . . like she's going to. The association posse caught him stealing cattle on Lamar Shelton's ranch. And what did she do? Married the man who sent her father to prison!"

Heat was gathering in Chance's head. He seemed transfixed by the hissing voice and the small blue eyes. She lowered her voice.

"When her father was marshal, he permitted . . . I don't know how to say this. . . ."

"Sporting girls?" Chance suggested.

Her eyes were turned away at last. "Yes. *That* . . . was the sort of man *he* was. And after he was sent to prison, she did everything she could to get him out. She insulted some of our best citizens before she quit. The wrong man, she said. Wrong man, indeed!" She sniffed.

"Maybe it *was* the wrong man."

Mrs. Coles narrowed her eyes. "Listen. Those things are in the blood. They say she and her husband drink whiskey and throw things at each other out there like crazy people."

"Maybe he drinks, and she throws things."

"I'm not asking your opinion. I know what goes on in this town. I'm telling you, as a friend, that the devil's brand is on

Arrowhead Ranch. If you go to work for her . . . it's at your own risk."

Chance picked up his parcels and the carbine. He spoke softly, but annoyance underlay his voice. "I'm a little wild myself, Missus Coles. Maybe she and I'll howl at the moon and tip over privies together. We might ask you along some night. Maybe you'll find hell-raising so satisfactory, you'll let up on the sinners for a while."

Mrs. Coles's face loosened. Then she turned her head and stared at her husband, speechless. Chance walked off.

The town closed around him. The big chinaberries sifted their leaves onto the crooked boardwalk. Rain had laid the dust. The air was clear and the sky blue. Chance had the thought that he would like to be a big man in a town like this.

He was pretty sure, however, that he would not enjoy being hanged from the big trees before the marshal's office. There was what looked like a scar of ropes over a high, stout branch. It stopped him for an instant. Standing there, he felt the blood running down into his fingertips, sodden and cold. He cleared his throat and, shifting the paper-wrapped carbine, walked on toward a corner building with the simple sign: **Hotel**. He heard a slow clangor of hoofs behind him, but he kept his gaze stubbornly ahead as he walked on.

A shafted horse passed him. It slowed to a walk, the buggy pacing him. Laurel Shelton was driving alone. She leaned forward. Her smile was faint. "Won't you let me drive you, Mister Chance?"

Ross wanted to shake his head; and he wanted even more than this to talk to her. He put his things in back and climbed up to take the reins.

"Of course, you know what this will do to your reputation?" she asked.

"Mustangers don't have reputations, Missus Shelton."

She was small and full-bosomed, vivid of coloring. The sun shone deeply in her eyes, and he saw the disturbance in them. He shook the reins, and the horse trotted ahead. In a moment they were at the hotel.

"I'll stop here," he told her. "Unless you wanted to talk about something."

"I did. Turn right beyond the hotel. We can drive to the canal and back."

The buggy ran on a narrow road between bare pits smoldering with burned weeds. Green truck fields stretched to the hills on the left, the *bosque* along the river on the right.

Laurel rested her head against the bow of the fringed top. "I wish you'd stay on with the ranch for a while," she said.

"You don't need a horsebreaker, Laurel."

"I need . . . something. I need somebody trustworthy. A man who doesn't smirk at me."

His fingers handled the thick limber lines. "Why would anyone smirk at you?"

"I thought you'd had that from Missus Coles and George Gunlock."

"I had some gossip thrown at me. I don't seem to remember it."

"You'll be the only person in town who doesn't, then."

There was nothing to say. He drove silently.

She went on deliberately: "I was friendly to you in El Paso because you didn't smirk at me the first time we met. I won't ask what Gunlock told you, because I know. That I didn't marry Lamar Shelton . . . I married his money. And now Lamar's gone, and his money is left, and they'll say I drove him to suicide. And maybe I did, Ross . . . maybe I did!"

Her voice broke. He was startled but kept driving, trying to outrun the panic in himself.

"You can't say you killed him," he said gruffly. "What

33

kind of foolishness is that?"

She was looking at him. "Just before my train left yesterday, I told him I was going to file suit for divorce when I got back. And the next thing I heard . . . he . . . he'd fallen from a catwalk . . . when he'd been walking them drunk and sober for fifteen years."

The numbness in his mind seemed to creep down his arms. He felt a compulsion to tell her what had happened — that Shelton had not died in grief, but savagely, drunkenly jealous.

"He loved me, I think," she was saying. "He got me the only way he could . . . with a lie. And I decided to make our marriage a lie. I made him as wretched as I could. I moved to town and gave him plenty of reason to be jealous."

"What do you mean . . . a lie?"

"You'd be the only one who knew this, if I told you. Do you think you could keep it that way?"

"Do I have to answer that?" Ross heard the horse's hoofs pumping steadily into the soft road dust.

"I married him to get my father out of prison," she said.

"Maybe if I'd finished school," Ross said, "I'd see the connection. Shelton wasn't a lawyer, was he?"

"He pretended to be more than that. It was strange . . . everything about my father's going to prison. He couldn't make out on a marshal's pay, and he was always in a prospecting scheme or something. Then Coles and the purity crowd voted him out, and he was desperate. He hadn't expected to lose the election, and he didn't have anything lined up.

"After he was out, he got into a deal with the Gunlocks. He wouldn't tell me what, but he was excited as a boy with a new rifle. He'd be gone all day, day after day, sometimes for a week. Coles became suspicious. I think he laid for him. Anyway, they spotted him on Shelton's land one day, and he tried to get away. They caught him. About a mile away they found a calf tied beside a branding fire."

Ross found no comment that was not banal. "Well," he said, "it's happened to better and worse."

"But not to less guilty. He was off-limits, that's true, but not to steal cattle. Only he wouldn't say what he was doing. All he would tell me was . . . 'It was a prospecting deal. I can't say more than that. But the Gunlocks will get me out after the money comes in. Coles and Shelton laid for me. They built that fire and laid for me.' "

Chance's mind moved ahead. "And you got tired of waiting, and Shelton said he could pull some strings."

She nodded. "He said there were a few things he could do. He said they'd mean a lot of expense, and he couldn't do them for a mere friend. But a relative. . . . Well, we made him a relative, and after a while he told me the man he'd counted on to help out had lost his job. I knew he was lying. He wouldn't even pay for a lawyer to reopen the case. And then Father died . . . in prison. About that time I decided to break my part of the bargain, too."

The horse had almost stopped. A mockingbird swooped low over the buggy. A breeze riffled the tough yellow grass along the road.

"What about Gunlock?" Ross asked. "Couldn't he help?"

She shrugged. "Gunlock," she said, "helps nobody but himself. He said it would spoil things, if he told all he knew, and it wouldn't help my father. Tell me something. Did he fight with Shelton on the train? I had the impression he was holding back."

Ahead a narrow bridge spanned an irrigation canal. Ross turned the buggy around. "No," he said. "Why should they have?"

She shrugged. "Do you think Lamar is dead?" she asked.

"Yes, I reckon he is. It's quite a fall from the top of a car to the tracks. And then . . . falling in the river."

They heard a horse on the road beyond the canal, loping toward them from the rough dun hills. Laurel turned to look back. She sounded pleased.

"It's Blade Ramsey," she said. "He's coming in from the horse camp."

It was as though something shining and smooth had been uncovered in Ross Chance. Things complex had been cut away by something simple and direct. He didn't look back but said, "Sure enough," and kept driving.

The girl was watching him. "I notice you've taken off your ring," she said. "Why did you do that?"

"I got tired of people asking me about it."

The horseman pulled up just ahead and swung his pony to await them.

"Howdy, Laurel," Blade Ramsey said. "The sun can start shining again, now you're back."

"As a matter of fact," she said, "it's been raining everywhere I've been."

Chance looked at him. Ramsey had not looked at him squarely yet. Blade was a big, limber fellow with a long jaw and thick brown sideburns, a smiling man and a reckless one. He was riding a fine rosewood bay gelding. His saddle was a Mexican tree crusted with silver.

"Say," he said, "I trapped out a little brown mare yesterday that's got your look all over her. I was thinking I might. . . ." Then he stopped. He stared. His pony backed a step as he set the bit with an involuntary gesture. "Well, by God!" he said.

"By God and good luck," said Chance.

Ramsey's face tried to decide on an expression. "Say!" he exclaimed. "Where you from fella?"

"Plaster Cast, Colorado," said Ross. "Why don't you ride

on and meet me at that big saloon? Let's have a drink on . . .
things."

Ramsey glanced at Laurel, frowned, and said earnestly: "I
wrote three times, Ross, but I never got an answer. There was
some trouble. It. . . ."

"Go on," Chance said. "I'll see you at the saloon."

Blade rubbed his chin. "OK, Ross," he said. He gave Laurel
a salute and spurred the pony ahead.

As they rolled on, Laurel laughed. "I never saw such an
expression on a man's face before. You've been following Blade,
haven't you?"

Chance winked. "I haven't asked you anything, Laurel.
Now, you do the same."

IV

Chance got off at the hotel. He watched the buggy roll away.
He watched her slender shoulders and dark head until she
turned a corner. There was a blunt ache in his body. It seemed
to him that there had been purpose behind his coming here,
yet it was obscured by too many things that should never have
occurred.

Two old men, playing dominoes in the lobby, watched him
with nearsighted inquisitiveness. A yellow-toupeed man with
black eyebrows put down the newspaper he had been reading
to register him.

"Number Seven," he said. "The girls will bring hot water if
you want it. Toilet in back. Room smells a little of sulphur,
but, by Joe, you won't come out scratchin'."

It was a neat little room with a chipped iron bedstead and

a muslin ceiling. There was a white candlewick bedspread and a bolster cover with the rather sinister slogan: *Sleep in Peace.*

After throwing his things on the bed, Ross opened the suitcase and took a blued-steel Colt from beneath several dirty woolen shirts. He shoved it into the hip pocket of his jeans. He rolled a cigarette. As he lighted it, he looked at himself in the mirror. There were fine tucks about his eyes. Lack of sleep had started those; worry had cemented them. His face was thin. With his roached hair he thought he looked like one of the faces on post office dodgers.

In the crisp late afternoon he walked under the chinaberry trees to the Frontier Saloon. There was a small crowd of cowboys, ranchers in with small beef herds, and townsmen having a drink before dinner. The place was dirt-floored, adobe-walled, with a low ceiling of willow rip-rapping. The pounded dirt floor had been soaked with linseed oil and rubbed. The bar was short and painted green. There were some game tables, a roulette layout, a couple of girls, talking at a table in the back. It smelled mustily of tobacco smoke and stale beer and the girls' perfume.

Excitement began to thump in Chance. He was eager for what was ahead. In the dusk of the smoky lamps he looked about until he found Gunlock and his brother and Guinn Campbell at the bar with another man who was big and dark and young — Blade Ramsey. Limping slightly, Chance walked slowly down the bar.

Campbell moved his glass away to make room for Chance beside the mustanger. Still smiling, Ramsey watched every move Ross made. He was eating a hard-boiled egg from a bowl on the counter. He called to the counterman.

"A double for Mister Chance, Harry."

The whiskey brimmed in the glass. Raising it, Ross spilled a little. He put the liquor down in two swallows. Ramsey put a coin on the counter.

Ross slid it back. "I can pay." He did, and all the men were watching him as he faced Blade. "That was a good-looking plug you were riding, Blade. A beautiful saddle, too."

"Thanks. When'd you get in from Colorado?"

"Today. Why don't you ask how I made the train fare?"

"All right. How *did* you?"

"Well, after I got out of the cast, I had a doctor's bill of forty dollars to pay. I swept out saloons till I could break horses. I made enough to pay my bills and hopped a freight to Albuquerque. It wasn't hard to follow you by the girls you'd been with. Knowing a man's habits helps. I found the saddlemaker in El Paso who sold you the saddle after you delivered the horses to the fort. I nosed around till I found out you'd been back twice with bunches of mustangs." He smiled. "And here I am."

Ramsey's good humor had drained off, leaving a slit of temper in his eyes. "Any reason we can't talk about this somewheres else?"

"A good reason. We aren't going to talk about it. You wouldn't begrudge me a little skin off your nose, would you?"

Ramsey's mouth twisted. "Not if you can take it."

At once he gasped and hunched over. Chance had kicked him in the shin. While he was bent over, Ross went in with a smashing swing at his head. It collided with his cheekbone. Blade stumbled back against Campbell and, catching his footing, shuffled away from the bar and got his arms up to catch the blows Ross was throwing. Ross saw the mark he had put on the dark face and felt a wicked joy — a wanting to slash all the reckless good looks away. The long, hard road from Colorado had laid mercy in its grave. He sent a hard hook around Blade's guard and saw his head jar. Blade threw off his pain with a shake of his head and stabbed his left out, then came in eagerly with a long right. Through Chance's grin his teeth showed a white splinter. He pumped his fist up from his hip.

Ramsey took it on the nose and cried out between his teeth. He covered his face with a hand while keeping his guard out. He began to back as Ross moved in again.

There was yelling from the small crowd, a community wincing when the mustanger's fists smacked Ramsey's face. Gunlock stood at the bar with one elbow on it, drank his whiskey, and soberly observed the fight. Across the narrow room Ross steered Blade Ramsey into a corner. Doggedly he chopped and slashed, feeling the slickness of blood between his fingers. Ramsey's face looked as though it had been spurred.

The bare arms of the corner suddenly closed around Blade. He looked startled. He put his head down and fought out of it. Ross threw off the blows, and, when he was ready, he took one step forward and smashed Ramsey to his knees. Ramsey started to get up, and then slumped onto his face.

Now that the craziness was out of him, Chance could feel where Ramsey had hit him. He had a hot, feverish cheek and a swollen lip. His ribs ached. Ramsey lay, breathing windily.

Gunlock came over and put a whiskey in Chance's hand. "Friend of yours?" he asked.

"Pardner of mine," Chance grinned. "Is there a back room here? He and I will want to talk over old times."

They deposited Blade on a rumpled cot. Gunlock's brother, Webb, sat on the foot of it and looked at him curiously. "What the hell were you trying to do?" he asked. "Kill him?"

For some reason both Chance and George Gunlock looked at each other. "No," Ross said, "I just wanted to come as close as I could."

"What the hell for?" Webb asked. His voice was slow and inflectionless, as wooden as his face.

"Over some women," said Chance. "The ones that got the twelve hundred dollars he owed me."

40

"Eleven," Blade said. He said that, raised himself up awkwardly, and began washing in a small wooden tub the saloonkeeper brought and put beside him on the cot. He raised his wet, blood-pink face to say: "Will you guys get out of here? Ross and I want to talk."

"I got a feeling," Gunlock said, "that I ought to be in on it."

"What gave you that feeling?" asked Chance.

Gunlock's smile was a big-man smile — lazy and self-confident. "Tell him, Blade."

Blade finished washing. He dried himself and tried to roll a cigarette. His face was sad. It was beaten, cut, discolored. It looked sick. But it did not look resentful, and that, thought Chance, was typical of his ex-partner. He knew when he'd done wrong. You could whip him for it, or try, and he didn't begrudge you the act. It made him a pleasant companion and a hell of a partner.

Ramsey stopped trying to roll the cigarette, closed his eyes, and tilted his head back against the wall. "I gave the money to George," he said.

For a while Ross didn't speak. He sat on a rawhide-seated chair, balancing on its rear legs. He looked at Gunlock, who looked back at him. He took the silver-and-onyx ring out of his pocket and tossed it on his hand.

Blade tried to put something special into a look. "You'll get it back, Ross," he said. "You'll get it back and ten thousand on top of it!"

"Blade," Ross said angrily, "nail it down for me. What is this?"

Gunlock stood up, solid and sure and angry. "He invested in a proposition," he snapped. "That's all you need to know."

"Invested . . . with my money! If this is a partnership, you can cut me in for Blade's share."

41

Gunlock's fists were on his hips. "It ain't the kind of partnership that you cut every Tom, Dick, and Harry into."

"All right," said Ross shortly. "How many horses have you got ready to go, Blade?"

"About a dozen. I shipped two weeks ago."

"Where's the money from the shipment?"

"Gone. I had a bad run of sevens."

Chance felt a blocked anger. He looked at them all and said: "I'll go out with you and see if I can't find a few hundred lying around that the gamblers didn't get."

Blade sighed. "Maybe I can figger something out between now and then. I'll pay you back, Ross. Somehow." He commenced again, trying to roll a cigarette.

Ross saw that he was too shaken to think. Gunlock looked satisfied with the way things were going. He punched Ramsey's shoulder and drifted out with his brother. After a moment Ross rolled a cigarette and put it in his ex-partner's lips.

"You damned maverick," he sighed. "You gave me the roughest four months a mustanger ever had. And here I am rolling smokes for you."

George Gunlock waited in the warm, windy dusk before the saloon. Leaves and papers scurried along the street. Mexican women screeched at their children, and there were odors of frying meat and chilis on the breeze.

"Staying at the hotel?" Gunlock asked as Chance came out.

"Probably."

"I might come up for a drink."

"I'll be busy," Chance said.

The rancher shrugged. "I'm going out to the horse camp with Blade in the morning. If you want to go along, meet us here."

"I'll be here."

"You might as well know," Gunlock said. "He gave me eight hundred for his interest in the company. We'll make a killing, or we won't make anything. *I* think we'll make a killing. And I reckon his share ought to go to you."

"So do I. Why'd you let him in on it, anyhow?"

"I needed him. The cash . . . well, I could use it, too. I needed him so a man could putter around on Shelton's Arrowhead Ranch without looking like a long-looper."

"This sounds more like cow stealing all the time."

"Nope. I was going to say, Ross, if you want to ace him out of it . . . I'll back you up."

Dropping his cigarette, Ross stepped on it. Then he looked fully at Gunlock. "If I decide to ace him out of it, I won't need any help. You know how I am about favors."

Gunlock's grin was assured. "So am I," he said. "I wonder if they've found Shelton yet?"

Ross watched him saunter to his horse and swing into the saddle. "I wonder," he said slowly, "if you got your foot in his way on purpose?"

Gunlock laughed and rode away.

The morning was clear and pink, with a pinch in the air. Mexican farmers brought dripping loads of vegetables from the river to freight trains, unloading up on a back street, destined for villages off the main line. After a breakfast of steak and potatoes, Chance came out to find five horses before the saloon. The Gunlock brothers and Blade were smoking while they waited for him. There was an extra saddler and a pack-horse.

Ross adjusted the stirrups on his rented horse. When he was in the saddle, Gunlock took the lead rope of the pack-horse and trotted up the street.

In an hour's time they were far out in the rimrocked hills. It was rough, hardy range. The hills were not high, but they were ribbed with bands of black rock, and in between these low ridges were sandy cañons mottled with oaks and yellow cottonwoods. The cattle they passed wore Lamar Shelton's Arrowhead brand. *Shelton had been no great shucks of a man,* thought Chance, *but he had been a particular rancher.* Salt was set out here and there, and the cattle looked thrifty. But in a melancholy way it made him think of the Bible — *I builded me houses, I planted me vineyards . . . and behold, all was vanity and vexation of spirit. . . .*

And behold, Lamar Shelton drifted down a sluggish river, nibbled on by catfish, or perhaps he lay on a tule-clogged Mexican shore. He had got little pleasure out of his possessions. And he had left little joy to his wife.

Chance struck the saddle horn and tasted the sawdust the rancher had left him. Guilt that rolled like a stone in his belly. Love that had its feet in its own kind of guilt.

They rode most of the morning and came unexpectedly on a camp in a little pear-shaped cañon that held an earthen tank surrounded by trees, a rope corral with a dozen horses in it, and a canvas lean-to moored to two trees.

It looked like a score of such horse camps Ross had lived in. Sourdough bread and sowbelly, thistles in your blankets, and no sugar for your coffee. He was ready to settle down. *And what a hell of a time for* that *mood,* he reflected.

Webb Gunlock, lantern-jawed cook of the crew, started whittling jerked beef into a kettle of water. Blade explained to Chance how he had been working.

"This here's the rump end of the ranch. Ain't much ranching

44

being done in this section, and the wild broncos have took over. Things are getting slimmer, though. May be through before long."

They ate from tin pans, hunkered down on their heels. Gunlock seemed perfectly adapted to the background: rough, durable, almost primitive. He said suddenly: "Chance, I'm going to tell you what we've been doing. You and Blade can work out whatever you want about a split. We're shooting at a hundred thousand dollars out here . . . gold."

"I'll settle for eleven hundred," Chance drawled.

Gunlock squared his jaw, but his eyes brooded pleasantly. "This is one of them treasure stories," he growled, "only we happen to have a man that's seen the treasure. Laurel's father, Marshal Smith, got the yarn first. An old Mexican he'd fed at the jail for ten years told him, after he'd got elected out. Guillermo Salazar. His daddy was a tax collector when this country belonged to Mexico. That was better'n forty years ago. He'd come down from the capital at Santa Fé and make tax collections in all the villages along the trail. Then he'd take it back to Santa Fé and get five percent of what he'd collected." He grinned. "Hell of a temptation, hey? It shore was to Salazar's old man. He staged a phony holdup one time with a pardner. They hid the money in a cave until the smoke cleared. Then they went out to collect it. Hanged if they didn't get to scrapping, and, when Guillermo found them a couple of weeks later, they were both dead. They're still there. So's the money."

"What's the matter with Guillermo?" Ross demanded. "Why didn't he take it?"

"Religious. He got to figgerin' that the money had the devil's curse on it. He told Smith how to find it, but he must've forgotten to tell him about the trap he'd set. Anyway, needin' help, Smith let me and Webb in on it. Webb went with Smith. When they found the cave, Webb went in first . . . and lost

45

some fingers. He was bleeding so bad they had to leave. But they saw the gold . . . at least they saw the box, but it was locked and too heavy to move. Coming back," he added, "they run into this holy-Joe posse of Marshal Coles's. Smith dropped back to give Webb a chance to get away. Webb was mighty sick. They took Smith, but they never did know about Webb."

"I'm a little slow," Ross said. "Why didn't you and Webb go back?"

Gunlock's glance at his brother was troubled. "Webb never was . . . well, strong under the hat. He nearly died of his injury, and afterwards he didn't remember much about it. But I knew better'n to mosey around Shelton's ranch any more until I had an alibi. I went pardners with Blade to get here. And, by God, we'll tie onto that money yet. We know where Smith was took, so we're working from there."

He got up and slung his pan into a wooden dishpan. He tightened the cinch of his pony and stood for a few moments, gazing down the short loop of the cañon, where it sloped behind a run of hills. He turned back.

"That's how she looks," he stated. "Are you with us?"

Chance looked at Blade's swollen face. "I'm in this," he said, "to the extent of eleven hundred dollars. That my liability. I'm just out here trapping horses, boys. When we trap enough to make that amount, I'm out."

That night Ross asked Ramsey about the mare he'd told Laurel he'd trapped for her. "I don't see anything but sausage meat in the corral."

Ramsey grinned sheepishly. "Well, I didn't exactly trap her yet," he said. "But I spotted her with a colt over near Carrizo Creek. It'd take a month to herd her into a trap, but a man might be able to crease her and stun her long enough to take her."

"Might have a shot at her myself," Chance said.

"I'll draw you a map," Blade said.

In the morning he got Blade's description of the country, put a can of sardines and a chunk of camp bread in his saddle pocket, and took off. He was not convinced that Gunlock was telling it straight. Gunlock was a forward-looking man, and it might pay a man who dealt with him to do some looking himself.

From the rim he took his bearings and looked for signs of horses. The hills were brown and gold. The beef shipping over, Shelton's cattle would soon be moved onto this back range for the winter.

As he rode, his eyes recorded that a mare and colt had passed down the cañon a few hours before. He pulled his carbine from under his knee.

He thought about Gunlock. He tried to reconstruct the instant when Shelton had reeled through the door onto the platform. He saw the bloated red face of the rancher, and he heard himself shout at Gunlock to catch him.

With a start Ross realized something. Gunlock had been standing so close that he could hardly have missed Shelton if he had tried. But he had missed him. *Was it because he had tried?*

And now Ross saw Shelton begin to catch his balance, but stumble, and in the middle of the aisle was Gunlock's boot. It had been Gunlock, not Ross, who was directly responsible for the accident. He was suddenly sure of it. But how could you bring back the smoke of a lost moment and put it together again? Shelton was gone; the caboose was gone; the moment was gone.

He heard a horse whinny not far ahead, behind a turn of the cañon. He pulled in his pony. He dismounted and jammed matchsticks into the rowels of his spurs to silence them. He went ahead, the carbine on set-trigger. Walking softly, he approached a rough angle of rocks at the turn of the cañon. He wiped his palms dry on his jeans, each in turn. He disliked creasing a bronc'. You aimed for the particular spot on the neck, where you could stun the horse without killing it. Then you prayed and pulled the trigger.

He came around the turn. The horse wasn't in sight. Something stirred on a ledge above him, at his right, and his head jerked. Metal shone, a gleam of cloth was visible. Ross swung the rifle and fired, and, while the thunder was still big in the cañon, he sprinted for a talus of rocks at the base of the bluff. He felt a sharp pain in his ankle and went down in a rolling fall.

The other man now fired, too. The bullet blasted a crater into the sand.

Ross was back of a rock with his whole body involved in the pain of his ankle and the sledging of his heart. He hunched there until he could breathe. He began to be angry, after that. He pulled back the hammer of the Spencer and laid the barrel in a rut on the side of the rock.

So you thought I'd come riding into it? he thought. *Gunlock, I've been ambushed better by ground squirrels.*

On the hillside the rifle roared again and dislodged a landslide of echoes. In the turbulence of it Chance leaned forward and saw the blur of black powder smoke fifty yards above him. He laid his sights down on the center of the smoke and waited.

Something that looked like horsehide became visible. He waited an instant longer, looking for the rifleman, but all at once the horsehide was gone, and he knew it had been the man himself — someone who wore a pony-skin vest.

He held his gun there until he discerned a glint of steel. The shot went off explosively. Chance heard a cry. He jacked another shell into the smoking chamber and heard the hot cartridge fall among the rocks. He waited, his muscles cocked.

After the cry there was silence, but in a moment he heard a man swear, and then groan. Now, in the rocks, he could see him. He saw the yellow hair, first, then the pony-skin vest over a gray shirt. With a loud clatter the gunman's rifle slid down the rocks. Chance started up the slope.

He made his way painstakingly, moving upward through the rocks, never taking his eyes off the rifleman. He could see him more plainly now, and all at once he saw his head turn and knew him.

It was Guinn Campbell, Shelton's foreman. Breathing hard, Campbell said: "Go easy. Go easy with that, Chance."

Campbell had been shot in the left forearm. The bullet had gouged along the outside of his arm, taking out a deep trough of flesh and leaving a vicious wound that filled itself with blood. He was frightened and in pain.

After disarming him, Ross rolled up his sodden shirt sleeve. He got a small fire burning and laid the barrel of the ramrod's Colt in it. Campbell stared as Chance did this.

"What the devil are you doing?"

Chance shrugged. "If you want screw worms and gangrene in that wound, it's up to you."

Campbell, perspiration in the spined stubble of his chin, twisted the rag about his upper arm.

"Was this your idea or Gunlock's?" Ross asked.

Campbell laid back and stared at the sky. He looked much younger than Ross had thought him. With his hat off his blond hair was revealed in a self-conscious bartender's part. His face needed lines. His mouth looked wide and spoiled.

"I was trying to scare you off," he said.

Ross looked at him. Then he smiled faintly. "Missus Shelton?" he asked.

Campbell kept his eyes closed. "Maybe. You ain't good for

her. You ain't good for anybody, mustanger. You were too damn' close to the old man when he was killed, too."

"You figure you might be better for her?"

"Better than a crew of mustangers robbing her blind. I never did trust this fellow Ramsey. Nor Gunlock, for the matter o' that. And I don't like the way you moseyed in."

"So you reckoned you'd mosey me out. The next time you want to see how close you can come to something without hitting it, what about picking a tomato can?"

Lying still, Campbell opened and shut the fingers on his left hand, and his face etched itself deeply with pain. "Git it over with," he said suddenly.

"Don't rush me. A warm iron will hurt worse and do less." He paused. "Well, it's a sorry business," he admitted then, kindling a fire.

"And getting sorrier. Missus Shelton sent me over this morning to fetch you. She drove out to the ranch last night. But she got word from Coles this morning to come back to town."

With a branch stirring the coals, Ross hesitated. "What's Coles want?"

Campbell looked squarely at him for the first time. He was wet with sweat. He was sallow. But his voice was soft and steady.

"They've found Shelton. He's coming back tomorrow night."

For a full minute Ross fussed with the fire, turning the gun barrel in it, fanning it with his hat. At last he asked: "Alive or dead?"

"She don't know. Coles had a telegram from the sheriff's office in El Paso. They said they were returning him. They never said how."

"So you hustled right over here and started shooting at me."

"I . . . I reckon you had enough on your mind so you'd take off, if a man threw a couple of slugs at you. But I didn't expect

50

things to . . . to go to hell that-a-way."

Chance wrapped his bandanna about the butt of the heated gun. The blued steel smoked when he raised it. His flesh tingled; the back of his neck prickled. "Feller, this is going to hurt like hell for five seconds. Then it'll slack off. After that, it'll just hurt . . . plenty, for a couple of days. But you won't get the screw worms."

Campbell had stiffened to the ordeal. *In the cow country a man might cry over the loss of a horse or a wife,* thought Ross, *but he would quicker die than flinch from pain.*

Then he saw Campbell, looking at him. His beard looked soft, and the blue eyes were pitiful. But there was a hot young anger in them.

"I hope he's dead, Chance," he whispered. "I hope to God he broke his neck and drowned. He was a pig. And pigs don't deserve girls like her."

You, too, Chance thought. *I reckon you've been hurt before this, then.*

When he was through, he had to pack the ramrod back to the horse camp with one arm around him. He fortified him with whiskey and coffee, and after a while Campbell mounted again. Chance could not dissuade him from riding back to the ranch. He watched him ride down the cañon.

He smoked four cigarettes, sitting on a rock at the edge of the pond to watch *guajalotes* swimming in the warm green water. From the marshal's message he tried to wring every drop of meaning.

Bringing him back . . . that could mean in a box. On the other hand, an injured man would need an attendant, too. Why had Laurel sent word to him? Because she suspected something had happened on the train, and wanted him to have time to make it out?

Chance gave it up and sliced potatoes into sizzling fat while

51

he waited for the rest to return to camp. When the others came back, near sundown, Ross had made his decision. He said nothing until, the fire dying in the post-supper darkness, Blade spread his tarp and bedroll and began preparing gloomily for bed.

"Shelton's coming back," he said suddenly.

Half seen in the dim light, they all looked at him. "How do you know?" George Gunlock demanded.

Ross told him. "They don't know whether he's alive or dead. But he's coming back on the afternoon train tomorrow."

Blade pulled off his shirt. "If he's alive, we've got to go easy out here. George, you'd better figure to move out for a while. Sure as hell, Shelton will be poking around again."

Smiling, Gunlock said: "You won't have any trouble spending all that money, will you?"

Watching the mustanger, Chance saw a curious expression flick across his face. Anger — suspicion — guilt — it was all these things.

"Webb will be here," Blade grunted. "Shelton's used to him helping me out when I've got a herd to run. You don't have to worry."

Gunlock chuckled. "You're techy, feller. Going down to meet the train?" he asked Ross.

"I'm taking off tomorrow. Like I expected, this four-flushing pardner of mine has got nothing but beer checks and lip rouge behind his ear to show for my money. I'm not the kind of fool to treasure hunt on another man's range until I get hung for a horse thief, either. I'll take an I O U, Blade. It'll give me a laugh now and then."

He thought Blade sounded tense. "I still say the money's out here. Stick it out another week, Ross."

"No. I'll go through Horsehead Crossing to see what kind of shape Shelton's in. Then I'll get on the same train and head

52

back to the horse country."

It was quiet then, the fire succumbing to darkness, the night settling thickly with the small cries of foraging animals in the brush.

Gunlock was in the saddle again before Ross could pack. Sitting big and affable on his pony, he reached a hand down to him. "Take it easy, Ross. I'll see to it that this hoss thief don't forget you when we strike it. Write us your address."

They shook hands, looking into each other's eyes.

"So long," Ross said.

It was an hour before he decided to leave. Back and forth his mind went. To risk it or not? Laurel was expecting him. But perhaps the marshal was, too. He thought of her, waiting alone for the train from El Paso, and all at once he knew he had to see her once more. He would tell her good bye and ride on up the valley to some whistle-stop where he could board the train without being noticed.

He struck cross-country to the wagon road winding from Arrowhead Ranch to the town. In the dust were fresh prints of a buggy, and he trotted his horse in the hope of catching up. But when he reached the green plain running down to the river, he saw only the town ahead, drab in fall colors, with no one on the road. He was too late.

For a few minutes he sat there. The rails ran fluidly along the river, south and east. Somewhere along those tracks, at this moment, a deputy sheriff from El Paso was traveling up the valley, bringing Lamar Shelton's remains or — Lamar Shelton. There was plenty of time to make it out. He could start riding and be in Mexico before they knew he had left. A day and a night and he would be in the country where only an act of the Territorial Legislature could bring him back.

Presently he split open his cigarette, gave the moist crumbs to the wind, and rolled the scorched paper into a ball which he flipped away. He put his pony down the wagon road toward the town. A man could die from too much wondering about too many things. This was one thing he must settle now.

VI

He came in by the road he and Laurel had driven over before. He remembered her warm, perfumed presence in the buggy. He remembered the things she had said and exactly the way she had said them, and he knew he would be remembering them twenty years from now.

He came onto the broad street between the chinaberries. More leaves had been stripped from the trees; the berries hung withered and yellow. The sky was fleeced with thin clouds that stole the blue. It was a melancholy day to tell a girl good bye. It was a day for hellos, not farewells.

By his watch it was twelve-thirty. The train would not be in until about sundown. He wondered where he would find her.

Riding on, he suddenly saw the bright blue of the Shelton buggy in the station yard. He rode past the marshal's office with a glance into the window. Coles was sitting in a rocking chair with a newspaper on his knees, but he was staring out the window. Pressure came onto Ross, cold and heavy.

Laurel was not in the buggy, but as he approached she came from the station. They gazed at each other across the yard. He saw her face change, lighting for an instant. But then she bit her lip and, putting her head down, hurried to the buggy, holding her skirt off the ground with one hand. Ross helped her up. He saw the tears in her eyes when she looked at him.

She was being torn to pieces by it. And he knew at once that he was going to tell her.

"Oh, Ross, Ross!" she said. "Why did it have to happen this way? Why do I have to be tortured with not knowing?"

"Is there ever reason in trouble, anyway?" he asked. "I got your message, Laurel. Did Campbell get back?"

"No. I thought he'd stayed at a line shack last night."

"Well, he'll show up. We had some trouble. Go easy on him. But have your husband fire him, if he comes back. He's got Chance's disease. Quick amputation is the only cure."

"Is that what you're doing . . . amputating yourself? And letting me get out of it the best way I can?"

He took her hands. "I've made a lot of mistakes, Laurel, but this time I'm right. I'm leaving . . . this afternoon."

The sage-hued eyes were steady. "Because of what happened on the train?"

He nodded, observing the quiet wisdom of her face. "You had an idea it wasn't a fall, didn't you?" he said.

"I couldn't help feeling something was wrong. There were too many corners that wouldn't lie flat."

A wood cutter with a burro load of *leña* passed with a finger to his sombrero for the girl. Ross tried to find the right words.

"What happened?" Laurel asked softly.

He held her hands tightly. "Believe me, Laurel. I was fighting for my life. Even so, I wasn't trying to kill him. He jumped me with a gun. I knocked it out of his hand. He came at me again, and I hit him. Gunlock tried to catch him, and missed. He fell backwards off the platform."

Laurel firmed her lips. Her voice was warm with anger. "If Gunlock had anything to do with it, it wasn't accidental. He hates Lamar."

Ross shrugged. "Who's to prove he missed saving him on

purpose? I told Gunlock I thought he'd tripped him deliberately. He shrugged it off. *¿Quién sabe?* That's why I'm getting out, Laurel. If he's dead, it may come out that I fought with him. If he's alive, Gunlock may side him and claim I started it. I'd go to jail for assault."

"What did you fight over?" she asked.

"What do you think we fought over? We talked about cattle, but we were fighting over you."

He saw her mouth tremble. He knew how close she was to breaking down.

"Just the same," she declared, "you didn't kill him! If Gunlock had only. . . ."

"And if I'd only seen you before Shelton did, and if Blade hadn't moved out on me. . . ." He sighed. "Some time I'm going to save up for a girl like you, Laurel. I'm going to have a ranch the size of Shelton's and a house with four maids to take care of it. And I'm going to bring her home in a buggy like this."

Her mouth tried to smile. Her face was breaking into crying lines. "It's no use, Ross. Because there isn't another girl like me, is there? You'll just have to find me again."

He suddenly pulled her face down to his. He kissed her, feeling her fingers in his hair. "I will!" he said. "Someday . . . when a jug-headed horsebreaker can start dreaming again."

They heard a horse on the road and drew away.

Ross told her quickly: "I'll be around for an hour. I want to make a deal with the stable for this horse and buy some food.

She moved back onto the seat. She was small and neat, and her eyes were large. "All right, Ross. I'll be back here in an hour. Start saving for that girl soon, won't you?"

He said: "I took four bits out of my left-hand pocket this morning and put it in my right. That's a start." He squeezed her hand and turned.

This was when he saw Marshal Coles, standing by his horse under a tree, watching him, with a Colt in his hand. Coles now came forward. His face burned with a righteous light that was wild in its intensity. He said: "Keep your hands away from your gun. Stand right there."

"Standing still is one of the best things I do, Marshal," Ross said. And now, that it was here, he found a core of steadiness in himself. He held it by both hands. *I'll bluff and lie and fight. This old buzzard and his pious-mouthed woman won't keep me long in that jail.*

Coles possessed himself of Ross's gun. In the buggy Laurel cried: "Marshal, what is it?"

Coles kept his stare on Ross. "Murder, Missus Shelton. George Gunlock just signed an affidavit that he seen this man kill your husband."

"Then why didn't he tell us before?" Laurel demanded.

"Because this feller threatened to kill him if he did."

Laurel was out of the buggy. "And you believed that? Gunlock is a liar, and you're a fool to believe him. I demand that you lock him up for perjury, if you lock this man up for suspected murder."

Coles's big mouth twisted in irony. "Excuse me, ma'am . . . was it me or you they elected marshal?"

"You, unfortunately. The disciple of keeping garbage out of Main Street. Store it in your back rooms, instead."

Coles's eyes narrowed. He looked at her with contempt and yet with relish — the prophet at last proved true.

"You Smiths seem to be specialists on garbage, Missus Shelton. Your father had a good first-hand knowledge of it, too."

Laurel saw Ross moving before he knew he had started. She clutched his arm and cried something to him, and by that time Coles had stepped back a pace and was waving his gun menacingly. Ross swore low and bitterly, and then stopped.

"I'll whip you for that, Coles," he said softly. "You'll crawl the length of Main Street to ask the lady's pardon."

"I'm asking no one's pardon," Coles bit out. "This is attempted murder . . . murder proper, if Shelton's dead. I'm telling you that, if you don't march straight up the walk, I'll drop you. I've got the power to do it. And I will. I'll do it for you, too, one of these days," he told Laurel. "You've run mighty close to tar and feathers this last year. You may run closer one of these nights."

He stepped aside, motioning Ross along. As he moved to the boardwalk, Chance heard the girl say, quietly menacing: "And if my husband turns out to be dead, Marshal, I'll use every dollar I own, if I must, to discredit you. Women like me, you know, have a talent for vindictiveness."

Facing the street, the marshal's office was a single room deep, with a corral in back, a wood rick, and a small adobe shack with an iron door that was the jail. An adobe wall enclosed the yard, and a cottonwood dropped papery leaves into the corral.

Coles prodded Chance into a cell that contained two bunks suspended from opposing walls on iron chains. Sitting down with a sigh, Ross began rolling a smoke, but Coles struck the sack and papers from his hand and turned his boot on them.

"I can do without fires in here," he snapped.

Banging the door, he departed.

In his mind Chance stood Gunlock up and smashed at his face with the butt of a pistol. *Why?* he asked himself. *What had brought the man to throw him in jail? He had taken off this morning by a back trail, reached town first, and gotten to Coles's ear early.*

Was it because he was afraid Ross would confess and implicate him, too? Finally he thought he understood. *Gunlock had been shaken by the news that Shelton was coming back. If the rancher*

58

were alive, he might put Gunlock himself in jail for withholding news of the fight. In sheerest virtue George Gunlock was commencing to establish his innocence.

After an hour Laurel came to the jail. Coles stood in the back door of the office while she talked with Ross.

"I've wired a lawyer in El Paso. He's coming up to handle it for us. I wired the sheriff's office again, but they wouldn't tell me whether Lamar's alive or not. I think it must be part of their strategy."

"It sounds to me like he's dead," Chance said gloomily. "It sounds a little bit like I'm dead, too. Do me a favor, Laurel. Take a nice room at the hotel and wait there until somebody comes to tell you it's over. Either he's alive or he's dead. If he's alive, leave and get your divorce somewhere. If he's dead . . . go back to the ranch and let your lawyer handle things. You've already had one shot at getting men out of jail."

"You're going to get out, Ross," she insisted.

"In case I don't," Ross said, "do you reckon a fellow could kiss a girl through an outfit like this?"

She put her face up to the bars. With the cold caress of the iron against her face, he found her lips — too warm, too sweet, too soft to believe. "I love you, Ross," she whispered.

"And that's bad, too," he sighed. "But if you didn't, I wouldn't care much whether I got out of here or not. That's how bad it is with me."

Just before dark he heard spurs coming through the marshal's office, and men's voices in angry conversation. The screen door banged open. On the stoop he saw George Gunlock — this big, darkly handsome man who never stopped figuring. He sauntered to the cell with another man behind him. It was Blade Ramsey.

Ross had one weapon left, and, when Gunlock's face was

close enough, he used it. The spittle struck Gunlock's cheek.

Softly Gunlock swore and clubbed at the fingers grasping the bars.

Ross laughed at him. "I'd give my right hand to have you in here for five minutes. Then they'd have something to hang me for."

Gunlock stared at him. "You don't give a man much chance to help you, do you? Damn it, Ross, I had to do it or be jugged with you for . . . for God knows what. I was going to tell you I'd hire a lawyer as soon as we find the money."

Ross regarded him levelly. "I'm saving spit again, George." He watched Gunlock step back.

"OK," Gunlock said. "This was your chance. There won't be another that I know of." He turned. "Comin' Blade?"

Ramsey shook his head. "Be with you in a minute."

Chance looked into the dark, reckless face. "Have I got to show you what I think of horse-stealing mustangers now?"

Blade's voice was hardly audible. "Shut up. There's things going on, Ross. I came as soon as I got wind of what he was doing."

"Fine. I'm willing you all the corral sweepings in Colorado, kid. Spend them wisely."

Blade lighted a cigar and passed it through the bars. Ross looked at it. "Does it blow up when it gets down to the ring?"

Ramsey seemed pressed. He spoke tightly. "Ross, will you ease up for a minute? I'm in a spot myself. Have been for a month. The Gunlocks have found that tax money. Sure as hell, though they wouldn't let me in on it. But they've kept quiet until they figured they could ace me out of my share. I reckon that's why George invited you into it. He figured you and I might get to squabbling and take each other out of it. Or at least you'd drop me, and he could set on it until he was ready to move out."

Ross's face was unemotional. "I'm looking a rope in the face . . . and you want me to get worked up over some tax money a Mexican hid forty years ago."

"Can't you see how it all ties in? You played right into his hands on the train. *You* didn't shove old Shelton off the train . . . *he* did! But all of a sudden the squeeze is on him. He don't know what's coming up from El Paso. He had to put you away for a while, and now he's going to try to do the same for me."

The cigar glowed as Ross drew on it. "Somehow it doesn't seem to worry me much what happens to you, Blade. Just don't try to borrow from me to pay the fiddler."

In the doorway Gunlock, watching them, tilted his Stetson to scratch his head, calling tersely: "Let's go, Blade."

Ross saw Blade's knuckles tighten on the bars. "This is the last chance you'll get, Ross. He's going to try to kill me tonight when we go back to camp. Then he'll load up with that money and take off."

It suddenly came to Ross that Blade was telling the truth. He was wound tight as a new rope. He knew the Gunlocks planned to kill him, and he was afraid.

"What do you want me to do?" Ross asked quickly.

"If you're with me, Ross, I'll get you out. I'll try to get out of going back tonight. If I figure George right, nothing's going to keep him from getting out of town tonight. Time's crowding. After Coles goes to bed, I'll come back."

Blade leaned forward. Against the deeper shadows his features had a sudden fire of readiness in them, an eagerness for conflict. His grin came briefly. Then he turned and walked back to the others.

It was not over thirty minutes later that the long, wailing cry of a locomotive floated up the valley. Ross was sitting on his bunk when he heard it. He came to his feet. His fists squeezed shut. A moment afterward he heard a door thud — Coles was hurrying to know whether he had a hanging prisoner or a jailing one.

In an agony of suspense Ross ground his fist against his palm and closed his eyes. *Be alive!* It was a prayer in his mind. *Be alive, you swine!* He broke out of it and strode to the rear wall of the cell. He cut back to the door, glanced out, took two strides to his bunk, and sat down again.

He heard a small sound in the darkness. Sitting straight, he listened. Someone was in the office. A match flared. The screen door rustily grated. A man was in the yard. Ross moved quickly to a corner invisible from the door. The treachery of George Gunlock might run as deep as murder.

"Ross!" It was Blade again. "For God's sake, wake up!"

Ross slipped to the door. "What's at the station?"

"I don't know. I told George I was quitting. I was fed up with treasure hunting. He's sore. I figured this might be my only chance to get back. I'll keep out of sight until he leaves. Coles is still at the station. Take this and stow it. I got it out of Coles's drawer."

Ross received the Colt through the bars. He shoved it inside his shirt. "How do I get out of here?"

"I've got a pick," Blade said. "I'll work on the wall till we hear Coles coming. If I'm not through, I'll leave the pick with you, and you'll have to work from the inside."

Blade disappeared, and immediately the soft impact of a pick against the adobe bricks began. The wall was a single course of adobe bricks. The mortar was the soft grout Mexican builders used. In about five minutes Ross saw the first brick stir under his bunk. Working desperately, Blade dislodged it. After that, he was able to work out other bricks.

Blade worked until he had made a hole about two feet long

and a foot high. He threw the pick across the wall. "Wait till the town's in bed," he said. "If Coles notices you're gone now, he'll have a posse whipped up in fifteen minutes. Give yourself a break." He began maneuvering the wide, flat bricks back into place. "Somebody's comin'," he whispered. "Lay low till the southbound passes, about eleven o'clock. Then cut and run. I'll be in La Gloriosa *cantina* two blocks south, facing the tracks. I'll have everything."

"Everything for what?"

"How's Mexico sound?"

"Lonesome. What sounds good to me is collecting that tax money before we go anywhere. I'm going to buy my way out of this, somehow. All a poor man can buy is trouble."

"We'd buy a little trouble collecting that money. The only chance would be if the Gunlocks take off for the cache tonight. Then maybe we could jump them."

"That's what I'm thinking. Jump them and run."

"They'd scrap, Ross. We'd catch hell before we got out of that one."

Ross's voice leveled. "Gunlock's got a little hell coming for this. Do what you want. I'm going to tie myself to his tail until I've got a stake."

He lay on the bunk then. After a few moments he became aware that Coles had lighted a lamp in his office, for the reflection shone faintly into the cell. There was little chance that the marshal would see the hole in the wall, unless he scouted thoroughly in the weeds outside. He heard him cough and move to the door. A moment later the light grew stronger, and he heard the marshal's lanky tread on the path.

He had hidden the gun under the straw pallet. He lay there, feeling the lump it made. Coles put the bull's-eye to the grille and turned it steadily about. "Wake up," he said.

Ross swung his legs overside. "What's the good word?"

"Do you want a lawyer?"

"I've got one ordered. How's our friend Shelton?"

Marshal Coles's long goat-face was split lengthwise by the lamplight. It looked white and meatless as a skull. "Our friend Shelton," he said, "was found in the river on the Mexican side last night. I just seen him in his coffin. Catfish had eaten his eyes out. He's rotted pretty bad, but you can still see where you hit him with the gun. I wish," he said, "we didn't have to go to the mess of having a trial. Why don't you plead guilty? Maybe you'd draw life."

Ross sat down, his legs half giving way. A shudder went through him. He said: "I've got a pretty slim hold on life right now, my friend. Thanks for the good word. If anybody asks about me, just say the prisoner ate a hearty breakfast."

VII

What Blade's plan had not taken into account was the marshal's weak kidneys. About ten-thirty Ross saw his lamp go out and heard him bedding down. In twenty minutes the lamp went on again. The lawman opened the screen door, trudged to the backhouse, and, returning, called: "You there, Chance?"

Chance delayed replying with purpose.

Just as Coles left the stoop to return, he called from his bunk: "What . . . whassat, Marshal?"

Coles grunted something and went back.

At eleven o'clock the lamp went on, and again he trudged to the backhouse. On his return he kicked the jail door and said grumpily: "Don't be trying nothing smart, mustanger. 'Less you want a rump full o' buckshot."

Far up the valley now Ross heard the iron whispers of the train. His body awoke to a grinding tension. Blade's timetable was set around the passing of the train. It could not be stretched far. He crouched to drag the adobe bricks in under the cot and clear the opening. He wished the hole could have been made in the rear, out of view of the back door. But that would have made the hole visible from the grille of the cell. He kept pulling the bricks in and stacking them along the wall, and now the train whistled two fading notes and rushed through the village.

Silence came down like soot.

For ten minutes Chance waited for the marshal to go back to sleep. Suddenly he crouched to thrust the Colt through the hole and placed it on the ground. He lay flat and began wriggling through the hole. He was just emerging when he grew conscious of a long underwear-clad form in the doorway. Coles was coming out. There was an explosion of nerves in Chance's body. He was almost ill when the shock passed.

He held the gun tightly in his fist. Across the yard the marshal called irritably: "Chance, what the hell you doin'?"

Very slowly Ross began turning back toward the hole. Hugging the ground, using every bit of weed for cover, he tried to get his upper body into it. Coles slammed the screen door open, and now the moonlight ran on the long barrel of a shotgun.

"Chance!" he shouted.

Ross took a breath and lunged halfway through the hole. His head was under the bunk. He coughed.

"Damn it," he called, "am I the one that's going to hang, or you? Go to bed and let me sleep, will you?"

After a long interval the marshal growled something about the train and added: "But don't try nothing. A mouse couldn't clear its throat without me hearing."

"No," Chance agreed, "and you can't clear yours without me hearing. If this is the kind of sleep I'm going to get, I'll die of rings under my eyes before you can hang me."

Coles let the door creak shut. Five minutes later Chance wriggled back into the yard and silently departed.

Standing outside La Gloriosa *cantina,* Ross heard the clamor of a small crowd of Mexicans. He stood on tiptoe to see over the green-slatted door. It was a typical Mexican drinking place with tiny square tables, a bar that was a mere plank, and streaked plaster walls. Two men were playing a coronet and a guitar in one corner. The bar was thronged with sinister-looking Mexicans who were, he knew, no more sinister than the plows they pushed in the daytime.

He went in and immediately saw Blade in a corner with another man whose back was to the door. Ross went through the clamor of the instruments and the fog of smoke to the table. He pulled out a chair and sat down.

Blade signaled the barman. *"¡Un mas* weeskey, *por favor!"*

Chance looked at the blond, ruddy man with him. It was Guinn Campbell.

Campbell looked pinched, and his arm was in a sling. He smiled. "Congratulations."

"Thanks. I'd like to congratulate myself, but I won't feel like it until I shake this place. Blade, I'm ready any time you are."

"Everything's set," Ramsey said. "But I want you to hear something. I ran into Guinn after I busted up with Gunlock. He's been telling me stories, Ross. You ought to hear them."

A wire of tension was jumping in Chance. He picked up the whiskey as the barman set it down and drank it in gulp. He kept his voice low. "In about thirty seconds Coles is going to come out to use the backhouse and discover I've left. And you want me to listen to windies."

"There's no wind in what Guinn's been telling me," Ramsey

insisted. "Talk up, cowboy."

Campbell put a forefinger against the table. "One thing, Chance . . . I'm no double-crosser. I went into this thing because I thought it was right. It wasn't. All I can do to square it now is to talk about it. Coles framed Marshal Smith," he said. "Gunlock and Shelton helped him. And Shelton made me help."

"Why didn't you talk a little sooner?" Ross asked. "This doesn't help Smith much now, does it?"

"I was afraid to. After he died, I didn't see where it could help him any to get myself shot. But now Gunlock's putting the same squeeze on you."

Ross leaned forward. "This gets interesting."

Blade spoke impulsively. "I wish that pig, Shelton, was alive to sweat out a couple of years in jail. He had the idea to begin with. And Coles and Gunlock trailed along with him."

In bitter retrospect Campbell went on. "We all knew Shelton was crazy for Laurel. And she wouldn't touch him with a buggy whip. Then he started thumping the tub for Coles for marshal. Coles was a part-time revival preacher who got by on commission buying. He was great for purity. I don't know how Shelton ever got Smith voted out, but he did. Even then he wouldn't quit. He started squalling that he was being robbed blind by cow thieves. I knew he was watching what went on back there where the horse camp is now, but he couldn't figure it out.

"One day he told me he and Coles were going to crack down on Smith. They knew he was in this cattle-rustling ring . . . had it in writing from one of the gang . . . but they'd have to take him in the act. Now that would be hard to do. So if they caught him on Shelton's range, would I see to it that the evidence was plain?" Sickness was in his eyes. He shook his head. "I figured they were telling the truth. I built a branding fire, roped down a calf, and left them there. That was what they used for evidence. I don't know what Smith was doing on the land, but he wasn't stealing no cattle. I knew that when things began to shape up later. Laurel marrying Shelton . . . that wasn't right. I hated her for it, at first. Then I . . . I admired her. After the old man died, and she began to cut up, I knew damn' well what the deal had been. Shelton had welshed on his bet, and she was welshing on hers."

"Where's Gunlock come into it?" Ross demanded.

"He was in the posse. I didn't savvy it until Blade told me tonight what's been going on out there. Gunlock was getting Smith out of it . . . after he'd been the man to start the treasure hunt in the first place. And I think George wanted his brother out of it, too." He shook his head. "Those Gunlocks! That's why I've been quiet, Ross. George will go to the smoke when he knows I've told this. And what help will Coles give me?"

Ross looked at Blade. "Maybeso a lot, if it's handled right. The place to start would be with Gunlock."

"Gunlock's left," Blade stated.

"Good. We go after Gunlock first. When we bring him back. . . ."

The *cantina* was suddenly quiet. A bell tolled in the night. A Mexican left the bar to hold the door open.

"*¿Qué hay? Incendio?*" someone called.

"*Creo qué no. . . . ¡Debe ser algo al jusgado!*"

Something at the jail. Ross stood up. "I'm getting out. There'll be time to make a deal with Coles, but this isn't it."

They let the crowd surge out and, following them, turned up the side of the building to where two ponies waited. The bronze strokes of the fire bell bonged steadily. Lights were coming on in the boxy adobe houses and in the windows of the two-story hotel. Campbell stood there, nervous and undecided.

"Want to follow this through?" Ross asked him.

"I wouldn't have started it if I hadn't."

"Go to the hotel, write an affidavit of what you know about Shelton and Gunlock, and send it over to Coles. Don't mention him in it. Let that come later. Get the hotel keeper to witness it for you and tell him to make Coles issue a warrant for Gunlock's arrest. Then hole up and wait."

Campbell said: "If you're going after the Gunlocks, you'd better have help."

Ross smiled. "After you know what to expect of a man, you can usually handle him. Do what I say. Keep out of sight, though, or we're apt to lose a good witness."

Campbell smiled then and put out his good hand. "The doc says I'll be able to rope a cow, Ross, so I guess it's even-steven."

Chance met his grip. He felt sympathy for this man who was just beginning to learn some of the things a man could only learn the hard way. "Don't get so busy roping cows you forget about the ladies," he said. "Give them another chance. Nobody ever told you falling in and out of love would be fun."

Ramsey, already in the saddle, wheeled his horse out onto the side street. Ross checked the saddler Blade had brought him, and, as they cut for the back road, he looked around to see Campbell, jogging toward the middle of town, a stiff and lonely figure.

It was near sunup when they dropped into the cañon where the horse camp was. They entered the dry wash a mile below it. The passing night was full of the small sounds of hunting animals. Mice foraged for insects. Raccoons hunted the mice. Bobcats preyed on the raccoons. It was not unlike a range on which men glided silently in the darkness, hunting each other.

"I think I know the day they struck the cache," Blade

69

grunted. "It was about a month ago. Gunlock couldn't put in too much time hunting before that, trying to follow the map. All of a sudden he began missing days. Then he went down and bought some good herd cattle, when he damn' well couldn't afford them on a spread the size of his."

"Then why haven't they moved it out by now?"

"Maybe they have. But I'm banking on his being afraid to move it until I was out of the deal. He knew I couldn't hang around Shelton's range forever. Shelton would get suspicious. He figured I'd drift along, and everything would be easy."

They rode slowly and cautiously on the bare sand between the rounded hills. A milky light was beginning. A small breeze sent branches to crackling. Suddenly Ross reached out to touch Blade's arm. There was smoke on the air.

They pulled over and dismounted, removing their spurs and hanging them on the saddle horns. Ross crossed to the far side of the wash, a hundred yards away. Pacing slowly, they walked toward the camp. Coming to the peninsula of trees that shielded it, they worked through to where they could see the murky pond and the canvas lean-to. The horses shifted about in the rope corral. Where the stone fire hole was, a pale feather of smoke leaned with the wind. There was no sign of the Gunlock brothers.

Ross walked ahead a short distance and halted by the carcass of a dead cottonwood. Still he could see nothing in the camp but the broncos in the corral. Yet a fire had been built here within an hour. Coffee had been boiled, and its fragrance was still on the breeze.

They walked into the camp, looked about, and said nothing. Moving around, Chance found horseprints leading up the cañon. They had stopped to rest their horses and refresh themselves.

"Maybe you're right," he told Blade. "They're going

somewhere, that's for sure."

"They've taken a couple of extra bronc's, too," Ramsey pointed out. "They're figuring on packing something out. We've got to stay with them." He stared up at the gaunt hillsides, stained with melting shadows. "I'll hike up that ridge while you go back for the horses. Maybe I can get a line on them."

In twenty minutes Ross was back with the ponies. From the rimrock Blade waved his hat at him. Ross climbed the slope as the mustanger hurried down to meet him.

"They just cut through that saddle. Gunlock told me they'd combed that Panther Valley stretch a year ago. Maybe he did . . . but he didn't happen to mention they found the money there. We went through once, and he kept me moving."

A half hour later and away from the windy pass, they looked down on a rough little valley with a stream threading the middle of it. Tough growths of ironwood and mescal tangled the hillside. Cattle trails switchbacked through the brush toward the water, and near the bottom they saw the horses moving toward the stream.

They started down, but in a few minutes Ross pulled up. "We aren't going to get far this way." He dismounted. On a shelf of rocks and weeds they left the horses. They sighted once more and saw the other horses — tied now, near the head of the valley.

"There's a little falls there where the creek comes down," Blade told him. "It's cave country."

Below them the valley lay small and tangled, dark with meaning. It seemed a dismal goal for the long trail Ross Chance had followed to find it.

Reaching the bottom, they began to hear occasional sounds — a ring of metal, a man's voice. They separated, taking opposite sides of the cañon. As he walked, suddenly Ross was startled by something that flapped up in front of him. He fell, excitement striking in him like a gong. He rolled onto his side and lifted his Colt. For one instant he was braced for the crash of the gun. Then he saw the ghostly shape of a horned owl, rising through the top of a tree.

Across the cañon Blade crouched behind a rock. George Gunlock said something sharply, and there was an iron silence. Then Webb's wooden voice said: "Just a damned owl."

After a couple of minutes Ross moved ahead. He saw Blade, gliding through the brush. The stream separated them, twisting among the trees from the broken bluff down which it fell. The bluff was of rusty black rocks, cracked and gaping with fissures. He came to a rough clearing that had been used as a holding spot for cattle. A branding iron and rags of harness hung from the branch of a tree. The bluff formed a barrier for the clearing. The horses stood at the edge of it. Brush tangled the base of the cliff. Through it he could distinguish the ragged mouth of a cave.

Blade found a vantage point near him and signaled: *Stay put!*

Someone was pounding inside the cave. Dull metallic blows resounded in a dogged rhythm. Four men waited in the cave to see what was inside the chest. Two were alive, two dead. And Ross saw that whatever men reckoned worthwhile, they would always be willing to die for it.

Now Webb was speaking excitedly. His brother said: "Take it easy! She'll come, she'll come!"

"You could shoot her off, couldn't you?"

Gunlock seemed to hesitate. "Sure," he said. "A little risky. You want me to shoot the lock off?"

Intuition touched Chance. He made a signal to Blade and slipped into the clearing. The dawn was golden behind him. He walked softly on the sandy ground, while Blade frantically shook his head and then in desperation moved to join him.

Webb said eagerly: "Stand back a bit, George. I'll lop 'er off like a turkey's head."

"No, no!" Gunlock said in alarm. "My God, you'll have chunks of lead flying all over the cave!"

"How would you do it?"

Chance moved faster, a sickness in him.

George Gunlock sounded patient and brotherly. "Like this," he said. The gun sounded flat in the cave.

Chance was running. Blade was just behind him, and they were bursting through the dead ironwood before the cave. They heard the hoarse cry.

"George!" they heard Webb say. "You . . . you hit me!"

"I know." All the feeling had leached out of Gunlock's voice. It was cold and level and emotionless. "I must have shot high, Webb. I'll try it again."

Chance breasted the tangle of brush and lunged for the cave. The dawn at his back was a misty gold light, slanting into the wedge-like cave. Powder smoke rolled on a faint draft. He had a blurred vision of Webb Gunlock with his chin locked against his chest and a hand clenching his shirt front. The light was brassy on the face of his brother. It was the most vicious countenance Ross had ever seen. Yet it was open and expressionless, waxen in its coldness, just a brown mask of flesh with eyes cut to black splinters. It was the lack of expression that horrified him. He was pointing a Colt at his brother with total absence of emotion.

Then Gunlock saw Chance, and his face loosened in shock — sagged, and bunched again in fury. He was on his knees beside a small wooden box, a mechanic's hammer resting on top of it. There was a wisp of smoke in the barrel of his revolver. Chance swerved to get behind the other Gunlock. He dropped to his knees and held Webb with an arm locked about him. He

73

heard the Colt crash. His ears rang, and the flash seemed to fill the whole cave. He felt Webb start and heard him cry out again.

He and Webb were falling sidewise on the floor. Blade was crashing up through the brush. Gunlock's hand was coming down on the recoil, the Colt cocked again. Chance pointed his gun like a finger. He shot and felt the kick lift his forearm. The cave was strangling on powder fumes. Sunrise burned in it, and George Gunlock was hardly visible. Chance knew that. He was coming forward.

Ross threw the gun down again but heard Blade fire first. He saw that Gunlock had not been coming forward, but falling. He had one arm out to sustain himself. Chance held his fire. He watched Gunlock stretch out on the floor. He lunged forward to knock the Colt from his hand with the barrel of his own. Gunlock did not look up. The smoking revolver spun away.

Blade crouched in the opening to the cave. "Ross!" he called. "You all right?"

"All right," Chance said. "I think he's done."

Blade came forward and turned Gunlock over with his foot. He looked down a moment and shuddered.

It had seemed to Chance that it would be easier to write all the things in his mind than to say them. While he was not much of a man with a pencil, he felt it would be harder to explain face to face to Laurel why he was leaving. He stayed in the hotel room — after the first business with the marshal and the bank — and at dusk, two days after the trouble in Panther Valley, he left the hotel and walked down to the station.

He had fifteen minutes to wait. He sat on the polished oak bench inside the waiting room. A fire snapped in the little iron stove in its sandbox. It had turned cold.

He smoked a cigar and gazed out onto the tracks. A suitcase and three paper parcels rested on the dock. His imagination found another suitcase, probably a large leather one — or more likely two or three, the truck women carried with them. He saw a rather short, blond man in a city suit standing beside a dark-haired girl in a gray gown. The man had the country look of a horseman, but the girl looked trim and attractive. They looked as though they might just have been married.

While his eyes were closed, the door of the waiting room opened. A girl came in, small and shapely in a pale-green, lightly hooped gown. She smiled at him, and said: "Oh, hello! I wondered if you might be here. At the hotel they said you'd left."

He stood up and indicated the vacant section of bench on his left. "I was going to write," he said.

Laurel sat down with her knees close together, smoothing her gown over them. "I should think so," she said.

"Because . . . it's hard to say, Laurel . . . it would be like moving into a room just after it was painted. It would be . . . too new and raw. It might not be right. And when I move into the room, I want to know it's for good. I'm a one-girl man."

"A man's man," she smiled. "Ross, the nicest thing happened today. Missus Coles . . . she's president of the Ladies Study Club, you know . . . asked me to join it. They're studying China this winter. They want me to make the first report."

"What do you know about China?"

She smiled, sparkles of light laughing deep in her eyes. "Nothing, but I can read. She thanked me for 'co-operating' with her husband, as she called it, and I told her I knew why he'd done it. He was just overzealous. He was so sure Dad was guilty of everything they said that he thought it was all right to . . . to plant the proof."

Chance grunted. "Co-operating isn't half of it. You could have sent him to jail."

"Yes, but I'd rather have done it this way. I like Horsehead Crossing. I like being the daughter of a man they all know now was a good marshal. Everybody's come to tell me how glad they are that Campbell cleared him. Some of them told me they thought you were fine, and I ought to thank you. Campbell told the marshal that he saw enough on the train before Lamar died so that he was certain Gunlock was really the guilty one, if anyone was . . . but, of course, there's no proof that he didn't fall."

Ross turned the cigar in his fingers, frowning at it. "Coles came to the hotel this morning and said he wanted to collect a reward for me, for trying to capture Gunlock. I told him, never mind . . . I didn't need the money any more."

Laurel looked at him intently. "How much was there? Someone said you found nearly a hundred thousand dollars!"

Ross chuckled. "The bank wired El Paso to find out what the stuff was worth. It came to seventeen hundred and fifty-six dollars. I gave Blade the price of a railroad ticket and kept the rest. He went down to El Paso this morning. There'd be a good pardner, if he wasn't a thief." He turned his head to listen. "That's her," he said.

They went out to the tracks together. "I'll count the days," she whispered.

"*You'll* count them! Listen," Ross said, while the train came clanking from a turn and clouded the evening with its cindery smoke, "I'll be back exactly a year from today. On the sixth of October I'll get off that train right here. If you aren't here, I'll know you've changed your mind, and I'll get back on and keep going."

She was crying, but smiling with it, and she said: "I might

miss it! I think I'll go back into the station and wait."

"That might be a good idea," Ross said. He chuckled, and Laurel laughed. When he kissed her, there was laughter in his heart as well as tears.

THE MAGNIFICENT GRINGO

"I have tried to avoid," Frank Bonham once remarked, "the conventional cowboy story, but I think it was probably a mistake. That is like trying to avoid crime in writing a mystery book. I just happened to be more interested in stagecoaching, mining, railroading. . . ." Notwithstanding, it is precisely the interesting and — by comparison with many traditional Westerns — the exotic backgrounds in Bonham's novels that give them an added dimension. He extensively researched the technical aspects of transportation and communication in the 19th-Century West. By introducing these backgrounds into his narratives, especially when combined with his firm grasp of idiomatic Spanish spoken by many of his Mexican characters, his stories and novels are elevated to a higher plane in which the historical sense of the period is always very much in the foreground. "The Magnificent *Gringo*" was first published in *Blue Book* (6/45), and this marks its first appearance in book form.

I

You could stand anything for a while, Lee Brian thought, but the smell of hides you could stand not quite so long as most other things. Hides, however, had been kind to him — from the trouble of buying them, having them cured, and selling them as half-tanned leather to the trading ships he had trebled his capital. By New England standards he would have been considered a young man of some substance. In California he was *un gran hombre* indeed.

He supposed he could keep right on trebling his capital, but in his twenty-eight years he had learned that only part of a man's energies could profitably be spent in making money. The rest should be spent in enjoying it.

There was nothing to spend money on at San Pedro. Civilization consisted of his own weathered shacks and stinking brine tanks — lost in a labyrinth of tidal marshes — and the native settlement on the green hill behind the harbor. At Lee Brian's stage of life, pleasure was closely allied with girls of his own color. The young ladies of San Pedro were of mixed California-Mexican extraction. They were squat and brown and snag-toothed. Aside from the paucity of girls San Pedro offered only crab-spearing and drinking. Lee Brian was tired of crabs and not quite ready for solitary drinking. So he was leaving his fulsome trade for someone with cooler blood and a less sensitive nose. He was going back to the States by the first steamer.

About noon Ignacio rode in. Ignacio was majordomo of the vast Los Arcos ranch, and he never missed rent day. He saluted Brian cordially, lying expertly and with a smile.

"I chanced to be in Los Coyotes this morning," he explained. "I said to myself . . . 'I have come this far. I will go a little farther and greet my good friend, *Don* Brian.' "

Not that he needed the lease money, Brian thought. Oh, no — he just chanced to be fifteen miles from home by twelve o'clock.

Ignacio accepted the American's invitation to share his lunch. He ate frugally, as an old man eats, chewing the boiled *carna seca* interminably, sipping his wine as though each drop were the last in the cup.

Then they went out and sat on a bench, squinting at the sapphire sparkle of the ocean, hearing the chatter of the Indians, fleshing hides on the beach. Lee Brian tried to think of a gentle way to tell the majordomo that after this month the income of *Rancho* Los Arcos would be less by twenty dollars.

Ignacio himself gave the opening. "Seagulls and Indians!" he remarked. "Not much company for a young man. Every month I think . . . 'He will go home soon.'"

Brian stepped into the opening. "As a matter of fact," he said, "I've been thinking about leaving. There must be other businesses where the returns are as good . . . and the smells better. Will you tell *la patrona* I won't be renewing my lease next month?"

Ignacio's wrinkled, dust-brown face showed, Brian thought, almost pleasure at this news. He nodded. "It was expected," he admitted. "I bring *Señorita* Graham's request that you honor her with your presence this evening."

Brian wondered with what effort the word *honor* had come out. Still, the old man seemed to like him, Yankee though he might be. But with Maria Catalina Arango y Graham the roots of Yankee-hating went deeper. Yankees had cut *Rancho* Los Arcos down to half the size it had been under the Mexican governors. Yankees would possess it yet.

The majordomo read the creases in Brian's forehead. "It is for business," he explained. He added, shrugging: "They do not discuss with me the *negocios grandes*. Just the little things . . . the cattle, the vineyards."

He was being ironic, and Brian liked him for it. He was saying that all he knew was how to raise cattle and grapes, how to press out the wine and care for hides and tallow — in brief, how to make the ranch pay. Maria and her grandmother were the ones who knew how to borrow foolishly and spend unwisely.

Well, it would relieve the monotony, and it might even satisfy

Brian's curiosity as to what lay behind the dark pretty face of this daughter of a Mexican woman and a Scottish sea captain — intelligence or dullness! He rode away with *Don* Ignacio, wondering what lay ahead besides the best food he had tasted since hitting California eighteen months ago.

The road ran through cattle range, much of it a jungle of semi-forest growth. Brian and Ignacio lost the sea breeze, and the hot air of the valley brought sweat out on them. From a hilltop they rode into pleasant acres of low-growing grape vines that lent a relieving greenness to the brown summer range.

Brian could glance to the left, into August Moxley's vineyard, and see why the Yankee prospered where the *Californio* failed. Moxley's fields were beautifully tended. At the moment Indian laborers were cultivating them. But on Los Arcos, the vines grew as wild as ivy.

Yet there was more than Yankee ingenuity causing the *Californio's* distress. There was sharp trading, and there was dishonesty. Moneylenders offered loans at from two to ten per cent per day — and found takers, simple *hacendados* who had hardly heard of any currency but hides before the *gringo* came. In this summer of 1854 only a few of the greatest ranchers were still afloat.

The hot July sun, scorching their backs, was on the rim of the hills when the two crossed Los Angeles River. Mosquitoes came out of the moist tropical thickets to assail them. Just at dark they mounted a long plateau where the buildings of *Rancho* Los Arcos sprawled in open-handed magnificence.

A long arch of sycamores led to the ranch yard. Indian stable boys took their horses. *Don* Ignacio accompanied the American as far as the long gallery of the house. Brian had the feeling that the whole place was alive with small inconsequential beings — the sixty or seventy artisans and laborers who alone were necessary to maintain the headquarters of Los Arcos.

At the foot of the steps *Don* Ignacio left him with a smile just seen in the dusk and with a murmured: *"¡Buenas noches, patrón!"*

It stopped Lee Brian, put him off balance. "Good night, boss!" Before he could decide whether or not it was a joke, he was being greeted by two women at the top of the steps. He ascended, took the hand of old *Doña* Berta — Maria Catalina's grandmother — and bowed. He had not intended to bow. He had come here with a chip of defiance on his shoulder. He knew their opinion of Yankees. He would not bow and scrape like a Mexican to change it. But the face of this old woman who had lived through the glory of the colonial days demanded courtesy and got it. She was thin and brown and erect. She was inflexible, even when she smiled.

She spoke in Spanish. "So good of you to come, *Don* Brian. We were not sure . . . the *Yanqui* is always so occupied with business."

Brian did not return her smile. He wouldn't take any sarcasm from them. He'd paid what they asked for the lease on the waterfront. He'd bought thousands of hides from them, tons of tallow, and all at the going rates.

Maria spoke courteously. "My grandmother means we were presuming to ask you to visit us on such short notice. Thank you for coming."

They went through a spacious main hall to a smaller sitting-room. Here it was cool, softly lighted by many candles. Brian thought of this room as the heart of *Rancho* Los Arcos. Here they must spend much of their time — in an atmosphere dedicated to the old regime. The furniture was of ancient rosewood. There was a harpsichord in one corner and good rugs on the floor. There were articles of silver and crystal in abundance.

They talked commerce, the only place their lives touched.

"I told this to Ignacio," Brian said finally, "but I might as well repeat it. I'm letting my lease go. I'm going back to the States."

The women nodded, looking pleased. Brian began to fret in his mind. Would they ever come to the point? Asking a *gringo* to dinner — Ignacio called him "*patrón.*"

He got to studying Maria. She was damned pretty. She looked anything but dull. Framed in silver on the wall were pictures of her mother and father — her mother was a rather plain-looking Mexican woman, her father a shaggy, fierce-eyed Scot. Her father's blood had pastelled the dark native characteristics. It had given her light brown hair and blue eyes, put gold in the tawny skin.

But Captain Graham hadn't put any Yankee ideas in her head. He was one of the first white men to settle in Los Angeles back in the 'Thirties. Foreigners weren't welcomed then, but a sea captain with goods to barter and hard cash to pay could always get around the authorities. Some, like John Calvin Graham, found the country so pleasant and the people so friendly that they married Mexican women and took the Catholic faith along with, perhaps, thirty or forty thousand acres of pasturage. But John Graham had died seven years too early, as far as the good of his ranch was concerned. Since the Mexican War, Yankees had flocked unchecked into California, squatting on the unfenced range, going to court with the impractical *Californios,* fleecing and shaming them.

Lee Brian compared the faces of the father and daughter. He thought: *I'll bet your father didn't call you Maria. I'll bet he called you Katie.* Probably it was the grandmother, that withered flower of a dying vine, who kept in this house the perfume of the great days.

The girl's hands were folded in her lap. She did not look up as she said: "I wanted to talk to you about business, *Don* Brian."

"All right."

"You may know that Los Arcos has lost much since my father's death. I don't want to lose any more, if it can be helped. I thought you might help me." She glanced up at him.

Sitting there with the candlelight on him, Lee Brian looked darker than the girl. He was a large man, and he did enough physical work to keep his flesh hard and his skin brown. He began to frown.

"You're asking a Yankee," he said, "to help you?"

The grandmother was severely silent, her eyes on Maria, prompting her.

The girl continued to look at him. "Ignacio is a good majordomo, but he isn't a trader. He buys when the market is high. He sells when it is low. Our people have not been concerned with the market before. It is ruining us now. I would like to hire you as my overseer, *Don* Brian."

Brian held her eyes steadily. "As we say in the States," he commented, "'set a thief to catch a thief.' I'm not flattered, *señorita*."

He saw the flush come into her cheeks. "Is it so unreasonable?" she countered. "To mend harness, I have a harnessmaker. To make wine, I have vintners. To make money, I need a Yankee. It is a talent we lack."

Lee Brian asked leave to smoke and held a thin-twisted Mexican cigar over a candle until it began to smolder. Then he turned back.

"Do you know," he asked them, "what the others would say, if I managed Los Arcos, and it failed? That I was filling my pockets, robbing you behind your backs, while you went broke . . . and, of course, I could do that, if I wanted. But I don't need to."

The women looked at each other. Here was a factor more complex than they had expected. Here was an American who seemed to have a quality unlooked for in a Yankee — pride.

The window was open. Through it came the sound of a horse jogging up the road to the house. *Doña* Berta, her ear turned to the sound, frowned.

"*Señor* Rockwell's horse," she murmured. "I did not know he was coming."

Maria smiled. "Do we ever know when he is coming, *abuela?*"

■■

Clay Rockwell was thin and dark, a man of forty who possessed the courtliness of a Californian. Lee Brian had met him a few times and had been unimpressed. Rockwell's mouth smiled while his eyes were as busy as countinghouse clerks. He said all the right things, the apt things, but to Brian they lacked the ring of good metal.

Brian shook hands with him, and they went in to dinner. By tacit agreement the discussion was temporarily ended. Clay Rockwell talked well. He seemed to go everywhere and know everyone. He was one of the few Americans who were popular with the *rancheros*, chiefly because he extended himself to flatter them and their beautiful daughters.

Rockwell glanced at Brian. "I was talking to Juan Bandini yesterday," he said. "He tells me he's going to slaughter two thousand steers next month. I think you can get the hides, if you hurry."

"I'll let them pass," Brian said. "I'm all through with hides."

Rockwell raised an eyebrow. "Retiring?"

Brian shrugged. "Call it that."

Rockwell said thoughtfully: "If you're giving up the San

Pedro lease, I might be interested. I've been thinking that I ought to get back into business."

Brian had heard that Rockwell had made money in a freight line out of Sacramento during the bonanza in northern California. At any rate, he seemed to have enough money to live without working.

Doña Berta gave the idea a push. Rockwell seemed to be a favorite of hers. "*Don* Brian had found the harbor profitable," she suggested.

"To tell the truth," said Rockwell, "I've already given it some thought. I'd like to double the size of the tannery and put up some extra buildings where the ranchers can store things they want to sell to the ships. I can see quite a future for the harbor . . . a real town there, maybe."

Maria's cheeks were pink with pleasure. "You talk just as my father used to," she told him. "Always planning improvements . . . and making them."

Brian asked: "What are you going to do . . . lease San Pedro, or buy it? You can't build a town for somebody else and make a profit."

Clay Rockwell pressed the base of his wine glass firmly against the cloth. "I thought of a ten-year lease," he said. "Of course, I would have a commission out of the trading."

Doña Berta and Maria were excited. They could see wealth pouring into Los Arcos from the ships that stood offshore, hungry for trade. But the girl glanced at Brian and saw his frown. It may have been that, or mere caution, that caused her to put off the decision.

"We will talk about it, *Señor* Clay," she promised him.

After dinner the men were deftly maneuvered apart. *Doña* Berta insisted that Rockwell play a tune or two for her on the harpsichord. There were only she and Maria to play, and they knew only the melancholy native songs. Rockwell played the light-hearted tunes of the American, Stephen Foster.

Maria said to Brian: "It is so warm inside. Shall we walk down the river path?"

The breeze from the river was warm and moist, stirring the flat leaves of the great sycamores. The moonlight gleamed on Maria's bare arms and shoulders. She walked close to him, neither of them talking. From the top of the river path they could look down on the *bosque,* whispering with the small voices of the river.

For Lee Brian this country possessed an intoxication. He liked the great reaches of it, the wide valleys, lying between the ocean and the towering San Gabriels. He liked the tempo of it, in tune with the pulse of a man who went through life at a walk.

Brian glanced at the girl. He saw reflected in her face the same emotions that were in him. But it was a love of the land, completely divorced from practicality — an instinct, you could call it.

Suddenly he said: "You said a while ago that your father was always making improvements. Why did you stop when he died?"

Maria said simply: "Because I don't know where it needs improving."

"Do you think it would improve the ranch to have Rockwell in possession of the harbor?"

She looked up at him, and he thought she smiled a little. "You don't like *Señor* Clay," she said. "You wouldn't like any improvements he made, would you?"

Brian's teeth locked for an instant. *No,* he thought, *she isn't stupid.* She had known that he was feeling jealous even before he knew it.

"If you know him as well as you seem to," he stated, "he's the man you should get to manage Los Arcos. He knows the natives as well as the Americans."

Maria shook her head. "He is our friend, but friendship should be kept out of business."

Lee Brian smiled. "So naturally you thought of me," he said. "Managing Los Arcos wouldn't interest me, *señorita,* but something else might. A ranch like this doesn't have to lose money. It can make a fortune for its owner, as *Rancho* Laguna does for Gus Moxley. I think I could do that for Los Arcos. But if I did, I'd want to share in the profits." He took a fresh cigar from his pocket and rolled it thoughtfully between his hands. "I'll manage it for you," he said. "But as a partner."

Maria stared at him. "As a partner?" she said quickly. "I don't think so."

Brian shrugged. "It would be a lot safer than hiring me . . . or any other American . . . as an overseer. Your one sure defense against a Yankee is to have a Yankee interested in your welfare."

They walked on down the path. Once his hand brushed her bare arm, and a tingling went through him. Brian had known many girls, but Maria Graham affected him in a way that none of the others had. He liked to think that he could spend fifteen minutes with any woman under the sun and be able to classify her as passionate, cold, or indifferent. But Maria was a word written in a foreign tongue. She had a remoteness, like the sea. Your mind could reach out, trying to learn what was hidden beyond the horizon, but you might never know the things she chose to hide.

Just before they reached the house again, she confronted him. "My grandmother will think I've lost my mind," she said. "Perhaps I have. But I think you are right. . . . In the morning we can talk terms."

Lee Brian was startled. He had hardly been serious himself when he suggested it. He said: "All right. But there's one condition . . . that you don't give Clay Rockwell a ten-year lease before we sign the papers."

Maria lifted a shoulder carelessly. "As you say."

There were in Los Arcos ten guest rooms, to one of which a house servant conducted Lee Brian at ten o'clock. Walking through the silent halls, Brian was touched with an uneasiness. It was as if the body of Los Arcos lay here, with the blood, the spirit, drained out of it. Los Arcos, and a score of *ranchos* just like it, had begun to die when a Mexican general signed his name to a treaty at *Rancho* Cahuenga seven years before. There would be no more of the glorious extravagance of the *dons*. The Lugos, the Bandinis, the Verdugos were learning to be businessmen, or else they were being ruined. It was sad, but it was just. The system had been out of balance. Too many had been hungry, too many gorged — there was no in-between. Out of the present turmoil would come a better life for the *pobladores*.

Brian thought of his own boyhood. It had followed the usual sheltered pattern until cholera took both his parents when he was twelve. His uncle, Tom Bixby, kept him out of an orphanage by taking him on Bixby's three-masted brig, the *Lafayette*, as a cabin boy. There were times before Lee Brian left the ship when he wished that he had gone instead to the orphanage.

Tom Bixby did not understand boys, nor did he care to. What he understood was how to make a sharp trade. There were those who said he was one jump from piracy, while others swore he was a couple of jumps beyond. He was a harsh, uncommunicative man, and Brian feared his violent angers.

When Brian was eighteen, Captain Tom Bixby put him ashore at Mazatlán with fifty dollars and some advice.

"Set yourself up as a trader or something. Fifty dollars will go a long way down here. You can buy a hundred dollars' worth o' goods from the natives for ten, if you're canny."

Brian got his land legs under him and took his uncle's advice. He bought cheap goods from the natives and resold to the shipmasters. It was such a profitable trade that he never quite got away from it.

He wondered if John Calvin Graham had missed the sea. There would have been times when he yearned for her moods, when he stood bareheaded in a storm and felt his heart torn out of him. But there must have been a greater bond that held him to the land, or he would have left it.

As he blew out the candle, Brian noticed the sea chest against the wall. Above it hung an old-fashioned glass. He went to sleep thinking of an old Scot who scanned his glass every morning and night and who called his little girl "Katie."

In the morning, after breakfast, Clay Rockwell left the ranch. *Doña* Berta, haughtily silent, withdrew to her room.

Maria smiled. "Grandmother is not pleased," she explained. "But the ranch is mine. Ignacio is waiting in the office."

The office, by the look of it, was the least-used room in the house. It needed dusting in the corners; it needed airing. At a warped desk of native oak Maria sat down across from Brian. Ignacio — uneasy, frowning, tugging at his mustaches — sat in an armchair beside the girl.

"Of course, you will want to know what the ranch is worth," said Maria. She turned a fat ledger toward him. "According to my father's last estimate, he owned forty thousand acres, worth about seven thousand dollars. Since then fifteen thousand acres have gone, in sales and foreclosures. There are twenty-five thousand acres left, valued at five thousand dollars. That includes the parcel at San Pedro."

Brian saw that no entry had been made for over two years. "What about cattle?" he wanted to know.

Ignacio came to life. "*Ganados del campo* . . . eight thousand head, at four dollars each," he recited with pride.

Brian said: "Where are the tally books?"

Ignacio scratched his head. Then he began to nod. "*¡Ai, sí!*

Los palos . . . the sticks." He brought from a closet two bundles of willow wands, notched their whole lengths. "Ten cows to the notch," he declared. "Twenty-five notches to the stick. Thirty-two sticks. Eight thousand head!" he finished victoriously.

Eight thousand head. No record of brands or earmarks. Maria was unaware of any flaws in their bookkeeping. She went on quietly reciting the number in sheep, the acreage in grapes — she did not know how many plants. She finished the account almost with pride.

"And only one loan . . . three hundred dollars to *Don* Gus Moxley."

Brian's spine went back against the chair. "What interest?" he demanded.

Maria glanced at Ignacio for help. "Six per cent, I think."

"Eight, *señorita*."

Brian relaxed. But he said: "Let me see the note. It will have to be paid off."

The note stated in Gus Moxley's square black handwriting: "Three hundred dollars, with interest at eight per cent *per diem*, to be paid on call." The date was sixty days earlier.

Brian closed his eyes. He said slowly: "The loan was at eight per cent . . . *per day!* You owe over fourteen hundred dollars interest as of today. You can thank your saints it isn't compounded daily, or Moxley would own Los Arcos."

Maria was stunned, though only her eyes and her color betrayed it.

Brian weighed it all for a moment. He had nine thousand dollars. It would take him far. But if he failed to save *Rancho Los Arcos*, he would have nothing but a few bundles of tally sticks by which to remember his fortune.

"I can pay you twelve thousand for a half interest," he declared. "Nine thousand cash, three thousand to be paid within a year at six per cent interest . . . *per year*. Satisfactory?"

Maria nodded helplessly. "I suppose so."

"I'll get a lawyer in Los Angeles to write it up. I'll pay off Moxley and deposit the rest in your strong room."

"There's one other thing," Maria admitted. "I gave *Señor* Rockwell a lease on San Pedro . . . but just for two years!" she added hastily. "I didn't think it could do any harm. He might do the land a lot of good."

Brian shook his head in despair. He had a long row to hoe if he were ever to teach this girl the ways of the Yankee.

"My guess," he told her, "is that the land will probably do him more good than he will do it."

Lee Brian never enjoyed his days in the pueblo the mission fathers had blithely christened "The City of Our Lady, the Queen of the Angels." If the angels ever came through, they would hold their skirts high! You ate dirt with your meals; you slept in the dirt; you drank from dirty glasses in the *cantinas*.

It was Sunday night when he stabled his horse in the corral of the Bella Union Hotel on Main Street. His room was a sort of stall with one slit of a window, letting light and dust through the adobe wall. By this pallid light Brian wrote a letter to the Rothschild Bank in San Francisco. He hoped he could expect the gold specie within two months. He specified that it be sent by steamer, since there were many road agents between Los Angeles and San Francisco.

For want of better banking facilities Brian always left his money in a moneylender's safe until there was enough to ship north. In the morning he withdrew two thousand dollars. He sought a lawyer and had an instrument executed, dividing *Rancho* Los Arcos. Then he thought of Gus Moxley.

Moxley had earned twenty-four dollars on his note while Brian slept. It was a wonderful way to make money, providing you had no soul. Moxley hadn't. Acting on that theory, Brian took his way to the yard of the jail. Monday was auction day. Most of the ranchers came in to pay bail on a few dozen drunken Indians and take them back to work the money out. On Friday night they gave them drinking money again and bailed them out on Monday. The system was pat. It was part of the scheme that was corrupting the entire Indian population and robbing the *Californios* of their heritage.

Brian's hunch was right. Gus Moxley was helping his foreman and a *vaquero* to load fifteen sorry workmen into a wagon. Brian steeled himself for Moxley's pulpy handshake. He was a beer-fat Swiss who spoke a linguistic hash of German, Spanish, and broken English.

Moxley held his hand, patting him on the shoulder. "My good friend!" he exclaimed. "You come not often out of your cave. *Wie geht's?*"

"I've got some money for you," Brian said. "Maria Graham sent it over. I understand you hold a note of hers?"

Moxley appeared surprised. In the bright sunlight his skin looked unhealthy, gleaming with a light sweat. He had gross Teutonic features in which his eyes were the most outstanding feature, with a translucent look to the blue irises, and the whites yellowish.

"I hold her note," he said. "Why is it you who brings the money?"

Brian said: "I'm associated with Los Arcos now. I'll ride back with you."

They departed by the San Pedro road, which traversed the sloping tableland. Trees were few, beyond the cottonwoods bordering the river. A few miles south of the pueblo they entered August Moxley's land. His cattle grazed wide on many hills, fattening on *afilaria* and grama. Still farther out Brian and Moxley came to the mustard thickets, covering the mesa on

94

both the Los Arcos and the *Rancho* Laguna sides of the river. Until late spring this section was golden with wild mustard as high as a horse's head. By July the blossoms were gone, the stalks brown and dry.

Here, again, Lee Brian found a difference in Moxley's way of doing things from the easy California ways. The thickets north of the river had been well trampled by cattle and horses. Southward, they were still a jungle where outlaw cattle could hide. And as they rode, he saw something strange, occurring across the river.

Eight or ten longhorns broke from the brush, plunging down the shelving bank to the river. Behind them, a moment later, appeared three *vaqueros*. They swung rawhide ropes over their heads, chousing the cattle on. Then they saw the wagon on the river road. They stopped still.

The first to move was a Mexican on a big palomino. There was blood on the horse's hip from a jagged branch. Brian could discern it from here. The cowboy rode wide to intercept the cattle. The others, following, helped to throw the cattle back into the thicket.

They were gone again. Nothing was left but an expression of mild surprise on Gus Moxley's face, and a small suspicion in Brian's mind. Perhaps they were merely moving the cattle from the thicket, but Brian's impression was that they had been taking them across the river.

The wagon stopped at a mud shack at the edge of the vineyard. Dogs ran out to bark. A litter of children, wearing only shirts that came to their navels, stood shyly peeping from various points of vantage. A dark-skinned Mexican appeared, smiling, bowing, holding his hat to his breast. He made the polite Castilian inquiries as to their health. He said fervently: *"¡Grac' a Dios!"*

Gus Moxley said: "A fine day for sleeping, eh, Manuel?"

Manuel, who was the vineyard foreman, ceased to smile. "No, *patrón*. But all is well with the plants."

Moxley shook a fat finger at the fields. "Vines dragging in the dirt! The whole vineyard a jungle! *Lieber Gott,* do I pay you to sleep? See that these things are remedied."

Moxley dumped the Indians and rattled on in the empty wagon, Brian's horse jogging along beside. The Mexican, Manuel, stood silent and shamed before the adobe. A fine maker of money, August Moxley, thought Brian, only he would never get his money's worth out of these people. They had pride, the humblest of them. They were sentimental and faithful and hard-working. What Moxley did with a club, he could have done better with kindness.

The rancher's headquarters, on a knoll overlooking the river, had a solid, permanent look. Inside, the main building was cool, dark, and dusty. Moxley thought first of wine, after the hot ride. He filled two glasses. He sat in a rawhide-bottomed chair with his fat legs spread apart. His hand held the wine to the light.

"Zinfandel," he grunted. "I import the cuttings myself. No other rancher in California can make such a wine. How do you like it, *Don* Brian?"

Brian sniffed it. He wet his lips. He put the glass down with a grimace. It had the same fault as its maker — it was crude. It had the heaviness of grape juice and the sourness of vinegar.

"I like it," Brian said, "about as much as I like the loans you write."

He had his saddlebag on the floor beside him. He opened it and stacked seventeen hundred and fifty dollars in gold pieces before the scowling Swiss. He added fourteen silver dollars. "Receipt," he said.

Gus Moxley took the original note from a strong box. He endorsed it at the bottom, dated it, slid it across the table to

Lee Brian. Then he gave a sheepish smile.

"These *Californios!*" he deprecated. "They are children. Finally they lose everything. Much better that their land goes to men who know how to build. *Zo?*"

Brian put the paper away only after examining it closely. "You won't be dealing with children any more at Los Arcos," he remarked. "I've bought in."

He walked out on August Moxley and his consternation.

Nothing had been said about Lee Brian's place of residence now that he was half-owner of the Graham ranch. But that night, when he returned, a desk had been moved into the bedroom he had occupied before he left for Los Angeles. An armchair also had been brought in and a round mahogany table with silver candelabra. It was gratifying, but quite obvious: this corner of the house was his domain. Beyond the door he was not expected to roam.

Brian looked the room over, his hands jammed in his pockets. The grandmother again . . . ? Or was it? Someone, at any rate, with far less business sense than sense of caste. Someone who thought Yankees should be kept in their place.

He smoked a cigar without tasting anything but his resentment. They must come to an understanding. There would be no working while they held daggers at each other's throats. Or, if that pride of the Arango y Grahams proved to be of the metal that shatters rather than bends, he would sell out. They could take their chances with the Gus Moxleys.

He hunted up Ignacio in the morning. "Have some food packed for a few days," he told him. "I want to go over every acre with you."

They rode first to the winery, about a mile from the headquarters. The winery was a large adobe building constructed in the style of a mission. The winemaker was a man proud of his trade. He saluted Brian cordially, and took the men down to the cellar.

Here it was cool, almost chilly. The rays of a candle reached out feebly to trace long corridors formed by barrels and hogsheads. Dust lay upon everything. Everywhere there was the sour aroma of wines.

The vintner drew a cup of wine for the *patrón*. Brian closed his eyes with enjoyment as he drank. He spoke the word that pleases the artist most: "Ah!"

The Mexican rubbed his hands. He made a quiet boast. "Any man can crush grapes, but it is given to only a few to make wine."

Brian had an inspiration. He saw that the butts of the casks carried only scrawled dates. That was too plain a dress for a wine that might go clear to Massachusetts, perhaps to a governor's table. Men ought to know what they were drinking, when they bought this wine.

"Burn our brand on every cask," he directed. "Have another branding iron made that says, Los Arcos Wine. Next year we'll ask fifty percent more, and get it."

They left the winery. The morning was hot and clear, without a rag of cloud to mar the sky. The hoofs of their ponies struck up puffs of dust as they rode.

Brian was thinking about the cowboys he had seen from the river road the day before. He asked Ignacio: "Who has charge of the cattle?"

Ignacio said: "I am responsible for everything . . . the cattle, the sheep, the vineyards. But," he admitted, "in each I have a subordinate. For the *ganados,* the corporal is Angel Rubio."

"Why hasn't he run the mustard thickets yet?"

Ignacio shrugged. "We will ask Rubio. His camp is not far."

Nevertheless, dusk had drawn deeply over the mesa when they reached the range camp. A dozen pole-and-mud *jacales* formed a rude village in the wilderness of mesquite, boulders, and tough plains grasses. Candles burned already within them, and the air was heavy with the fragrance of evening, the tang of wood fires, and the rousing odors of Mexican cooking.

Ignacio, sitting his horse by the stone corral, raised a shout: "Angel!"

Dogs had heralded the visitors, and now a horde of children appeared, and behind them a few *vaqueros*. One of the men raised his hand. *"¡'Tardes, compadres!"*

Ignacio introduced Brian to the range boss. And Brian knew as he took his hand that this was the man who had reconsidered driving the cattle across the river yesterday.

III

Angel Rubio took them into his house. The women — his wife and an unidentified ancient crone — stood silently beside the brick stove as the men ate. The cabin seemed to squirm with children.

Rubio had black, noticing eyes. He was swarthy, pock-marked, and dirty. Every finger of his long hands wore a ring. About his neck went a thin silver chain that supported a medallion hidden beneath his shirt.

Brian, feeling some responsibility as a guest, did not mention the purpose of their visit until after the last gray cup of coffee. He said through the smoke of their cigars: "How goes the *rodeo*, my friend?"

Rubio raised one eyebrow. "The *rodeo*," he said, "finishes itself six weeks past. Ignacio has the tally sticks."

"I mean the other roundup," said Brian. "The *corrida*."

Rubio knew what he meant. In this country a man had to conduct two roundups a year, or half his cattle were born, lived, and died in the mustard thickets.

"Ah! The *corrida!* One day soon," said Rubio, "we must get to it. Last year we are running the thicket too soon. The branches are green, and they trip our horses. We lose time and have to run it over again."

"They're dry now," Brian declared. "We'll run it tomorrow."

Rubio agreed gravely: *"Muy bien,* tomorrow."

Hospitably he offered his floor as a bed, but Lee Brian preferred to roll himself in his blanket under a liveoak. The night was cool; the sky was star-frosted jet. He heard a man singing softly a song of unrequited love — their songs all seemed to be of unrequited love and untimely death, these people who made happiness out of so little. The song caused him to think drowsily of Maria. He was sorry for her, trying to preserve a little kernel of a day that was gone, but another side of his mind was uneasy, afraid.

He wished she had been stupid and homely. He wished there were other girls around to interest him. It was a bad sign when a man's thoughts drifted to the same woman every time his mind was unoccupied. It was an omen still worse when he found himself thinking of her the last thing at night.

It was all wrong, the whole picture. They had nothing in common but Los Arcos and a stubborn vein of pride. Lee Brian was thinking that a man never fell in love so hard as with the wrong woman, and he was thinking that a man in love was apt to forget his pride and everything else. He would have to watch out. He would have to take himself in hand like an unbroken horse, pulling his nose against the snubbing post every time he found himself getting foolish. However, he decided with relief that, as long as he recognized the danger, he need not worry.

He had not been asleep an hour when in his dreams she

came to him, her hands held out, her red lips parted, laughing at him — laughing Katie Graham.

Sounds of movement woke him. Cowboys were cutting their horses out of the *caballada*. A woman was screaming at a child to come out of the corral. Lee Brian washed his face in cold water and felt the tough black stubble on his jaws. He had coffee with Ignacio and Rubio, still gloomy with sleep. They ate fried beans rolled in corn tortillas, and then tucked a few of the papery tortillas and a little jerky in their pockets for the midday meal.

This day the *vaqueros* took care that their saddle girths were snug. There would be hard riding — undoubtedly a few falls. Their saddles were the high wooden trees of Mexico, rawhide-covered with horns as large and flat as plates.

They rode west to the edge of the hot, stifling brush jungle. Rubio dispersed his men in a wide crescent, one end of the line touching the river, the other extending south. They began to push into the thicket, yelling, beating the brush with rawhide ropes. Brian was near the center. A hundred yards from him, on the right, rode Angel Rubio. Ignacio was at a like distance on the left. Soon they were out of sight of each other.

Cattle began to move. Their crashing progress, their bawling, added to the clamor of the drive. Lee Brian dropped his coiled rope back over his shoulder and rode ahead. There were some things he wanted to know about the cattle before they were allowed to filter onto the range.

He found a lane through the brush, one of a hundred of cow paths that criss-crossed the area. He surprised a few shaggy longhorns, but never got a throw. Then he came without warning into a small arena.

Cattle had been worked here, many of them. A dozen lanes converged in the round clearing. There were the ashes of old branding fires. There was a small heap of scorched sacking. Lee Brian did not have to look at the sacking to know what he would find, but he dismounted and picked up one of the coarsely woven bags.

It was a typical article of the cattle thief's trade: a sack that had been held, water-soaked, against a steer's hide while the *fierro* was made. It caused the iron to blister, rather than to burn. It gave the effect of an old brand within a few days. The brand that had been made at this fire was an Arrow and Circle. It was the brand of August Moxley.

In this bedlam of shouting cowboys and moving cattle, small sounds were not easily picked out. Thus Lee Brian did not sense the reata dropping over his shoulders until the throw was completed, and he was jolted to the ground.

He was conscious of the hard earth raking away the skin on one side of his face. He was in motion, skidding over the ground, slewing into the brush, not feeling any pain, but conscious of a choking terror. Suddenly his motion stopped, and, looking up the taut length of the twisted rawhide, he saw that it was caught in the cleft of a mesquite stump and that beyond it, swearing savagely through his white teeth, Angel Rubio tried to flip the rope free so that he could drag the American on.

Lee Brian flung his arm outward, loosening the rope. He came up on his knees, the dragoon pistol he carried coming out of a dirt-choked holster. Rubio saw him, and he saw the gun. He released the snagged rope and spurred into the brush.

Brian fired. The horse stumbled. It went down with the corporal pitching headlong over its head. Brian ran down the path so that, when the Mexican rose, he was looking into the muzzle of a .44.

Rubio began to talk, choking with defeated rage. "We don't need a damned *Yanqui* here! Three years I am foreman for *Don* Juan Graham. He does not meddle. The *señorita* does not meddle. Then why do *you* come meddling?"

Brian answered: "Because you're a damned cow thief. You've been branding Los Arcos cattle and turning them over to Gus Moxley."

"We brand the strays as we find them," said Rubio. "So there is less work at the *rodeo*."

Brian made a gesture with his gun. "Loosen your gun belt and let it drop."

Some of the fear went out of Rubio's eyes. He was not to be shot. A man did not disarm his enemy and then shoot him.

Brian kicked the gun into the brush. He holstered his own pistol. "In the States," he said, "this is the way we tell a thief he's fired." His hand went out like a flicked rope.

On Rubio's face there was blood — and hatred. He lunged at the American, reaching for Brian's gun. Brian slugged him on the ear, bringing him to his knees. He was in close as soon as Rubio staggered up. He pumped a fist into Rubio's belly. He stepped in to break the long hawkish nose with a chopping blow.

Blinded, Angel Rubio fell back, holding his hands out in front of him. Lee Brian had the taste of savagery on his tongue. He had no pity for this man who knew nothing of fighting with his fists. He felt no emotion but a brutal urge to see him on the ground, whipped.

When Rubio lowered his hands, Brian jolted him with a blow to the face. He sank a short punch into the man's body, and Rubio turned green and began to gasp. With two more blows Brian finished him.

Ignacio came plunging from the brush. "*Don* Brian!" he was shouting; and then he saw them. He took in the rope and the skinned, dirty *gringo*, standing over the corporal. He said: "I am glad you shot him. I wish I had seen it, to do it myself. He is a stupid pig. Why did he try to kill you?"

"He isn't dead," Brian said. He began to wipe blood and dirt from his burning face. He told the older man what had happened. He added: "We'll finish the roundup. He can find his way back. He's through, and so is every man at the camp. He's had accomplices, so they'll all have to go."

In the tally that afternoon there were three hundred head of unbranded cattle. Brian himself jammed the smoking irons against each red-brown flank. A *vaquero,* armed with a sharp knife, deftly made the *señal* — the earmark. Ignacio stood by, frowning.

They spent the night again at the range camp, but this time Lee Brian spread his blankets far out, with his gun at his hand.

IV

They took a looping route back to Los Arcos, cutting through the vineyard, two hundred acres of almost untended vines. The plants sprawled recklessly across the ground, so that it was difficult to tell which way the rows ran. Already the bunched grapes were becoming dusty purple, but there would be only a fifty per cent crop, unless the grapes were soon rescued from the ground.

Brian thought of Moxley's vineyardist, the mustachioed man full of bows and gentle phrases. He said: "That man of Moxley's . . . Manuel, the vineyard-tender. Get him for me. Offer him fifteen dollars more than Moxley pays him. Moxley's been stealing our cattle. We'll steal his man."

As they approached Los Arcos, Ignacio remarked: "*¡Mire!* A visitor who rides a burro!"

The burro, bridled but without a saddle, stood rein-tied

outside the corral. Brian's foot was on the step when he heard a loud, familiar laugh. He hesitated, caught in a rush of almost forgotten emotions and memories. Dark nights, when he was tossed about in the forecastle of a shoddy, disreputable little brig. Days of wind and sleet, while he tried to set a new block high in the rigging with his uncle, bellowing from the safety of the deck.

He went inside. *Doña* Berta and Maria sat side by side on the sofa, glancing around as he entered, to stare at his scratched face and dirty clothes. The room was blue with the smoke of rank pipe tobacco. Brian looked at the visitor, sitting carelessly in an armchair.

He said: "It's been a long time, Uncle."

Captain Tom Bixby stood up. "Lee, lad!" he exclaimed. He shook hands warmly, and his eyes sparkled with amusement at Brian's stiffness. They stood a moment facing each other, then Brian abruptly turned and walked to a chair.

"Where did you hear of me?" he asked.

"I was speaking with a friend of yours only yesterday," said Captain Bixby. "Mister Clay Rockwell. I dropped anchor yesterday and came ashore to see what was to be bought hereabouts. Rockwell mentioned you. 'Saints be praised!' said I. 'Is the lad playing at being a great rancher now?'"

Tom Bixby looked much older, more careless of his person, than his nephew remembered him. He had a head of disheveled gray hair, growing far back on each side, and his sideburns were ragged and almost covered his large ears. Brian remembered the sensuous lips and the brows like a black bar. He recalled how the whole face could light up like a madman's when the captain was in one of his furies.

Brian thought Bixby's eyes looked harried. They couldn't rest. Brian wondered how many ports he daren't put into by this time. He asked casually: "What are you calling your ship now, Uncle?" and watched the quick thrust of anger into those eyes.

But Tom Bixby retained his good humor. "The *Clementine*," he said. "Had her overhauled and refitted two years ago. I hope you aren't forgetting the fine old days in the fo'c'stle, are you, boy?"

Doña Berta murmured an apology and rose. "I will see what ails that lazy thing of a cook," she said. Maria departed with her.

Lee Brian leaned forward with his elbows on his knees. "Now," he said, "what in the devil are you after? You wouldn't ride fifteen miles on a burro to say hello to me."

Captain Tom Bixby crammed coarse flakes of tobacco into his gnarled pipe and, walking to the table, took up a candle. When he had it going, he turned back.

Brian had crossed and was standing just behind him. Brian pulled the pipe from his uncle's lips and flung it into the corner fireplace.

He was relishing the situation. "I think you used to forbid smoking on the *Lafayette* when you were displeased," he said. "You can consider that you're before the mast in this house. And this time I'm the master."

Bixby's broad face with its deep corrugations turned red. He began to swear, as only a sailor can swear, and as only Tom Bixby among sailors, but he kept his voice down. Brian waited with his hands in his pockets. He was the one in his prime now — his uncle was the one at a disadvantage. The captain knew it. He hated his nephew for it, but he was still a canny one. He went back and sat down, clutching his knees with his hands.

"Let it pass," he said. "I come on business. I've been out of Salem two years, and I go back soon. I want hides and tallow . . . and good wine, if there is such a thing in this country."

"There's wine on Los Arcos," said Brian. "But you'll pay

for it. You can get wine from Moxley fit to pickle a boot in. None of the other ranchers are making much beyond their needs. As far as hides go, we've got a few hundred. The slaughtering won't be for a month yet." He added: "But you'll pay in gold for everything we sell you."

"I've got gold," said Tom Bixby. "I suppose this damned slaughtering proposition means I'll have to hang around all summer."

"I hope not," said his nephew.

At dinner Captain Bixby ate hugely, appreciative of the fresh vegetables and beef. He smacked his lips over the wine. Brian was glad when the food and liquor began to make him drowsy. His uncle stretched.

"I find the bridge of a jackass more wearing than that of a brig," he announced. "If there's a spare corner where I can rest a watch or two, I'll be obliged."

When Brian came back from settling his uncle in a guest room, he found Maria alone in the parlor, displeasure pinching her brows. She had some half-finished fancywork on her lap, but her hands now lay idle.

"Ignacio tells me there was trouble at the *corrida*," she mentioned. "He says Angel Rubio tried to kill you."

Brian said: "We found in the brush three hundred *orejanos* that he was hiding."

Maria glanced coldly at him. "Was that any reason to fire all the rest of the men?"

"Certainly," Brian said. "At least half of them must have been in it with him. How can you tell the thieves from the loyal ones by looking at them?"

"It wasn't fair!" Maria declared. "Those men need the work. They have families. *Rancho* Los Arcos has always taken care of its own. I told Ignacio to keep them on."

Brian leaned on the mantel, one hand tucked in his pocket.

He could see that she had fortified herself for the encounter. He smiled and saw her eyes drop, but still the high color of anger was on her cheekbones.

"That means," he said, "that I'll have to countermand the order. Did you get yourself a Yankee partner just to override his suggestions?"

"But this is cruel! My father would never have done it this way. He would have fired Rubio and trusted the new corporal to watch the rest."

"On twenty-five thousand acres a man needs good eyes to do that," Brian told her. He took a gold piece from his pocket. "In the States," he said, "we settle an argument with a coin when we can't decide it any other way."

Maria sat with her hands clenched in her lap. She said: "All right."

Brian poised the gold piece on his thumb. "Heads, they go. Tails, they stay." He sent the coin up in a shining arc. They both watched it strike the carpet and come to rest face up.

The girl made an exclamation and arose. She turned to the door, but Brian was there to block her way.

"We've got to come to an understanding," he said without rancor. "We can't go on settling arguments with a coin. If you want to buck the Yankees, you've got to use Yankee methods. I'm not being cruel. I'm only being practical."

She bit her lip. "I suppose so," she said dubiously. She looked very young and very perplexed and, suddenly, very desirable. The candlelight behind her kindled a shower of sparks in her hair. The creamy skin above her bodice looked warm and alive. He had never stood so close to her before, and the experience was making him breathless.

He said: "How can a man ever keep up with you? A minute ago you were Maria Arango . . . proud and haughty and impractical. And all of a sudden you know you've been wrong, and now you're Katie Graham."

She started. "*Katie* . . . why do you call me that?" she asked.

Brian knew he had guessed right. He knew by the way she had caught her breath. "Someone else used to call you Katie, didn't he?" he said. "He hoped you'd have enough of his blood to carry you through the days that were coming. I think you have. But you'll need a little pushing."

There was a challenge in her eyes. There was a dare. "And you think that you're the one to push me, *Don* Brian?"

All the good resolutions he had made under the stars the other night had died with the stars. He took the last step.

"Yes," he said softly. "I think I'm the one, Katie."

Within the hard circle of his arms she was passive. It was too surprising to her for her to react normally. Her body was against his, melting to him. Her lips were parted, and he kissed them roughly. In that moment, while it lasted, there was only desire and fulfillment.

Then Maria pulled away, her face flaming. Brian waited, not triumphantly, but with a kind of desperation in his eyes. He had not wanted this to happen any more than she had. The thing he had greatly feared had come to pass.

She went back to the sofa. She picked up her fancywork and returned. She paused beside him, looking down at the embroidery.

"You mustn't do that again, ever," she said. "I suppose you drank too much wine at dinner. If it happens again, we'll have to break the partnership."

He watched her move down the hall, her footfalls hurrying, carrying her away from something she could not have escaped on the fastest horse on Los Arcos. *Too much wine,* she had said. She was mistress of the art of self-deception!

Brian blew out the candles, and for a long time he stood at the window. In the moonlight the road led away into the darkness. He could ride down that road right now, forgetting the partnership. He could stop payment on his draft. But the places the road took him would be colored by the memory of Los Arcos. He would know he had left something half finished. He would wonder if it had been the same with Katie Graham as it had been with him. Katie — she would never be Maria to him again.

He went upstairs. He would stay through the fall shipping, at least. If he could straighten Los Arcos out, if he could instill some trading sense in Katie and *Doña* Berta, they might be able to hold out.

In the morning Captain Tom Bixby and his nephew talked business. "I can use," said the master of the *Clementine*, "about ten barrels o' good wine, at a good price, all the hides you've got on hand, and all the tallow."

The thought uppermost in Lee Brian's mind was to get rid of Bixby. He could best do that by selling him some merchandise so that the captain could profitably weigh anchor. They rode to the winery. The vintner brought red earthen cups of a dozen different wines.

Bixby sampled them all, with much smacking of lips. He selected three — a muscatel, a sweet red wine, and a dry.

"How much the barrel?" he asked.

Brian calculated. "Thirty a barrel," he said.

"Thirty!" Bixby spat on the dirt floor. "Moxley will sell me wine for twenty."

"Moxley doesn't make wine," Brian said. "He makes

vinegar. In ten years he may make a decent wine. . . . The price is thirty."

The captain, hands in his pockets, rocked on his heels. He was silent for half a minute. "Laddie," he said at last, "you've forgotten the trials of a seafaring man. How much do you think it costs me to carry a cask of wine back to Salem? No York shilling, I can tell you! Why," he said, chuckling, "you'd keep me around here, haggling, until you died of old age and old Tom Bixby inherited half of all the wines on Los Arcos."

Something caught Lee Brian around the heart like a cold fist. It was the fear that had been trying to make itself articulate to him ever since he first laid eyes on his uncle in the parlor — the chance that, if anything happened to him, Tom Bixby would step in and claim his nephew's half of the ranch. Brian could guess the rest — Bixby would gorge himself on plunder as a man might gorge on meat. But he could not let his uncle see that he was shaken, for Tom Bixby fought best when the other man was on his knees.

"If you're for cheap wines," Brian said, "we've got them too. Feliciano," he told the vintner, "bring us some of the green." He imparted a wink to the Mexican who had been standing speechless at the possibility of Brian's getting ten dollars a barrel more than he had ever seen wine sell for at Los Arcos.

"*¡Ai, si!*" Feliciano disappeared into the cellar.

Bixby complained about carrying second-rate merchandise back to Massachusetts. But the wines Feliciano brought pleased him — and why not, since they were the same he had just drunk? Too, there was Brian's logic to convince him.

"If I know the *Clementine*, it'll be a year yet before you reach Salem. By that time the wine will have a bouquet like Napoleon brandy. You'll get your money out of it . . . twenty-two dollars for a fifty-gallon barrel."

"Ah, well," Bixby growled, convinced he was getting a bargain but unwilling to show it.

They rode to a barn adjoining a series of corrals. Within the poled enclosures the earth was dark, enriched with the blood of thousands of cattle, for these were the *matanzas*, the slaughtering corrals. There were giant iron kettles suspended on tripods above the ashes of rendering fires. There were lengths of rawhide stretched between cross bars like clotheslines, where the *carne seca* was dried before baling.

The barn was gloomy and echoing, rank with the odors of uncured hides. It was nearly empty. Laborers dragged a hundred or more hides onto the floor.

"Four dollars apiece," said Brian.

Bixby did not question this. It was a standard price, fluctuating little more than the value of a silver dollar. He stipulated: "These are the prices on the beach. Is that right?"

Brian said: "Of course."

Before noon the whole cargo was loaded into eight *carretas* and started in the direction of San Pedro. After lunch Brian started for the harbor with his uncle. It was usual for the seller to pay the customs. And, besides, it would be comforting to see the *Clementine*'s canvas disappear beyond Dead Man's Island.

They rode with the sun on their faces. The earth was hot, the smell of sage stiflingly sweet. They passed the range camp. Of Rubio and his crew there were no signs. The new men, under a new corporal, were out of camp. A new harem of women, a different horde of children, had taken over the shacks.

They passed the slow-creaking carts with their plodding oxen and somnolent drivers. Late in the afternoon they came across the sand dunes to the welcome coolness of the ocean breeze. Beyond them lay the lagoons, the marshes, the tannery. At the customs shack the collector was hauling down the flag. Beyond the rocks the *Clementine* rolled ponderously at anchor. She

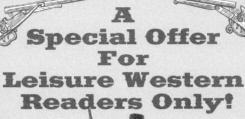

GET YOUR 4 FREE* BOOKS NOW— A VALUE BETWEEN $16 AND $20

Mail the Free* Book Certificate Today!

FREE* BOOKS CERTIFICATE!

YES! I want to subscribe to the Leisure Western Book Club. Please send me my 4 FREE* BOOKS. Then, each month, I'll receive the four newest Leisure Western Selections to preview FREE* for 10 days. If I decide to keep them, I will pay the Special Member's Only discounted price of just $3.36 each, a total of $13.44 ($14.50 US in Canada). This saves me between $3 and $6 off the bookstore price. There are no shipping, handling or other charges.* There is no minimum number of books I must buy and I may cancel the program at any time. In any case, the 4 FREE* BOOKS are mine to keep—at a value of between $17 and $20!

*In Canada, add $5.00 Canadian shipping and handling per order for first shipment. For all subsequent shipments to Canada the cost of membership in the Book Club is $14.50 US, which includes $7.50 shipping and handling per month. All payments must be made in US currency.

Name _____

Address _____

City_____ State _____ Country_____

Zip_____ Telephone_____

Tear here and mail your FREE* book card today!

If under 18, parent or guardian must sign. Terms, prices and conditions subject to change. Subscription subject to acceptance. Leisure Books reserves the right to reject any order or cancel any subscription.

Get Four Books Totally F R E E* — A Value between $16 and $20

Tear here and mail your FREE* book card today!

PLEASE RUSH MY FOUR FREE* BOOKS TO ME RIGHT AWAY!

LeisureWestern Book Club
P.O. Box 6613
Edison, NJ 08818-6613

AFFIX
STAMP
HERE

looked dirtier than ever to Brian, her rigging out of trim, her furled canvas gray with mildew.

Clay Rockwell stood in the ruddy sunset light before his cabin. There was a horse tethered in the salt grass behind the house. Brian looked more closely and discovered the heavy shape of August Moxley in the doorway.

Rockwell was casually cordial. He had a boy take Brian's horse and Bixby's rented burro.

"Los Angeles is becoming quite a crossroads," he remarked. "I dare say, if you stayed at this harbor long enough, you'd meet everyone you'd ever know. Fancy your encountering your uncle out here."

He laughed, but Brian was sober, watching Moxley advance with that waddle of his. Rockwell introduced Moxley to the captain. They stood about, making pointless talk.

Moxley said with a sly look at Brian: "I suppose I can't sell you some excellent Zinfandel, *Herr Hauptmann?*"

"Loaded up," said Tom Bixby. "The stuff will be down sometime tonight."

It couldn't be too soon, thought Brian. The *Clementine* couldn't shake out her mainsail too early in the morning to suit him.

Rockwell was speaking to him with a warmness that went only as far as his lips: "Of course, you'll stay here tonight?"

"I'll check in the stuff at the customs and head back," Brian told him. "I might as well go up and get the general in a good frame of mind."

Gus Moxley spat and wiped his lips. "There is," he stated, "one small matter . . . about using the harbor facilities." He glanced at Clay Rockwell, a smile turning the corners of his mouth.

Rockwell's color darkened. He said resentfully: "Damn it, Brian, I didn't know Gus was going to be in on this. Trust him to turn a dollar where he can. You see, he advanced the money

113

to make the improvements I plan. Now I find he's my senior partner."

The Swiss spread his hands. "Can I loan money to a man who wants to give it away? So I tie the string around it. For a little while, my friends, we will have to charge for the privilege of the harbor. I thought of a fifteen percent usage charge."

Tom Bixby whistled. He cocked an eye at his nephew. "On the beach," he reminded, "was the understanding."

Lee Brian's face had not changed. He had not moved. "You didn't tell Katie Graham where you were getting the money, did you?" he asked Rockwell.

Rockwell shrugged. "She didn't ask. I tell you," he insisted, "it came as a surprise to me. I don't like it any better than you. Of course, I can see Gus's point, too. He wants to make something on his investment. Only fifteen percent seems a little steep."

"You're a coward as well as a liar," Brian told him. "You wouldn't come right out and admit you're going to rob the citizens, would you? No, you'd hide behind a pig like Moxley. Do you think Los Angeles is going to let you get away with this? It's the only port within a hundred miles, as you damned well know. You'll take your fifteen per cent out in tar and feathers."

Rockwell was edgy, his lips pale. "You can talk to Gus," he snapped. "I'm not setting the rates."

"I'm talking to both of you. It's a great idea, but the heel's going to come down on it. I expected you had something like this in mind when you asked for the lease. You've played the dog at rich men's tables so long you can't even look honest."

He was taunting him, daring him to challenge anything he said. Rockwell's mouth hardened. His eyes hated Brian. He looked fully into the dark, angry countenance and said nothing.

"Youth," sighed August Moxley. "Hot blood. So many

things we say when we are young and angry. You will find, my friend, that your fifteen per cent is well spent . . . with the money I shall enlarge the harbor, build a dock, warehouses."

Brian spoke gruffly to his uncle. "It's no deal," he said. "I'll take the stuff back."

Captain Bixby looked placidly out at sea. A longboat had set out from the *Clementine* to take him aboard.

"Well, well," he said. "Hazards of the trade. Still and all, I want the wines. Tell you what, lad. I want to haul 'round to Santa Barbara while the wind is favorable. I may be gone a month. No doubt you'll have settled your differences by then."

Brian watched him walk to the edge of the water, just clear of the dark margin of wet sand. Then he turned, without a word to Rockwell or Moxley, and walked toward the custom collector's shack.

VI

The general was a throwback to the days, not so long gone, when the seal of Mexico was embossed on every paper he signed. The general — Juan Antonio Baca — had taken out citizenship at the coming of the Americans and gratefully accepted thereby the retention of his position. His office was a white-washed frame building on the hill, distinguished from the less important shacks of the village by the flagpole and a brass cannon.

Juan Baca was a portly little man who wore dirty white trousers and shirt and gold earrings. He had a brave white mustache that he kept honed to saber sharpness.

"So you leave me," he said sadly to Brian. "You leave the

poor old general to the crabs and the *indios*."

Brian sighed for the uncomplicated days of the hide trade, when Katie Graham was no more than the memory of a girl he had once seen.

"A *gringo* never knows when he's well off, General," he declared. "Last month I was *hombre rico*. Tonight it seems I'm going to lose everything I made down here. If the tax stays on for two years, *Rancho* Los Arcos is finished."

The general let his glance turn darkly down the hill in the direction of Rockwell's shack. "They think they shall make a fortune," he said. "But I think they will make nothing. It is in my mind that we go back to the old days of smuggling."

"Ah!" Brian nodded. This unlocked the very door he had been contemplating with some interest. "I've heard," he admitted, "that there are caves up the coast where they used to hide goods they were going to smuggle out to the ships."

"Many of them. There are two within a few miles of where we sit." Juan Baca twirled a spike of his mustache. "Though not since Pio Pico do I see any smuggling."

Lee Brian cleared his throat. He tried to frame his thoughts so that the general would understand without taking offense. "As long as the stuff was duty paid, I suppose you wouldn't care whether it went through here or not," he suggested.

The general did not immediately reply. Neither did he look at Brian. The brown flesh about his eyes crinkled. He watched the waves curl in, pink froth and sapphire in the sunset. He was studying it out, testing the idea as he might test a coin.

"I do not see," said the general finally, "where it would be dishonest. So long as I am paid the duty."

He began to nod solemnly, and Brian nodded with him.

"We understand each other," he said, smiling. He watched the rim of the sun drop through a spray of mist. Darkness, and the cold evening breeze, rose from the sea. The darkness hid many things, Brian was thinking, the bad as well as the good. It hid the boats that might pass in the night. It hid the beaches where smugglers and sea captains made rendezvous.

"About the caves . . . ?" he said. "Could a man store a few loads in them without waking up everybody in San Pedro?"

"By the cliff trail," said Juan Baca, "they are three miles. There is no danger. I myself will take you."

Between Portuguese Point and Point Fermin the waves rode in arrogantly, with a rising roar, to end in magnificent disaster on the rocks. There was a trail, almost lost in purple sand verbena, which led to a stairway in the face of the cliff.

By moonlight they lowered the hides and the casks of wine to the caves. There were old stains of candle grease on the floor and a few rotted hides. Standing on the ledge before the cave, Brian tried to chart the passage through the rocks. There was a single stretch of beach where a boat might land.

Risk there would be, of life as well as of cargo, but in the end it might be the only way out. Probably there was nothing they could do legally to pry Moxley from his hold on the harbor. Brian was not sure that he could arouse the other ranchers to unified action. *Californios* weren't natural fighters. They had never needed to fight, and he doubted that a Yankee would be the one to stir them.

All he did know was that they couldn't give away fifteen percent of their profits and still exist. There was an American invention called the tax that made certain of this. It had the eroding force of the ocean itself. It came disguised as state tax, county tax, jail tax, school tax, and even grazing tax. Profits might hibernate, but taxes roamed summer and winter.

You could never count on Katie Graham's reactions. When Brian brought her word of the situation at the harbor, she took it petulantly.

117

"Why couldn't Clay be telling the truth?" she inquired. "That fat one, Moxley, has him in his hand . . . just as he has us. Would it be to Clay's profit to be no more than a majordomo at San Pedro?"

Doña Berta, stitching a pillowcase, did not look up. But she frowned at her work, and her needle punched the cloth more slowly. Brian threw his cigar at the fireplace and started for the door. He stopped to confront the girl. His patience hung by a slender thread.

"I'm not surprised that you can still stand up for him," he declared. "What surprises me is that you haven't given him power-of-attorney over the range a long time ago. You've done almost as well by giving him the lease. But there's one port still open to us, and I'm going to use it."

She looked at him questioningly.

"I expect you to keep this to yourself," Brian told her. "I've made a deal with the customs collector. He'll let me smuggle our goods out to the ships if I pay duty. And I'm going to try it, if every hide on the place goes to the bottom!"

He talked over the matter of slaughtering with Ignacio. Ignacio knew cattle, even if he needed a little prodding to make use of his wisdom. "We've got about six weeks to get ready," Brian told him. "After October no ship is going to stand off shore waiting for the weather. How many cattle can we slaughter in that time?"

Ignacio considered the sky. He pinched his nose with thumb and forefinger while he calculated. "I think a thousand *ganados*," he said. "A month for the killing, another week to cut wood for the fires." His eyes kindled. "When it is all done . . . the fandango!"

"We may have our fandango on Smuggler's Beach," Brian told him curtly. These *Californios* . . . in the midst of disaster, they could still think of fandangos.

Then on a sweltering day in September Manuel, the vine-yard-tender, brought in the first groaning *carreta* of grapes. Now the tramping-out began, scenting the air with the rich fragrance of the purple juices. Feliciano lived between heaven and hell while he alternately despaired of a batch, then glorified in its fulsome progress.

In the *matanzas* the grim work of slaughtering cattle went on. To Ignacio there was beauty in the blood-soaked corrals, but Lee Brian never went near them without speaking sternly to his stomach. It brought death a little too close. Cattle bawled under the knife and expired bawling. The clothes of the butchers were dyed in blood, their arms gory to the shoulders. There was beauty only in the efficiency with which each operation was performed. Hides were skinned cleanly off the carcasses and dragged away to be cured. Long strips of meat hung on the drying racks under the brilliant sun. The dried jerky was packed in sixty-pound bales for shipment.

Movement was what Brian wanted most. As fast as the hides were cured, he had them carted, by night, to Smuggler's Beach. He went himself with the first loads of wine. Wines needed careful storing, away from moisture and sun.

They left a couple of hours before sunset, passing by daylight through heavy plains growth that hid the ox-carts from view. By the time they were within sight of Moxley's ranch house, across the river, full darkness hid them. Brian lay on a pile of hides with his arms across his face, dozing.

Suddenly he felt Ignacio's hand shaking him.

"¡Patrón!"

Brian sat up. He found his hand on his gun. It had been that kind of awakening — sudden and violent.

"Horses," whispered Ignacio. "In the barranca ahead. They wear our brand."

A cold salty wind was clearing Brian's head. He could not

believe they had traveled as far as the palisades, but somewhere in the opalescent mist waves crested and crumpled with a distant kettle-drumming. He went forward with the major-domo, past the other stalled carts. The barranca was a dry wash that hugged a few twisted trees to itself. The fog and moonlight did not make for good vision, but in the bottom of the wash four horses could be seen.

Standing there, Brian heard a sound from the beach. It could have been a wave larger than the rest, dashing on the rocks. But to Brian it sounded more like a cask of wine falling from a height.

VII

Brian knew they must hurry if they were to retain the element of surprise. He followed the cart trail across the barranca, holding his dragoon pistol low before him. Ignacio was a stride behind. His only weapon was a single-shot musket converted for linen cartridges, and he carried it at the port, like a foot-soldier.

Beyond the wash the terrain was brushy, a broken slope, falling away to the cliff a few hundred feet to their left. A man's silhouette now appeared above the cliff. Behind him came a second man, and then two more, their hats gray cones against the limitless black of the sea.

Brian stopped behind a shrub, half hidden. The first man was only fifty feet from him. He was walking slowly, a pistol in his hand. His face was a dark smear, but it was the high-shoul-dered frame of Angel Rubio.

Brian said: "Get your hands up, Rubio."

Rubio stopped still, his head jerking around. He brought his pistol up — and in the same instant Brian fired. The Mexican's gun spat flame toward the ground. He went to his knees and then rocked forward on all fours, crumpling against the earth.

One of the men behind him yelled, and raised a gun. Flame striped the darkness. The sound of the shot was like a physical blow. Brian found himself amazed that he had not been hit.

Behind him Ignacio's musket roared. The man who had fired went backward into the brush, impelled by a leaden slug as big as a man's thumb.

The other men, panicked, plunged into the brush. Brian raised his pistol again, but at the instant of firing he found he could not do it. His hand began to tremble. Death was something you could joke about until it took the guise of a man you had shot, moaning softly in the darkness, his blood soaking the earth. Brian let the men escape, into the sand dunes, into the night.

There was yelling from the direction of the ox-carts, but no one seemed to be in a hurry to cross the barranca. Ignacio finished reloading his musket. They went forward. Angel Rubio was the man who was groaning. Ignacio stayed with him while Brian sought the other. This man lay on his back, half supported by a salt bush. His head lolled gruesomely, the mouth choked with blood. Ignacio's bullet had killed him instantly.

At the majordomo's call the *carreteros* ran across the barranca. Ignacio left them with Rubio, guarding him with his own revolver. He and Brian went down the cliff trail to estimate the loss of goods. An inventory of the cave showed two barrels of wine left of the ten that had been hidden. The rest lay shattered on the rocks. But they had broken up the raid before the hides could be thrown into the sea.

"It is a thing of sadness," Ignacio declared, "but what is lost cannot be brought back with sighs. There is still much wine left, and I think it will now not be molested."

The carts were brought to the top of the cliff and each cask moved with care to its resting place in the shadowy coolness of the cave.

Angel Rubio was still alive when they had finished. His eyes were open, but he could not — or would not — speak. He made no attempt to move when they raised him to the bed of an ox-cart. His face was streaked with perspiration.

Throughout the whole thing Ignacio retained the earthy logic of his people. The mere fact of death did not stir him, nor that death had been administered by his hand and Brian's. What did interest him was the disposition of the casualties.

"This one," he said with a jerk of his thumb toward the dead *vaquero,* "shall be left in the thickets. The coyotes and buzzards will perform us a service. But Rubio" — he wrinkled his nose in disapproval — "cannot be left here to die."

"If he lives," Brian conjectured, "how much trouble can he make us?"

Ignacio grunted. "Our brand was on the casks as well as the hides. It is you, *Don* Brian, who can make trouble. But I do not think he will live."

And there was someone else who could make trouble, Lee Brian feared. Had Rubio observed the comings and goings of the ox-carts, or had he been sent to Smuggler's Beach by another? There was no way to tell. A guard could be set, they could hope, and that was all.

They left two men on the beach, armed with the dead bandits' guns. Not far from Gus Moxley's Angel Rubio died. They left his body deep within the trampled tangles of the mustard thickets.

It was twelve days later when Clay Rockwell and Captain Tom Bixby appeared at Los Arcos. Brian had just come from the *matanzas*. He was in his shirt sleeves, hatless, the sun harsh on his skin. He stood at the foot of the steps as they dismounted.

"The road leads out of here as well as in," Brian stated. "I'd recommend that you try it the other way now."

Rockwell smiled. He could be as brash and insulting with a smile as most men could be with a stevedore's vocabulary.

"Your damned stubbornness," he said pleasantly, "will probably get you into more trouble than it will get you out of. I came to see Maria. It appears that Moxley may be brought around."

"Maria," Brian declared, "will be away for about two months."

"Don't be silly," Katie Graham said. She had come quietly to the open door. "Come in, Clay."

Brian watched Rockwell take her arm as they went inside. The blood came up hotly through his face. It was her say as much as his as to whom Los Arcos entertained, but for Katie's invitation to throw Rockwell down the steps Brian would have given much.

With a grunt Captain Bixby sat down on the porch steps. He laid his white master's cap beside him and mopped his forehead with a polka-dot handkerchief.

"Those Santa Barbara *padres*," he declared, "are sharper traders than any Armenian I ever lowered boom on."

Brian let him talk, not listening. He was thinking about Katie, sitting cozily in the parlor with that dancing master of a man, blushing at his elaborate compliments, and believing everything he told her, amorous or otherwise. What kind of game was he playing now? Brian found some comfort in the knowledge that this time she could not endorse any paper without his co-signature.

"What kind of horse trading is that fellow up to?" Brian asked suddenly.

"He don't talk much about his affairs," said the captain. "Some kind of a contract, I think."

Brian snorted. "He won't be making any more contracts with Los Arcos . . . not without my name on the paper!"

"I ain't sure," Bixby remarked, "that this particular paper would require your signature."

Brian glanced sharply at him, but he did not question his uncle further, and presently Katie reappeared. Rockwell held her hand. He said something which Brian could not hear, and Katie laughed softly.

Rockwell came down the steps. "Shall we go, Captain?" he said. "I thought of staying over in Los Angeles tonight."

Bixby clapped his nephew on the shoulder. "Fair winds, lad. It may be I shall have those wines yet!"

Brian caught Katie in the hall. "What's this about a contract?" he demanded.

In Katie's eyes there was a sparkle. "*Don* Brian, there are a few small things about my life that were not included in our contract. This happens to be one of them."

Brian's mouth was dry. He was being clumsy and stupid, and it made him no less angry to realize it. "If it touches the ranch," he stated, "you may assume the contract covers it. I saw to that. And I wish to heaven you'd quit calling me *Don* Brian. You make me feel like an eighty-year-old *ranchero*, sitting around with a blanket over his knees."

Katie laughed. She was unnaturally gay. "I'm not so sure Clay would like my calling you Lee," she said. "But if it will make you happier. . . . Yes, the contract concerns Los Arcos very much. But I hardly think the *padre* would require your signature."

"The *padre?*" A finger was laid on Brian's heart, stilling it.

"*Señor* Clay has asked me to marry him. He says he can force Gus Moxley out of San Pedro simply by paying back what

124

he owes him. But he hasn't the cash yet . . . two thousand dollars. He is going to try to raise it somewhere. If he can do it, he wants my promise to marry him at fandango time!"

Brian could not keep the sunken feeling out of his face. "That's fine," he said, "that's great! I'll have him for a partner, then. We could probably make Los Arcos into something big." Then he asked the question his pride was not strong enough to block: "What did you tell him?"

"What does a girl tell a man?" Katie returned. "I promised him an answer . . . at the fandango, of course."

"And do you know what it will mean if you tell him *yes?*" Brian asked. He was rushing headlong into something he knew would be disastrous. "It will mean you're selling yourself for the ranch. You're putting Los Arcos above your own happiness. Because you're afraid of what Rockwell will do if you don't agree."

In the pale oval of her face Katie's eyes darkened. Her hands, hanging at her sides, clenched. "Is it so terrible to marry a man like Clay Rockwell?" she asked. "To marry a gentleman who understands the courtesies, as well as business?"

Brian's mind groped, trying to compass it. He found no words in him, nothing to express his despair, and he turned back to the porch, knowing she was despising him. There was a sense of catastrophe in him too deep for expression, a wave of jealousy that sickened him.

He had made the same discovery a million men before him had made: you could play with a hundred girls and keep your head, but the minute the right one came along, all your experience and your wisdom vanished.

VIII

The harvest was finished. On Los Arcos a hundred natives prepared for the fandango. To them, it made up for the toil and deprivations of the whole year. A late-summer haze bronzed the sky, turning the edge of the heat. Already the nights were touched with coolness.

Brian had seen to the stowing of the last of the merchandise in the caves. Juan Baca had accepted the final installment of duty money with forebodings.

"This I do not like," he had remarked, "this carrying of too many eggs in one basket. Today I think . . . only two little men to guard it, and so many large ones to steal. I look at my cannon. I think . . . that is the answer. Tonight," he added, "I move it up to Smuggler's Beach. I have powder, shot, fuses."

Lee Brian had not smiled. *Let the general dream!* The powder must certainly be long since spoiled by the damp sea air. But it cost nothing to humor him. "It would be appreciated," he had replied. "Tell the guards to help you."

Now, on his return, he found the ranch transformed. Strings of red chili pods brightened the house. The adobe walls had been freshly whitewashed that day. In a dozen pits fires were being laid for the barbecuing of steers and goats. Perspiring native women worked endlessly in the kitchen, laughing and chattering. On the patio the hard-packed earth was being swept clean in preparation for the *baile*.

From the fields and from the range camps of Los Arcos' rolling empire the workers came in, all afternoon and half the night. Before dawn the taste of wood smoke and tangy *salsa de*

126

chili was in the air. It was hard to resist the spirit of fiesta, but Lee Brian had enough troubling him to offset it.

For some time he sat watching the barbecue, the cooks stirring gray-red beds of coals and spreading over the browning carcasses with mops gallons of sauce scarcely less hot. Suddenly he was aware of *Doña* Berta's approach.

He stood. There had been a sort of truce between them these last few weeks. *Doña* Berta was almost polite. She now surprised him by taking a seat beside him on the hewn bench.

"A great day, *Don* Brian," she remarked pleasantly.

Brian agreed. "A fine day for the fandango."

"Perhaps also a great day for Maria," *Doña* Berta continued. "It is today she gives her answer to *Señor* Rockwell."

Brian glanced at her. "It was *Señor* Clay two months ago," he reminded her.

"Two months ago," said the grandmother, suddenly harsh, "I trusted him. I liked him. I enjoyed the music he played. I ask myself now whether there is any music in his soul, or whether it is all clamor and greed."

Brian leaned back. All at once he began to see intelligence in this sharp-faced old woman with her stiff black satins and her code of living that was prone to protest when disturbed.

"I've known the answer to that for a long time," he told her. "So it was the Moxley thing that started you thinking?"

"Only partly," said *Doña* Berta. Her black eyes, full of the wisdom the years trade for beauty, turned to him. "Partly," she murmured, "it was comparing him with you. I have seen Los Arcos change during the last seven years, but never for the better until you came. You are as capable as my son-in-law was. You treat our laborers as they should be treated . . . with justice, but with firmness. For these things I like you. You are a *gringo*, yes, but a magnificent *gringo*. And because of these things I ask your help."

Somehow Lee Brian divined what the favor was. He said softly: "You don't want Katie to marry Clay Rockwell. You want me to get rid of him."

"A girl's heart is wax," *Doña* Berta said. "Rockwell is a man who understands how to mold it. I ask you not to let her marry him." She began to smile, so faintly that the gesture did not go beyond her lips. "I would not object," she pointed out, "if Maria were to marry you, *Don* Brian."

He could be frank with *Doña* Berta. Probably she had long known the trouble with him anyway. "Nor would I object," he admitted. "But I'm still a Yankee to Maria. I happen to be proud of being a Yankee. I don't care to do any of the things to soften her toward me that she might like me to do."

"Pride is a fine thing," said *Doña* Berta, "provided it does not break one's heart."

Brian spoke in desperation. "Don't you see that I can't simply walk up and ask her to marry me . . . after she has all but announced her engagement? Maybe she really loves him. Either way, it's her business." He arose, thrusting his fingers through his dark hair. "I don't want Rockwell for a partner any more than you do for a grandson-in-law. But I don't know what we can do about it."

Doña Berta folded her hands in her lap. "Such things are for a man to decide," she said quietly. "Woman proposes, man disposes. But there is not much time."

Troubled, Brian went into the house. *Escapists!* he thought. *Trouble-dodgers, every one of them! Drowning their worries in a fandango and allowing another to shoulder their problems.*

About noon, Rockwell appeared from the direction of Los Angeles. Today he rode a fine black stallion. He was dressed like a San Francisco banker, with a gray broadcloth coat to enhance his slender build, with checked pants and a black string tie. *Doña* Berta did not appear to greet him.

Lee Brian, from his window, watched Katie give him her hands. Katie was in a gown to make the angels jealous, a gown of pure white, with her skin tawny velvet. Her hair was catching the polish of sunlight, but the light of the moon was in her eyes. It caused him to turn sharply from the window. He could hear the natives singing, while the younger ones danced the *tapatia*. The fandango had started. But all Brian could think of was Katie and Clay Rockwell.

Through the open window the brisk clop of hoofs came to Brian. Against the glowing stripe of roadway, running to the *bosque*, there was patterned the dull gray coat of a burro. A pack animal jogged in the rear, loaded with *aparejos*. The rider was bearded — a white beard cropped close to his jaws, and he wore a white master's cap.

Lee Brian remembered the gold coin consigned to him from San Francisco by steamer. Hurriedly he shrugged into his coat, went downstairs, and himself conducted the seaman into the parlor.

The captain's name was Anderson of the steamer *Mary Casey*. Captain Anderson cuffed dust out of his beard. "A relief it will be to sign this cargo off, I can tell you," he declared.

He sat in the parlor with his coat open, fanning himself with his cap. He complained about the suffocating inland heat and the disadvantages of burro travel. Using the top of the harpsichord as a desk, Brian signed his release. He stowed the money temporarily under the desk in the office.

"A bad summer for trade, young man," said the captain, reluctant to leave the coolness of the house for the sweltering road. "Every wholesaler in 'Frisco is clamoring for merchandise, and nothing to be had this side of the States. If I had known, when I left Boston, what I know now, I should have carried nothing but picks, shovels, and washbasins for the madmen in the gold fields."

"Your first voyage to the Coast?" asked Brian.

Captain Anderson agreed. "And perhaps my last. At my age a man begins to think more of family and home than of fighting a helm in a snowstorm."

Presently Brian produced a decanter of wine. Captain Anderson said: "Ah!" and rubbed his hands.

Lee Brian hoped that Los Arcos wine would pound in the wedge he was about to set. He had reason to believe it would, when he heard the captain's loud belch of appreciation after draining his glass.

"That, Mister Brian, is wine!" said the captain. "Your own?"

Brian nodded. "We have about fifty casks we might be persuaded to sell. Also hides and tallow to founder your ship."

"Indeed!" The shipmaster allowed Brian to refill his glass. "At . . . er . . . what rate each?" he inquired.

He was a Bostonian with a trader's keen eyes. Brian pegged the prices high, knowing they would be mercilessly pounded down. But the captain put up less fuss than he had expected. They agreed on a price. Brian agreed to deliver what he wanted within twenty-four hours.

"There is just one thing," he remarked. "Our relations with the lessors of the harbor are not what they might be. All the goods are on the beach now, duty paid and ready for the longboats. But there is one small obstacle."

Captain Anderson listened intently as Brian delineated the situation. Once he interrupted tartly: "I met the man, Moxley, at the harbor. I must say I have never cared for Germans myself. Go on."

Brian continued, ignoring the fact that Moxley was Swiss. When he had finished, Captain Anderson was on his third glass of wine. Outside, the sounds of music and laughter grew in volume.

"Well, sir," admitted the captain, "this is unusual, indeed. However . . . not impossible." He scratched ferociously at his underjaw. "But, of course," he pointed out, "I shall have to discount the value of the goods somewhat. The risks are not small." And all the time his eyes were saying that for a seafaring man the risks only spiced the bargain.

In the end, the prices still remained a point or two higher than Brian had hoped to get.

Captain Anderson dabbed at his lips with his handkerchief. "I shall expect you to accompany the first boat," he remarked. "Payment will be made as each boatload is put down. I don't care to pay for merchandise on the bottom of the sea."

Lee Brian watched him ride away, a little more erect than on arrival. So it was ready! He went upstairs and smoked a cigar, striding up and down. At dusk he would leave with Ignacio and a half dozen men to help load the boats. This could be the last act in the story of Los Arcos, or it could be the first of the new Los Arcos he wanted to build.

"The risks are not small," Captain Anderson had said. Brian was not deceiving himself that they were. If Tom Bixby, aboard the *Clementine*, got scent of what was going on, he would most certainly put in his own oar. If he had left the stuff alone so far, it was because Rockwell had kept an eye on him. Rockwell still hoped to come into possession of that treasure along with the rest of Los Arcos, by the simple expedient of putting a ring on Katie's finger.

The risks are not small. The phrase hung in Brian's mind until an old fear came to life. *What if he did not come through it alive? It was bad enough to die, but to leave misfortune above your grave for someone you loved — like it or not — was sorrier still.*

Brian thought of what *Doña* Berta had told him. Yes, there was a way out. There was a way to protect Katie Graham, after all. If Katie did not like it, that was unfortunate. But she was going to follow his lead in this one thing, if she never did in another.

Lee Brian lay on the bed and rested for an hour. Later he went down and sought Ignacio. Then he returned to his room and began to brush his coat and trousers. A man who was about to be married should not go looking as though he had just left the fields.

IX

It was necessary to enlist the help of *Doña* Berta. He could not march out among the dancers and say to Katie: "I'm taking you to the church. Come along."

Doña Berta recited to Katie the story upon which Brian had coached her. The money from San Francisco had arrived, but there was a misunderstanding. It would be delivered only into the hands of Maria Catalina Arango y Graham. Tomorrow the steamer would pull out again. There was only tonight to secure the money. She must hurry to the harbor and prove her identity.

She looked as beautiful as Brian had known she would. He helped her up into the Spanish sidesaddle, turning away while she arranged her skirts to hide all but one ankle. In the dusk he saw her face as they rode, pouting, impatient at leaving the fiesta. But not for an hour did he explain the real reason for taking her from the fandango.

He said: "Do you know *Padre* Armando at San Pedro?"

In the almost complete darkness Katie glanced at him. "Certainly. Why?"

"*Padre* Armando is going to marry us tonight."

Katie pulled her horse to a stop. "For a drunken man," she

declared, "you speak very plainly."

"I'm going to keep on speaking plainly," Brian told her. "We've got to be married, or you may find yourself partner to Captain Bixby tomorrow. Tonight we move the hides to the *Mary Casey*. If I don't come back to Los Arcos, my uncle will come in my place . . . as sure as I know his black heart. We've got to be married, so that my share of the ranch will go to you. Just making a will wouldn't do. He'd manage to have it set aside . . . and . . . well, people would say you . . . should have married me."

Katie's voice could have sounded much angrier. It could have been outraged or frightened, but it was neither of these. It was plaintive. It was bewildered. "Is this what a Yankee calls a proposal?"

Brian kept his eyes straight ahead. "The kiss that night was a proposal," he said. "And you gave me your answer when you said I'd been drinking too much wine. But don't worry. Tomorrow, if I come back, you can have the ceremony annulled. I'll lie to the *padre* about my faith. I don't know what I am . . . a Presbyterian, I guess, like my parents, but I'll tell him I've been confirmed a Catholic so that he'll marry us. He'll cross it off the books soon enough when I tell the truth."

He rode on. Katie did not try to turn back, but hurried to keep to his stirrup.

The road led through the dunes, winding over drifted mounds of sand and verbena tangles, and then it came out above the sprinkling of lights that was the village of San Pedro. In the moonlight the white walls and small belfry of the chapel were depicted faintly against the dark slope behind the village. It was then that the pride of Katie Graham broke.

Brian turned in surprise as she began to sob. Just as naturally he swung down and lifted her from the saddle. She came against him without any vestige of demureness.

"I can't do it!" she said against his breast. "I can't make a farce out of it. Oh, Lee! Lee! Haven't you the eyes to see that since the day you came to Los Arcos, I've . . . I've thought much of you? Only I was afraid of you, at first. And then you were always frowning at me, or laughing at me."

Brian's voice, breathing into the warm silk of her hair, was rough with emotion. "All I could ever see was a girl who hated every Yankee in California. Was that some other girl, Katie?"

Her face, below him, turned upward. "It must have been, *querido.* It couldn't have been Katie Graham. Katie Graham is going to marry a Yankee . . . in every church in Los Angeles, if he likes!"

Brian carried her down the hill in his arms, the horses trailing behind. He thought of the years that had seemed so full, years of danger and achievement and of disappointment. They were a part of his life that had been vacant. He could conceive of no joy now that did not start or end with Katie.

He went around to the tiny parish house behind the church. No one answered his call. Within the church there was only the somnolence of somber candlelit gloom. Brian left Katie in the church while he walked down the road to the village. Candles burned within a few houses, and Brian selected the nearest one to hail. A man opened the door.

"*¿Sí, señor?*"

"The *padre?*" Brian asked. "Is he in the village?"

"What a pity!" the man replied. "At Bolsitas a man was kicked by a horse. The *padre* will not be back until morning."

Brian returned to the church. The one possibility he had not figured on, the one hitch that could spoil the whole plan, had occurred. He told Katie, whispering, as a man does who does not visit churches often enough. But Katie smiled and took his chin between her thumb and forefinger.

"I am glad! Now you will know you must come back."

Brian brought her saddle blanket and made her comfortable on a bench. He forgot his awe of the wooden saints on the walls in the poignance of leaving. His arms imprisoned her. His hand was in her hair. He felt her own arms go about him, prolonging the moment, holding its sweetness.

Gently he ended the embrace. Beyond the church nothing seemed real, nothing important, but Brian knew that reality waited on Smuggler's Beach. This was the dream.

This one night, of the many that were foggy at this season, had to be clear. And now the full moon had risen above the hills. Brian crossed the barranca. He halted on the bluff to study the sea, a running tide of silver and black. Far out he discerned the massive hulk of the *Mary Casey*. Closer in, the *Clementine* rode the swells off the harbor.

Someone spoke, not ten feet from him: *"¿Quién es?"*

Brian started. Then he smiled, recognizing the voice of the general. "The *patrón*," he said.

Juan Baca rose from the heart of a thicket, a hooded lamp in his hand. "You are late, *patrón*," he responded. "The work goes not quickly enough. *¡Mire!*"

Brian followed him into the brush. The old brass custom house cannon squatted on the cliff, like an ancient bulldog making a boast with his throat that his teeth could not back up. Juan Baca had Brian sight along the top of the piece.

"At seven o'clock," he declared, "the brig lay under the muzzle of the gun. Now it stands fifteen degrees off! Captain Bixby is letting the *Clementine* drift. The tide will carry him between the beach and the steamship. Also," he said, "there is this . . . when Captain Anderson left for Los Arcos, Rockwell sent a boy who brought Gus Moxley. At sunset Captain Anderson returned to his ship. But his ship did not leave. Thus, they know he waits for cargo. At eight o'clock Moxley and Rockwell boarded the *Clementine*." He shook his head. "It is not comforting."

Brian said: "Let her drift. She may be closer to the beach, but she's also closer to the rocks."

Still, he was worried. His uncle could handle the brig like a ship in a tub. She drew far less water than the *Mary Casey* so she could safely move in to intercept the longboats. Seven men in a bobbing cargo-laden boat would be no match for a crew like Tom Bixby's. And with the *Mary Casey*'s crew neutralized, Bixby would put his own men to carrying off the trade stuff.

Baca raised the hood and let the lamp burn steadily into the darkness. An answering glint showed from the *Mary Casey*. Brian descended to the beach. Here everything was commotion. Ignacio, scolding like a fishwife, kept the men trimming the piles, preparing them for transfer to the boats the instant they reached shore.

In twenty minutes Brian was able to discern four longboats, moving in. And now the *Clementine* began to drift with perceptible speed. Captain Tom Bixby was a man who could bide his time, but he was also a man who could strike. The lantern had told him the treasure was ripe for plucking. There was an offshore breeze, tempering the tidal pull and furnishing impetus for a quick run.

Out there the longboats were now between ship and shore, riding in fast with the thrust of the rollers behind them. A few hundred yards above and below Smuggler's Beach, the same rollers cannonaded into the rocks under mountains of spray; but the boats were making squarely for the beach. Loaded, they would go out sluggishly, with the chance of being swamped in the breakers. But it was beyond the breakers that the real danger lay.

Upon the beach came the first of the boats, riding a crest of foam. The seamen, piling overboard, ran the longboat far up the beach before the wave receded and dropped her on the sand.

Ignacio yelled one word, and his men ran to meet it with cargo on their backs. Lee Brian helped stow cargo as it was piled beside the boat. The boatswain, a Swede with features like rough wood, saw to the stowing of each hide and barrel. Before the longboat was ready to shove off, a second and a third boat grated onto the beach beside it.

The stockpiles seemed to be depleted not at all by the flow of material, but Brian knew that each boatload the breakers claimed would cost Los Arcos five hundred dollars.

The boatswain raised his arms. "That's all, mates!" He saw Brian, standing by, and gave him a nod. "If you're Mister Brian, you can go back with us. Captain Anderson will pay by the load. Sit in the bow, if you like. You'll get a dousin', and maybe something worse. But I guess you know about that."

Brian waded in six inches of water to step into the boat. The seamen, three at each side and the boatswain in the rear, began to work her out of the sand. The apron of a wave slid beneath, and Brian felt the smooth downward glide to deep water. The men ran alongside, giving it a last thrust before it took the rollers.

Brian's eyes raised beyond the surf. Ignacio was standing by himself, waving his hat. The boatswain yelled. Soaking wet, the men came piling aboard. Beyond the boat a wave crashed, roaring mountainously toward them. Foam poured in, but the longboat went up, up, found a new level, and wallowed ahead.

Out of the darkness a breaker came, sweeping for the beach, a glistening palisade of black water. Foam appeared along its crest, presaging the moment of its crumpling. Brian's fingers clutched the thwart. Sluggishly the boat turned bow up to climb the breaker.

Dark water poured into the longboat, and for a moment the

sky seemed to be hidden by the overhanging wave. Brian stood up, ready to jump clear. Then, miraculously, they were through the wave and racing down the long slope in its wake.

The boatswain said: "Well done, lads!"

Brian began to breathe again. Once more he gave his attention to the *Clementine*. *She was in close, dangerously close,* he thought. What brought him up straight was the realization that a gig was pulling away from the ship to meet them. Brian held his gun under his coat to protect the loads from spray. He glanced at the Swede and saw that he, too, had discovered the gig. The boatswain grinned. "It's your party, mate!"

Tom Bixby's voice came across the water. "It's hold up, lad, or be run down!"

Brian shouted: "Come ahead, damn you!"

The gig was large and carried six oarsmen and the captain. The longboat, with hardly ten inches of freeboard, would capsize if she were rammed. Brian knew this, but he had some faith in the dragoon pistol he had drawn from under his coat.

The moon was behind Captain Bixby's boat. It silhouetted the men, straining at the oars, and brought into sharp relief the master himself, hunched over the tiller. The sound of water, sloshing off the bows, broke the quiet.

Again Tom Bixby shouted. To Lee Brian he sounded excited, apprehensive. "Will you stop, now?" he challenged.

Brian rested the barrel of his gun across his forearm. "It's the same answer," he retorted. "And I'll back it up!"

A gun flashed from the dark hulk of the gig. The ball chunked solidly against the longboat's bow. Brian fired and heard a man cry out. He cocked and fired again, but this shot was high. Again the gun in the captain's boat spoke. Water spouted directly before Brian. It was almost point-blank fire now, but the rocking of the boats forced the gunmen to depend on luck.

Now Brian saw that it was his uncle who had been firing, one hand on the tiller and the other holding a long pistol at arm's length. He had the sights almost true when the Swede yelled. In the same instant he swung the longboat a-starboard, causing her to roll.

Now the gig was on them with a crash of timbers and the shouting of angry men, and the ocean was pouring in upon them. They were gone! That Brian knew, hearing the shouts of the seamen and feeling cold water climbing to his knees. There was suddenly nothing beneath him but water.

Somehow he kept from under the boat. Somehow he held to the slippery keel when the boat came to rest upside down. The cargo was all gently sinking to ruin, but what was important was that the boat had not been swamped and taken down with it. Heads began to appear above the water like bobbing apples. These men were too used to duckings on the rocky California coast to be caught beneath any boat.

The gig was slewing about. This time it would be a clubbing with oars until no one was left to be rescued by the following boats. Helplessly Brian held the gun up and let the water drain out of it. He prayed that by some stroke the powder had not been wet.

The gig was in line with the *Clementine*. As Lee Brian watched her bear upon them, he saw a strange thing. A great spout of water lifted about a hundred feet from the brig. His first thought was of a whale, but it was too great a spout for any fish that ever swam. And then the sound came, and Lee Brian understood.

All the powder in the kegs of Juan Antonio Baca — called the general — was not wet. For the thunder rolling from the cliff was that of his brass nine-pounder.

Captain Tom Bixby did not see the spout, but he heard the roar of the cannon and then the shouts from the *Clementine*.

Instantly he forgot the longboat in the more urgent business confronting him. He bore hard on the tiller, putting the gig about. High in the rigging of the brig a lookout began to yell.

Now a second longboat, heavily laden, pulled alongside the capsized craft. The Swede had not lost his head, even though he had lost his cargo.

"Three of you may go with her," he directed. "The rest of us will catch her empty, on the way back. See that the gig is sent to tow this hulk to the ship."

Brian was too intent on the general's marksmanship to think of leaving the capsized boat. He saw another spout of water appear, closer to the brig but abaft of her. Bixby's craft took the swells from the shot, rolling crazily. Brian watched her pull up to the *Clementine*. The falls caught her, lifted her neatly from the water. Brian was despondent, knowing his uncle, now aboard, would instantly haul the brig out of range. Royals and topsails were already going up.

Suddenly he saw splinters fly from the *Clementine* and close to the waterline. And he heard the voice of the cannon on the bluff. The general had his range.

The brig was shipping water by the hogshead as she rolled her wound under. She was listing to starboard, so that the gigs hung far out on the davits. Canvas was slatting with a noise like thunder. Faintly the voice of Tom Bixby came through it. He was a fighter, Brian knew, if nothing else. Crippled as the *Clementine* was, she might still be taken into deep water. On the proper tack his uncle could keep her wound above the waterline until she was repaired.

But tonight there was a more powerful factor than Tom Bixby at work. There was the general. He had bombshell as well as shot. The next ball he lobbed to the brig trailed a fuse. A moment after it struck, orange flame burst from every hatch and port forward of the beam. Bits of flotsam began to fall to the water. Mortally hurt, she was burning.

Lee Brian kept watching the firelit deck for Rockwell, or Moxley, or his uncle, but he saw none of them again. The *Clementine*, her sails vanishing as a series of sheeting flashes, heeled over and began to sink. Smuggler's Beach had claimed another too-adventurous crew as her own.

In the small hours of the night Brian rode back to San Pedro. He was dog-tired. He was wet and cold. But in his heart he was warmly impatient. He was again the groom, hurrying to his bride.

When he reached the harbor, the sun was poised just below the hills. In the still predawn every color and outline was softened. The houses of the village lay sleeping, lay shadowless on the slope, and in the wide embrace of the harbor the water was leaden, without a highlight. Lee Brian's eyes found the church. Someone appeared in the doorway of it. Someone waved. Brian waved back. Just as he started down the road the sun broke over the hill.

THE CAÑON OF
MAVERICK BRANDS

Frank Bonham would arrive first at the characters in a story, character by character, and then plot it out half way, incident by incident, before with a prayer he would begin writing and let the characters take over the stage. "The Cañon of Maverick Brands" was showcased in *Lariat Story Magazine* in the January, 1945 issue. In many ways it demonstrates just how much Bonham had learned from authors he had chosen as his models. The hard-boiled protagonist, Rance Kirby, is very much like the protagonists in Luke Short's serials, then being published in *The Saturday Evening Post,* a market Bonham very much hoped to make his own and eventually did. In fact, Libby Caddo in this story is very much of the same stripe as Connie Dickason in, arguably, the best of Luke Short's Western novels, RAMROD, serialized in *The Saturday Evening Post* in 1943, published in a hardcover edition that year by Macmillan, and released by United Artists as a film in 1947. A reference is also made to Eugene Manlove Rhodes's masterpiece serialized in *The Saturday Evening Post* in 1926, *"Páso Por Aquí,"* and, interestingly, a line spoken by Rance Kirby to Nora Clay in this story would later be echoed in dialogue between Jason Robards and Claudia Cardinale in Sergio Leone's ONCE UPON A TIME IN THE WEST (Paramount, 1968).

1

The breathtaking vistas of the trail to Skyline Ranch had always held Rance Kirby, but tonight there was something poignant about all the old, unforgotten sounds and odors that his throat felt tight, and he had to stop at a bend and get his breath.

Two years! he thought. *Two years in heaven and hell, but never a spot like this!* They had a saying down in Three Rivers that the man who held Skyline Ranch held the Big Bend. From up here, a quarter mile above the big ranch house, you could see why. Not a horse, not a cow, could go down the cañon or across the hills into the badlands without being observed. No one could approach the grim, fortress-like ranch house without coming under the sights of the man who held Skyline. He had an empire of water and grass for his cattle, and there was Smoky River Cañon. You could call this an asset or a menace. So long as you left alone the men who called its wild vastness their own, it was an asset, for they paid well for the privilege of privacy.

Rance Kirby listened to the roar of the falls, like wind in the tops of tall pines, rising a sheer half mile from the juncture of the Blue and the Poverty. Here Smoky River blended with their waters and roared down the gorge, as brash and reckless as the men who inhabited this land.

Rance Kirby rode on, filled with memories, regrets, and a few satisfactions. He came out of the buckbrush and juniper growths into the clearing before the ranch house. It was dark; the windows were shuttered. The Skyline ranch house was a forbidding block of masonry rooted in the granite ribs of the mountains. There was only one high point to the square structure, and this was the water tower, rising thirty feet from the enclosed patio.

Rance raised his hand toward that tower. "Hello!" he called. "You there, Guss?"

Rudy Guss's voice came from the door of the house that Rance now saw was slowly opening. He said in that thick Teutonic speech of his: "Rance Kirby! I never t'ought you'd come back. Come in, my boy."

The shade was raised from a hurricane lantern. Rance went up the heavy plank steps and crossed the solid puncheon porch. Once Rance entered, the rancher barred the door and went around the living room, lighting wall lamps. Rance Kirby stood with his hat in his hand, letting the smell and the look of the room go into him, stirring something deep and strong. It was as though he had walked out of here only a week ago and now had come back, for not a thing was different.

The same Indian rugs hung on the walls. The same bear and lynx hides covered the floor, and the furniture on it was the handmade of juniper and goatskin, the furniture of his boyhood. The mounted lynx, that had had its eyes shot out by Rance's father, was still over the great fireplace.

"Live alone up here?" Rance asked.

"Who else would I be trusting, but myself?" Guss laughed. He was a big man, full of years as he was, his belly big with eating and drinking, and his long, pointed mustaches were white. His eyes were sharp little blue chips, but the lines radiating from them were full of worry. "My men live below, in the Falls House, near the work. I see my foreman once a week. You remember Rocky Taylor, *ja?* You scrapped with him as a boy." Rudy Guss laughed again as he put a log on the fire.

"Maybe we'll scrap some more," Rance said, smiling. "Is he still courtin' my girl?"

Rance let himself into one of the deep chairs before the fire.

He was a big, solid-looking man with full lips and a jaw to break a man's fist. He had brown eyes, guarded by heavy, dark brows. His face was sunburned and pleasant, except for a certain deep restlessness that showed through.

Rudy said: "*Ja*, but that Rocky courts every girl in T'ree Rivers." He poured two big glasses of elderberry wine, and, as he handed one to the other man, he said: "Why did you leave, Rance?"

"Why not? I had a two-bit stake in Hooligan Cañon and a hankering for travel in my feet. I've seen a lot of country in the last two years and hugged the *señoritas* from here to there. So, now I'm back."

He did not add that the thorn that had made life unbearable here was still just as sharp — his love for a girl who was so far above a Hooligan Cañon ruffian she could not see him for contempt — nor that he had some plans that would raise him farther than any man from Poverty Creek, in wild Hooligan Cañon, had ever climbed.

"Where did you go?" the German asked as he sat down.

"Mexico. I reckon I'll go back some time."

Guss leaned forward, his old eyes shining. "Tell me about it," he said. "You know, Rance, I was always one to travel. But now I'm old and fat, and all I can do is talk about it."

"I was in Tehuantepec most of the time," Rance Kirby said. "I got mixed up in railroads and politics. Everybody had a knife in everybody else's back and the other hand in his money bag."

He talked on, telling of high adventure and danger, of steaming jungles and blizzard-swept plateaus, and the cattleman listened with greedy ears, his eyes full of the remembrance of escapades of his own youth. The stories, the wine, and the fire made him sentimental. He reached over and patted Kirby's knee.

"Always I have liked you, Rance," he said. "You vass different from them other Hooligan Cañon cutthroats."

The dark-skinned man from below the border had been rolling a cigarette. He now lit it, blowing smoke at the ceiling as he mused: "Hooligan Cañon. Her men are looked down on more than anybody in the Bend. And so they're the proudest men in Texas. They drink and steal cattle and kill a man, if they don't like him. But they do it openly, so they'd never make out on Blue River. And they aren't far enough across the line to ride down the Smoky."

Guss now lit his big calabash pipe. "*Ja*," he said. "Most of them ain't worth hanging, Rance. But you . . . you're different. Maybe it's the blood. You were born in this house, weren't you?"

"Lived ten years in it. You're the third man to hold it since the old man died." He stood up, abruptly. "Do you want to sell Skyline Ranch, Rudy?"

The cowman started, then smiled. "My boy," he said, "on forty dollars a month, would you be buying ranches?"

"On thirty thousand dollars I might."

Rudy Guss regarded him narrowly. "Then it was true, about Tehuantepec! Whose money bag was you into, Rance?"

"I gambled," Rance said. "With my money and my life. And I came out with a stake. I can pay you cash. You can't hold it forever, you know. And when you go, it will be like Dad did . . . a shot in the night."

Guss nodded, thinking about the gun trap Rance had walked through as he climbed the porch steps. This last year he had felt that his candle was burning out. The Smoky Cañon rustlers — the unseen men who were known only by their work — had been cutting deeply into his herds. One night they would come up here and test the legend that he had a fortune locked in the strong room under the house. He would be ready for them.

Under the steps of the porch were two sawed-off eight-gage shotguns that would blow the belly out of any man who came creeping up. They would have killed Rance Kirby tonight, had Guss set the trap. But that was the last thing he did before going to bed, like winding the clock. His strong room was similarly protected from inside.

But they would come. When that happened, they would stay to fight it out, and what was one man against — well, how many? Enough to have driven out four strong men in turn who had tried to hold this place. Rudy Guss thought of the Fatherland he had left forty years ago. He had a chest full of good American dollars, worth millions of marks. He would be a big man in his homeland. *Ja* — a big man.

He said: "Let me see the money."

Rance went out and turned his horse into the corral, carrying the heavy saddlebags inside. He dumped the contents onto the floor before the hearth. Rudy screamed: "*Lieber Gott!* T'irty t'ousand, in real gold!"

It was too much for him. The scales were forced down. He went to the back of the house and returned with a crude sort of deed. It had been given to him by Sheriff Cave Jackson when he bought the ranch at auction after the murder of the last owner. The German signed it over, made out a receipt, and quickly, greedily, like a child, gathered the money into a strongbox.

"Now," he said, "you own Skyline Ranch. What you going to do with it?" He smiled — the smile of old age watching youth make a foolish error.

Rance smiled back. "I'm going to be king of Hooligan Cañon," he said. "And I'm going to open up the Smoky."

Guss laughed softly. "*Ja,*" he said. "Once I t'ought I open up Smoky River Cañon. I rode down to the Narrows, and somebody shot me in the leg, and I decide . . . what man needs so much water and grass? I leave the boys alone, and every month there is t'ree hundred dollars in silver left in the grain shed." He filled the glasses again, raised his against the light. "I wish you luck, my boy."

Rance stayed at Skyline Ranch that night. When he left him in a little room in the southeast corner of the house, Rudy shook a big key at him. "I lock you in, see? You are a goot boy, but . . . so I know where you are."

"All right," Rance said. "I guess it's time you got out, Rudy."

Rance opened the window and looked down into the whispering gorge of the Smoky. He had dim recollections that lay, like dusty silver coins, back in his mind. Memories of a day he had ventured down that forbidden cañon and had seen a pack train of burros disappear into a vast cave. Even then he instinctively knew that the original owners of the train had been Mexican traders or smugglers, and that they now lay somewhere along the moss-covered trail. That day he saw parks and cañons filled with stolen cattle. He saw only a few men, and they did not see him. It set him on fire with a desire to be lord of the Skyline some day and take possession of every acre of it.

But most of Rance Kirby's memories were of Hooligan Cañon, of the tough, uncurried men who rustled and killed and stole along Poverty Creek, and yet barely made a living in the rugged valley that God seemed to have forgotten. If they had been good ranchers, they would have worked for a stake on Blue River, across the ridge, where the grass was green and high, and the cattlemen were proud.

After his father's death Rance had hired out for board to one of the ranchers on Poverty Creek. There he learned to fight and to stalk, to rope and butcher in a hurry, to swear and drink, and live for the moment at hand. A young tough like Rance Kirby should have known better than to go a-courting on Blue

River, but he began to find occasion to speak to Webb Clay's daughter with the dark blue eyes, Nora, when they met in Three Rivers, and one day he rode out to call on her. Clay owned the big Block B ranch just above the falls. He was a big man in the Bend, but prideful.

Nora had been gentler. "I like you, Rance," she had said. "Come back some day, when you own Skyline Ranch again." And she had smiled.

Shortly after that the Smoky River crowd began to hit Webb Clay's herds pretty hard, and, of course, Hooligan Cañon got credit for it. Clay was a good rancher, but not a fighter, and finally he sold out to John Caddo, all except for a small strip up on Dutchman's Flat.

Now Rance Kirby owned Skyline Ranch, and he was going back to call on the Clays again.

II

Sometime after midnight Rance came awake as though a door had been slammed in his room. He sat up, unconscious that he had brought his Colt from under the pillow. It came to him suddenly what the sound had been, and he reached for his boots in a sort of panic. Death was abroad in the ranch house, and he was locked in his room.

He heard someone run by the room, and he yelled: "Guss! What's the matter?"

The man did not stop. He passed to the front of the house. The building was a hollow square built around a patio, a hall separating the rooms from the patio. Rance's room was at the rear, at the end of the hall from the German's. He began to

150

kick at the lock, but the oaken planks were as solid as stone.

There was another shot. It had the force and hollow thunder of a cannon blast, and immediately afterward a man screamed. Rance turned to the window and climbed out that way. He heard horses crossing the front yard. With his gun cocked, he slipped along the wall to the front.

Three horses were running past the corral toward the trail, but the saddle of the lead horse was empty, and there was a sodden-looking form thrown across the swell of the first rider's saddle. The horse, frightened by the burden and the odor of death, was throwing its head and trying to buck-jump, but the horseman kept a tight rein and spurred savagely.

Kirby shouted: "Hold it!"

The rear rider twisted in the saddle, and a gun stabbed flame and lead across the yard. The bullet snarled off the adobe wall close to Rance. He fired, hearing a solid *thunk* as the slug struck the man's saddle. The brush took the men, and then they were riding desperately down the cañon trail.

Standing at the corner of the ranch house, Kirby sorted the sounds that came to him, after the clatter of the horses faded. He found only the faint noises of the night, horses moving in the corral and coyotes along the ridge, and over them all the muted roar from the black cañons.

The front steps were a welter of blood. Rance slipped in it as he went up the stairs. He smelled powder smoke, heavy and warm. He went through the open front door and lighted one lamp. Walking cautiously, he trod down the hall to Rudy Guss's room. This door also was ajar, the lock shot away. In a big juniper chair, like a throne, a blanket wrapped about him and a shotgun across his knees, sat the erstwhile owner of Skyline Ranch. From the appearance of the bed, devoid of blankets or pillows, Rudy Guss had apparently been accustomed to sleep in this manner during his last years.

151

Not all his shotgun traps or locks could shut out death, for the dark angel's heavy hand had struck him as he sat there, asleep. The bullet had entered under his left eye and torn out the back of his head as it went into the wall. Rudy Guss had stayed in the Bend one day too long.

In the morning Rance found how it all had happened. The killer had tossed a rope over a *viga* and climbed across the roof, dropping into the patio and prying a window open. He had shot away the lock of the rancher's door and sprung through, while the old man was still dull with sleep and wine, and put a bullet through his head. Then he ran through the house and unlocked the front door to let his companions in. One of them had walked into Rudy's gun trap and had had his belly blown open. Hearing Rance's shouts, they had decided to leave.

Rance wondered about the gold he had given the old cowman. The saddlebags were not in his room. He remembered the wine cellar, and descended the stone stairs off the front room. There was a door now, at the bottom, a slab of concrete banded with strap iron and locked with three gigantic padlocks, to which Rance had not yet found the keys. It would be a day's work to break those locks.

He saddled and took the trail, following the blood sign. There was blood on the brush beside the trail and dried puddles of it on the ground. He was not surprised when suddenly the blood sign petered out. No man could have bled like that for long.

Skyline range was worked from the headquarters known as Falls House, a cluster of adobe cabins and pole corrals among the poplars and *alamos* along the river, just below the falls itself. The roar of falling water was close and constant. Rance raised a shout, and a Mexican came from the main building.

The man wore a flour-sack apron and no shirt. He was short

and bald-headed, and he had long gray mustaches. *"¿Mande?"* he called back.

Rance remembered him. It was like finding a little part of the old days untouched. He dismounted, calling: *"¿Cómo te ha ido, Casoose?"*

Jesús Corrales raised both arms as if to embrace him, and the fervor of his smile lighted every part of his face. *"¡Señor Rance!"* he said. "Thou art indeed back. *¡Grac' a Dios!"* He held him by the shoulders and kissed each cheek, and stood back, tears in his sentimental old eyes.

Jesús was as much part of this country as the cañons. He had been born here, and he had herded goats, and roped wild cattle, and even acted as range foreman in the days when Rance's father owned the ranch. He was Casoose to all the Anglo-Americans, that being close enough to the native pronunciation of his name and a lot easier on the tongue. He had taught Rance a lot of the lore of the country that only his people knew. Now he was back on the Skyline Ranch again, a humble pothooks for ungrateful cowboys.

Over a cup of coffee Rance told him about the beauty and dangers of the big land south of the border, and also of how it got into a man's soul.

Casoose listened, enthralled, and finally he said: "So now you come back to Hooligan Cañon." He sounded a little sad.

Rance said: "No. I've come back to the Skyline."

Casoose shook a finger at him. "Is not good. Rocky Taylor is foreman. He does not forget the whipping you gave him."

"Taylor's quitting," Rance said. "I bought out Guss last night. I'm firing the whole crew, Casoose, except you."

He told the Mexican about the deal with Guss, and about the murder. "I promised myself seventeen years ago that a Kirby would come back. It's happened now, and a lot of changes are going to be made. I'm going to hire men I can trust. You'll have your old job of range boss. I suppose the boys are out now on the calf roundup?"

Casoose shrugged. "*¿Quién sabe?* They ride much. They talk little. Rocky went to town. Maybeso he go to see a girl."

"I have a notion I'll run into him," Rance said. "When the boys come back, you can tell them they're done. Pick out any you think are worth keeping. And meet me at the ranch house tomorrow."

He crossed the Poverty a half mile above the falls and cut over the hogback to Blue River Valley. Here the cañon was narrow. A little way up the crimson sandstone walls fell back, and the cañon was a wide valley, full of sunlight and green grama, criss-crossed by sparkling feeder streams. He could see John Caddo's Ladder cattle, ranging wide from the Calamity Mountains on the west — separating the valley from Hooligan Cañon — to the clay mesas on the east. All this range had once been Webb Clay's, and now he had been crowded back to Dutchman's Flat, the gateway to the badlands.

That was the trouble with being honest, Rance thought. Clay had been one of the first Anglo-Americans in this district, and he could have held half of Blue River Valley by now, but he had trusted in men's honesty rather than his own six-gun. So now he was beating a living out of the salt grass with his fists, and a twisted cripple had usurped his place — John Caddo, who had a body that was a curse, a mind like a knife blade, and a daughter as beautiful as a black panther.

Rance reached the Block B in the afternoon. He looked at the unwhitewashed adobe buildings and ocotillo corrals, at the dozen-odd ponies in the corral, and he knew that Webb Clay was finished. This was his last stop this side of bankruptcy.

Nora heard his horse and came out of the house. There was no porch, and she stood in a blue gingham dress against the light wall, the sun in her blonde hair and her hand raised to shade her eyes. When she recognized the dark-skinned, heavy-shouldered man, holding the horse, she caught her breath.

"Why, Rance Kirby!" she said.

She put out her hand when Rance approached, and he took it, and all the things she had meant to him before were in him again, filling him with the same hunger for things that were above a Hooligan Cañon long-looper. She was gentleness and fire, steadiness and unpredictability. The man who won her would never win her completely. Even when she was in his arms, he would know that part of her was not his, a part that was strong and proud, and he would love her the more for it. All this Kirby knew, but he was going, nevertheless, to remind her of an old bargain today.

"You're just in time," she said. "Rocky stopped on the way to town. We're about to eat. Dad will be glad to see you."

"Rocky, too, I reckon."

They went into the cabin. The main room was small, with mud-plastered walls and a small corner fireplace. Some of the fine pieces of furniture from the big house on Blue River were being used. Webb Clay and Rocky Taylor got up from the dining table as the couple entered.

Clay offered Rance his hand. "Glad to see you back, Rance. We've often wondered about you." He was a small man who always reminded Rance of a bantam rooster. He wore a goatee and had eyes of a very pale and innocent blue. His frail frame was stiffly erect.

Rocky Taylor merely said: "Howdy, Rance." He still wore the marks of Kirby's fists. His nose was flat and had a white scar across the bridge. He was a stolid, stockily built 'puncher somewhat shorter than Rance.

Nora set a place for Rance, and he ate the big plate of stew. The conversation was conventional and formal. Clay told Rance about the changes in the three valleys and asked him some questions about Mexico. Taylor smoked cigarettes and watched his former adversary narrowly.

Webb Clay asked: "What will you do now, Rance? Go back to Poverty Creek?" He was ever the tactful Easterner, referring to Poverty Creek rather than to Hooligan Cañon.

"I reckon not for a while," Rance said. "I've got two aims. One is to open up Smoky River Cañon. The other is to take Nora home with me."

Clay's face turned red, and Nora turned sharply to Rance. Then she began to blush, and her eyes seemed to take on a darker, angry blue. She said: "Whatever else you've learned while you've been away, you've certainly haven't forgotten how to be presumptuous."

"Not so presumptuous as you might think, Nora. You told me to come back to you after I owned Skyline Ranch again. Well, I bought it last night. And here I am."

"That's just what I mean," Nora stated. She was blushing even more intensely. "I was only joking when I said that, and *you* would take it seriously."

"Is this straight?" Taylor interrupted.

"You'll never hear anything truer," Rance told him. "Or that you're looking for a job as of now."

Clay carefully laid down his knife and fork and, moving his chair back, stood up. "You may own Skyline, Rance, but you've chosen a brutal way to fire a man who was here, paying us a friendly visit."

Rance overreacted. "If I had a million dollars, I'd still be a blue-jawed tough to you, wouldn't I? Because I was born on the wrong side of the Calamity Mountains. You've got to be born on Blue River to marry a white girl, don't you?"

He hadn't intended to say it. He hadn't even planned to bring up the subject to Webb Clay and Nora in front of Rocky Taylor, but Taylor's silent contempt and Webb Clay's social disapproval of what he had done in telling Taylor he was fired had aroused him.

Nora looked strangley at Rance, not entirely in anger.

Rocky stood up. "This looks like your cue to leave, Kirby."

Rance said: "Would you like to make me?"

Rocky Taylor took off his gun belt and laid it on the table before walking outside.

Nora seized Rance's arm as he rose to follow. "Don't do it, Rance!" she said. "Fighting isn't the way a girl wants to be courted."

Rance silently unbuckled his cartridge belt, laid his Peacemaker on the table beside the other man's, and started out. Taylor was waiting beside the door. As Rance came into the cramped opening, Taylor stepped in and swung a haymaker at Rance's face. Rance could only partially duck it. Knuckles bruised his cheekbone, and he lurched outside.

Taylor was after him with his left fist, stabbing, and his right cocked. He had the black-haired 'puncher off balance, and he crowded him savagely, cutting his face with short crosses. Something sharp ripped Rance's cheek, and, when he fell back and instinctively touched it, blood was pouring down his face, warm and wet. He saw the silver horseshoe ring Taylor wore.

Taylor's right fist came in, and Rance ducked, but he was sluggish as a result of that first punch, and the blow caught him on the side of the neck. He went down, paralyzed. The ground was warm under the palms of his hands, and he felt its roughness against his cheek. He heard faintly a sort of sobbing sound, realizing finally that it was his own labored breathing, as he dragged air painfully through his paralyzed throat. Rance crawled to his hands and knees and saw Taylor, standing there, his hands on his hips, his mouth turned vicious.

Rance stood up. Rocky came after him again, aggressively

but not without caution, for he had dreamed of this moment for three years, and he would not have it spoiled by overconfidence. Rance saw that, and he knew what it meant — a long slaughter before the kill.

The 'puncher stabbed him with a short left to the heart. Rance gasped, and Taylor began to jab at his face, driving him back. Again the horseshoe ring slashed, and Rance's chin was cut diagonally. Taylor kept after him, rocking him occasionally with a hard one to the head, ripping continually at his body.

Rance Kirby weathered it somehow. It never occurred to him to let the other man drive in the finisher and take the easy way out. He began to notice something — that Rocky was breathing hard, unhurt as he was. Taylor had always liked his whiskey, and he had never been one to work if there was a cowhand he could order to do a job. He was snorting and sweating like a green hand, tying a steer.

Rance took the next blow on his shoulder, falling back as though staggered. Taylor waltzed in, right shoulder rolling as his fist went out. But Kirby side-stepped, letting the blow go by and slamming the 'puncher's jaw with all he had. Rocky's eyes crossed. He stumbled and tried to rig up some kind of defense against the blows that, now suddenly, hammered and slashed at his face. When he raised both hands to shield his face, Rance began sledging at his stomach. Rance found the soft spot under his ribs, and Rocky Taylor was done. He groaned, staggering away, and Rance put a thunderous blow into the side of his jaw. Taylor lay on the ground with his bloody face in the dirt.

When Rance went back for his hat and gun, Webb Clay said stiffly: "I don't think I need to tell you that you'd best not come back here. There was no call for this kind of brutality, especially in front of Nora. After all, Rocky was a guest in our home."

158

"Did it ever occur to you," Rance asked, "that maybe this was the kind of brutality Rocky deserved for throwing in with the Smoky River bunch? He was in with them three years ago when we had our last fight. He's not to be trusted, however charming he may seem, particularly to women. You've lived by a code all your life that just doesn't work in this country. At the rate you've been going, you'll be farming the badlands in another couple of years . . . if you're still alive. You'll be pushed and pushed until you've got no place left to go, or like Rudy Guss or my dad you'll be finished by a bullet. I fight for what I want and for what I believe is right."

"Rudy Guss is dead?" Webb Clay asked in shock and fear.

"Shot in his chair, last night," Rance told him.

Nora said: "It's terrible about Rudy, Rance. But there are some things you can't win by violence. You'll probably never learn what they are . . . until it's too late."

"Perhaps you're right, Nora," Rance admitted, pausing at the door. He gazed steadily at her and then looked at her father. "Or maybe you just haven't been pushed far enough. When that happens, look me up. That's one thing Rocky Taylor and the Smoky River bunch are sure to know about me. When I'm pushed, I fight back."

III

It was near sundown when Rance Kirby rode into Three Rivers. The town lay in a little cañon of one of the creeks that fed Blue River. Incense cedar and juniper grew down the cañon sides to the sandy wash, and up on the slope, out of reach of spring floods, the town occupied a clearing. As a town, it was strictly utilitarian. Three Rivers claimed a *cantina* where Mexicans could get drunk on tequila, a saloon where Americans could take on a load of whiskey, a post office, a doctor, and a few stores to supply the necessities.

There was also a lawyer who profited by frequent range squabbles when there was no call for sheriff or coroner. This squabble did call for both, and Rance Kirby visited Sheriff Cave Jackson after the doctor had taken some stitches in his cheek and chin. Rance was not perturbed by the fact that there would be permanent scars. There was more ruggedness than beauty in his countenance to begin with, and a few nicks would not weigh much against one of his breed.

Cave Jackson heard his story. He said: "My God, again? This makes the fourth time I've had to go up there and look at a corpse." He pulled a bottle out of his desk, took a pull at it, and handed it to Rance. "I can preach, and I can hang," he told him, "but I'll be damned if I can make murder unpopular in the Big Bend. I wonder who I'll bury up there next."

"I can tell you who's taking over," Rance said. He showed him the deed Rudy Guss had given him.

Cave Jackson regarded him closely. He had a florid face with many broken veins in the cheeks, and a mouth that held a smile or the rim of a glass with equal grace. He had been sheriff of Three Rivers for twenty years, partly because he personally counted the ballots in all local elections.

"Guess you see where this puts you," said Jackson.

"I told you Rudy's gun trap got one of them," said Rance. "After you see the blood spilled around, you'll know it wasn't me. I'm going down now and see Jim Lonnergan. I'll meet you here in the morning, and we'll ride up."

Jim Lonnergan was a paradox in this country of hard work and low wages, a man who made more than most cattlemen without hardly ever leaving his office.

"Well, what's your trouble?" he asked as Rance entered.

Rance looked at him, wondering how far it was safe to trust a lawyer with something as big as this. Lonnergan was in his forties, a dark-skinned man with a black military mustache and a strong mouth. He dressed carefully in city clothes and always gave the impression of saying a lot less than he knew.

"No trouble, Jim," Rance told him. "I bought the Skyline iron last night. I want you to take care of recording the deed and fixing it up right."

Lonnergan's face was blank. Then his brows pinched together. "*You* bought it! With what?"

"With thirty thousand dollars in gold. It was forced on me in a card game in Mexico. Here's the deed the German gave me. He was killed a few hours later."

Jim Lonnergan examined it. He had a crooked smile when he looked up. "Well, I'm damned," he said. "Every man in the Bend out for it and a Hooligan Cañon roughneck wins it."

"The Kirby clan started it," he said. "It's just a homecoming. And I'm going to run cattle on every acre I own. You can pass that around if anybody asks you."

Jim Lonnergan knelt before his safe in the corner and started to put the deed away. Rance walked over and studied a big wall map, tracing the extent of his holdings. He was in such a position that when John Caddo entered he saw only Lonnergan before the safe.

"Jim!" Caddo said. "Hell's on the loose! They're sayin' Rudy Guss has been killed."

Lonnergan looked at him. "Yes, I know," he said. He closed the big wooden safe and snapped the padlock.

Caddo walked to the desk, threw down his hat, and sat down in a chair. The only thing beautiful about him was his daughter. Caddo's back was a twisted thing that put lines of pain in his

161

face, and his mind was equally distorted. His head was over-large, his face long and lantern-jawed, with a nose like a thin ridge of bone. He had schemed his way into one of the richest ranches in the Big Bend.

"Look here," Caddo said. "In about a week somebody's going to move in up there and dare us to throw him out. You remember I was dickering with Guss last fall to take it over?"

The lawyer shook his head. "It's too late," he said.

"Why is it too late?" Caddo sounded driven, desperate. "You can fix up some kind of trust deed, can't you? Hell, if he's got any heirs, I'll pay 'em a couple of thousand, and they'll think they're rich."

Rance Kirby began to laugh. "You get around, Caddo," he said. "But this time I got there first. What's more, nothin's got to be rigged up. I own it."

John Caddo stood up, leaning on the back of his chair. He had a faculty of covering his feelings with a cold-blooded exterior like armor plate, and he showed only a surly, contemptuous face to Rance now. "You won't last a month," he told him. "They'll get you like they did Guss."

"It's not them I'm afraid of," Rance said. "It's the ones who slap your back by day and steal your cattle by night that I'm worrying about. When I clean out Smoky River Cañon, I'm going to drag out a man for Cave Jackson to hang that we've all drunk with and heard pray out loud in church. It might even be somebody with Blue River water on his feet."

"That's a big mouthful for a man who rode a Mexican pony two years ago," Caddo remarked. He occupied his quick, nervous fingers with a cigarette. Rance had the feeling that his rapier of a brain was moving recklessly. When the cigarette was finished, Caddo wadded it up and threw it on the floor.

"Guss had no more legal right up there than I do," he said. "That paper he gave you is a hand receipt . . . no more. Skyline comes under some Spanish grant . . . every acre in this part of the country does. I'm going to find out which. And I'll make my deal with the legal owner." He turned to Lonnergan: "I'm going to sue to make Kirby prove ownership. Do you want the case?"

Lonnergan said: "You're crazy. Suppose you come back when you've cooled off a little?"

Caddo hobbled toward the door. "Then I'll take it to Job Hatfield."

Later, when he left, Rance ran into Libby Caddo. She was dressed in a divided skirt and wore a flat-crowned Stetson, hanging down her back by a string. Her dark eyes glistened.

"I knew you couldn't stay away," Libby said to Rance, smiling broadly. "I told Dad you'd be back someday and turn Three Rivers upside down."

Rance grinned. "Whose door you been listening at?"

Libby ignored the question. "Rance, is it true . . . you've got Skyline Ranch?"

Rance Kirby pulled her to him and pressed a hard, quick kiss on her lips. She was warm and vital against him, and for a moment she did not try to free herself. Then she pushed him away, but she was laughing.

"Now we can talk," Rance told her. "I never could talk anyway to you but tongue-tied, for wanting to do that."

"You're a devil, Rance," Libby said, laughing. "Now, what about Skyline Ranch?"

Rance looked at her. Her hair was black, and she knew how to wear it, with an artful carelessness that caused it to fall in natural waves to her shoulders. Her eyes were the deepest brown, and her mouth was red, provocative, scornful. She was a slender, full-breasted woman, with a hard cast to her features. She appealed to Rance because of her openness with him. Maybe that's why he liked her, because there was no pretension about Libby Caddo.

"Your dad will tell you about it," Rance said. "I've bought the iron. That's all."

Libby said: "That's only the start. I knew you'd be back up there some day. And now don't let them scare you off. What are you going to do?"

"Run cattle. What else?"

"I've always thought running cattle was a sideline with Guss."

"I don't know how it was with Guss, but it will be cattle with me . . . all the way down to the Rio Grande."

Libby's eyes were on him, shining and full of wonder. "You'll be in the middle of the biggest feud that ever hit Texas," she said. "You didn't buy the ranch just to make a living. You bought it . . . well, why did you buy it? Because you like a game where the stakes are big? Or to show somebody?"

"A little of both."

For a moment Libby studied him, and the expression in her eyes was no longer that of the capricious hoyden, but something deeper and more purposeful. Rance thought she was about to say something, but, when he glanced up the street, following her gaze, he saw John Caddo approaching.

"I've got to talk to you, Rance," she said quickly. "When can I meet you?"

"I'll be with Cave Jackson most of tomorrow," Rance told her. "Wednesday night?"

Libby squeezed his hand. "At Hanging Rock!"

IV

After one of the Russian's steaks at the café, Rance shot a few games of pool at the saloon. He looked up to see Job Hatfield, sitting alone at a table, his glance on him. The lawyer beckoned Rance with one finger, calling: "Come over and have a drink."

Rance went over, finding pleasure in the encounter with the lawyer. Hatfield ordered whiskey. He was a large and fleshy man with a pouchy moon face and big, pulpy hands. His color pointed at a sluggish liver, and his eyeballs were yellow-white.

"I hear you're a big rancher," Hatfield said with the manner of one humoring a slightly backward child.

"Well, I guess there's bigger," Rance told him. "But not around here."

Hatfield laid his hand on Rance's forearm, shaking his head. "My boy," he said, "let me give you some advice. Don't try to set the world on fire. I've seen them come, and I've seen them go. You've had some luck. Never crowd it. You're bound to roll snake eyes sometime."

"In the Bend," said Rance, "you've got to crowd it or quit. But you've got to use some savvy. Caddo's crowding his . . . and look where he's heading."

"Where's he heading?"

"He's climbed higher than anybody ever did around here, except for me at the moment, but all he's got under him is a rotten framework of called loans and blotched brands. He's got an eye on Skyline, and right now there is where his little tower is going to come crashing down. It's too weak to hold as big a man as he thinks he is."

"No, no!" Hatfield shook his head, leaning his bulk on the table with both elbows and linking his fat fingers. He smiled, but no longer in that condescending way. There was unsureness in it now. "John knows you're in solid up there. I admit he had some crazy notion this afternoon of trying to oust you. But I talked him out of it."

"What are you working into?" Rance demanded. "I suppose he wants to ride for me?"

The lawyer's right index finger tapped on the table. "You're a man that likes adventure. You take your battles and your women where you find them. All right. All John Caddo wants is more water and more grass."

"Only he wants them like some men want whiskey," Rance interrupted. "He starts having the screaming horrors if he doesn't get his daily shot."

Hatfield's mouth twitched. "What you think about him is beside the point. I'm trying to tell you that Caddo will pay you five thousand dollars for all of the Skyline above the Smoky."

Rance threw back his head, and his laughter filled the room. "He wants to give me five thousand for what I just put out thirty for, is that it?"

"No. You get the thirty back. I suppose it's still up there in Guss's safe, isn't it?"

His eyes had an edged intentness that Rance caught. "I wouldn't know," he said. "I think he spent it all on candy last night. But you can tell Caddo for me that he isn't going to scare or buy me out. I may even decide to take his daughter away from him."

Hatfield finished his drink at a gulp. "Then the chances are he'll go back to his original plan," he told the cowboy. "Lawsuits can cost money. You've got to fight them or lose them by default. I can slap you with enough papers to make your head swim. And I guess I'll have to."

Rance stood up, putting his fist under Job Hatfield's bulbous noise. "The first time I see a subpoena, I'll hang this right here," he said. "I'll whip you till you don't know your Blackstone from a second-hand copy of Diamond Dick. Think about it."

He walked up the boardwalk, the crispness of the night air bracing him. The battle ahead of him was beginning to shape up. He would have Caddo to fight openly — the Lord only knew how many who would come in the night anonymously. Rather than discourage him, Rance found the thought of it a spice.

He started back to the café. There was a light in Jim Lonnergan's office up the street. It went out with such suddenness that Rance started. A moment later the sound of a gunshot reached him.

He saw doors open along the street and a couple of men step out. From the direction of the livery stable a Mexican hosteler's voice called: "*¿Señor Lonnergan? ¿Qué hay?*"

Rance was striding across the street, his heels hitting hard and his Chihuahua spurs jangling. When he reached the lawyer's office, he stood and listened. Someone was moving about inside, then a door closed. Rance said quickly: "Jim?"

A match flared, and Rance saw Jim Lonnergan, lighting a lamp. He went in, watching Lonnergan sit down behind his desk and mop his face. He had a rueful grin as he looked at an old cap-and-ball .44 lying on the desk.

"I've been meaning to get a new gun for a long time," he said. "This cinches it. I was changing the loads, and one of the damned things went off. Luckily I had already removed the balls. The concussion blew the lamp out."

"Well, thank God," Rance said. "I thought maybe somebody was settling a case with you out of court."

Lonnergan was in his trousers and boots, as though he had been preparing for bed. He had his living quarters in a small

167

room in the rear. "Don't worry about me," he told Rance. "I haven't had anything but enemies for fifteen years. But I'm the sort that nothing ever happens to."

"Not more than once, anyway," Rance said.

He went outside, explaining to the men who were gathering what the commotion had been. After they dispersed, he crossed the road, walked a hundred feet, and again crossed and approached the lawyer's office from the rear. There were some things Lonnergan had not explained. Why the powder hadn't burned him, and why the door to his safe was open?

He could see into Lonnergan's bedroom through a flimsy green shade. John Caddo sat in an armchair, and the lawyer stood over him, talking in a hard, intense fashion, his hands on his hips.

"This is the last time I ever stand between you and the law," he told the man with the twisted back. "I've closed my eyes to too many of your shenanigans, for your daughter's sake more than yours. When it comes to the point where you start cracking my safe to steal a paper, I'm all through. And the next time I won't shoot to knock a gun out of your hand. There's an easier way. I just wonder whether you'd have tried to use that thing on me."

Caddo's fingers tried to make a cigarette, spilling the makings on his shirt. He looked up at Lonnergan, shaking his head. "I don't know what got into me, Jim," he admitted. "I want that Skyline iron like it ain't decent to want anything. But I mean to get it legally."

"Do you want my opinion?" Lonnergan asked. "You were happier when you owned thirty sections up the valley than you've ever been since. You'll never be big enough to satisfy yourself. You've started something you can't stop. But if you bother that boy, I'll drag a few things to light for a judge to look at."

Caddo said something that made Rance almost sorry for him, something that caused him to see for the first time the vast difference between him and other men.

"When you've got a body like mine, you don't worry about happiness," he said. "All you want is to show stronger men you're as big as they are. I guess the only cure for me is to grow six feet tall and lick a few men with my fists."

Before he moved away, Rance heard the lawyer say: "There's another cure, Caddo. And if you don't pull in your horns, someone is going to show it to you. It's done with a six-gun."

Old Casoose had a big dinner of *chilis rellenos, enchiladas,* and *frijoles* ready when Rance and Sheriff Jackson unsaddled at the Skyline at noon the next day. Jackson preferred to eat before inspecting the body of Rudy Guss, now reposing in state on a shelf in the spring house. Rance was used to the gamy Mexican dishes, but Jackson drank a bucket of water with his meal and swore the devil had stuck his finger in Casoose's kettle.

Casoose grinned. "Eat much *chilis,*" he said. "Have much hairs on chest."

Jackson grunted. "Have much ulcers on stomach," he said. "Where's this here body now?"

They looked at the blood-stained chair in which Guss had died. Then Rance took him to the spring house, and he and the sheriff carried the German into the small picket-fenced graveyard up on the hillside where Fred Kirby and the two other past owners of the ranch also slept. They buried Guss. Jackson finished tramping on the mound to firm it and stood, looking at the reddish, loose earth.

He said, feeling that the ceremony lacked authenticity: "Well, *adios amigo*. Dust thou art, to dust returneth."

They went back to the house.

After inspecting the gun trap under the gallery, the sheriff went to the corral to saddle his pony. "You want to watch out for more of them traps," he warned Rance. "He's likely got them stuck all over. There must be some place he kept his money."

"I'll be careful," Rance told him. "But it will take dynamite to get into his strong room, unless I find the keys." As an afterthought, he said: "I'll ride down to the falls with you. I'm going up and see Uncle Ad today."

"What do you want with that old varmint?"

Rance threw his saddle onto his sorrel and took up the latigo. "I'm hiring cowhands. Nobody in Hooligan Cañon would ride for me if he turned thumbs down on the idea. They don't believe in God, but they sure believe in Uncle Ad."

They forded the Poverty an hour later, and Jackson rode up Blue River toward town. Rance followed Poverty Creek's twisting gorge. A mile upstream the cañon widened into a sandy valley with little islands of hackberry and black oak dotting the sun-struck wash. There was grass on the mountains to the east, across which lay Blue River, but westward a frowning barricade of red rimrock offered scant vegetation. Hooligan Cañon ranchers ran their cows in the valley in spring, when the grass was green and tender. The rest of the year the cattle foraged in the Calamities, cropping the tough burro grass down to the roots in the straggling cañons.

Up one of these cañons Uncle Ad Cooney ran a scrubby herd of cattle with his two sons, Cain and Abel. Uncle Ad was a patriarch with a full, rusty beard and the strength of a Percheron. He liked to preach, salting his conversation with quotations from the Book, and he liked corn whiskey, which he made himself.

Rance found him hammering a mule shoe in the smithy. He saw Abel Cooney piling a load of block salt onto a wagon behind the barn. Above the barn, on the hillside, was a little cemetery plot outlined with colored rocks, two forlorn headboards standing crookedly.

Uncle Ad Cooney came out of the dark shack, the sledge across his shoulder. He looked steadily at Rance Kirby, grubbing through his memory. Then he said in that gruff voice of his, that was like rocks going down a chute: "Well, howdy, Rance. Didn't reckon you'd come up thisaway no more. Now that you're a big man."

"Where'd you get that notion?"

"News travels. Own the Skyline, don't you?" Uncle Ad wore no shirt, and his white skin was sweaty. It was an old man's skin, loose and flabby, but the muscles underneath were tough. He had sharp eyes of the palest of blues, and he had brown-stained, large teeth.

Rance dismounted. "That's why I came up here," he told the cowman. "I've fired the whole crew, from Rocky on down. Maybe they're all right. But maybe their loyalty has already been bought. So I'm looking for men. Reckon you could spare one of your boys?"

Uncle Ad sat down on a chopping block. He bit off a chew of Mexican twist and masticated it thoughtfully. He said: "Well, I might. What're your plans?"

"To run cattle where I damn' please. I need some boys that don't scare easy. That's why I thought first of Hooligan Cañon."

Cooney turned his head. He called: "You, Abel!"

Abel came over, an indolent, black-haired man built on a narrower, less rugged last than his father. It was Uncle Ad's often-voiced opinion that Abel was no good for anything but

171

getting drunk and fighting, but, when their Fiddleback herd began to run understrength, Abel always managed to scare up a few head somewhere to fill it out. He was sleepy-eyed, slouching, and always smelled of sweat and whiskey.

"You want to work for Rance for a spell?" Cooney asked him.

Abel stood with his thumbs thrust under his cartridge belt. He looked at Rance without expression. "What's the pay?" he asked.

"Sixty a month."

"Gunhands' pay," Abel Cooney said.

Rance said: "That's right. You may have to earn it."

Uncle Ad Cooney hooked the fingers of his right hand through his dirty beard. "'Whoso sheddeth man's blood,'" he quoted, "'by man shall his blood be shed.'"

"And whoso stealeth my cattle . . . !" Rance remarked.

Abel looked Rance over critically. Then he said: "All right. I'll be at the Falls House day after tomorrow."

Uncle Ad tossed the sledge hammer over by the shed. "This I don't like," he said. "Your father tried to open up Smoky River, and he died for it. It's the scum of two nations you'll be fighting if you go in there, Rance. The Book says . . . 'Out of violence cometh bloodshed and grief.'"

It seemed to Rance that all of Uncle Ad's quotations had to do with blood. Maybe he had it on his conscience. Rumors connected him with a lot of unwholesome transactions in Hooligan Cañon.

"I'm not going looking for trouble," Rance told him. "But I'm not stepping aside, if I see it coming. When we get through, a Hooligan Cañon man will be able to look anybody in Texas in the eye."

Rance was able to enlist eight more men from Poverty Creek.

Some were not the kind he would care to ride the river with, but they could all use a rope and a gun. He thought with a smile that he would have to take away their running irons or they'd be running their own brands on his roundups.

He cooked his own supper at the Falls House. He ate on the doorstep, watching the late afternoon sunlight slant through the trees, setting fire to the mist above the river thickets. He smoked a cigarette and drank his coffee, letting the peacefulness of it go through and through him.

A rider jogged from the cottonwoods into Rance's view. The man was slender, erect, clad in a gray suit and wearing a dove-gray Stetson, flat-crowned. Until he pulled up, Rance did not recognize him. Then he grinned and called out:

"What's the matter, Jim? Did your office burn down?"

It was the first time he could remember seeing Jim Lonnergan out of Three Rivers. The lawyer's face was ruddy with wind and sunburn from the unaccustomed ride. He left his horse under the trees that shaded the bunkhouse.

"Not quite," he said. "How're you fixed for coffee?"

They went into the kitchen, and Rance poured a steaming cup of Arbuckle. They talked about beef prices, and how many cows could be ranged to the section in that untouched grama and buffalo grass down the Smoky, but Rance knew there was something deep and troubling on the lawyer's mind.

Lonnergan said finally: "I've just been to Webb Clay's. He's finished, I guess."

"Finished?"

"Caddo's running him out. He's been living by a code written in a language that we don't savvy down here, especially men like Caddo. Caddo's boy, Hatfield, thought up a good one. It seems somebody that owned the Block B twenty years ago let his taxes lapse. It was finally bought by another man who never heard about the taxes . . . the slip-shod way they run things here, no effort's ever been made to collect. Hatfield found it on the books, Caddo paid them up, and now he's got a paper from the county demanding repayment of five hundred in taxes and twelve percent interest, compounded semi-annually. I rode over to warn Clay today."

"What's he going to do?"

"*¿Quién sabe?*" Lonnergan's shoulders moved. "I fear he's forgotten how to fight. Why don't you lend him a hand, Rance?"

Rance was surprised at the suggestion. "All I could do is offer him gun help. He wouldn't want that."

"I'm not so sure. He's pretty disgusted with the position his soft-handed methods have put him in. And there's another thing." Lonnergan's eyes smiled, though his lips barely turned. "You'll catch a lot more flies with sugar than with vinegar."

Rance began to blush, but he countered: "Meaning what?"

"You'd kind of like to see Nora Clay in your pasture, wouldn't you? I should think the quickest way to melt her down would be for you to help her father out of this. You could do it. If he can hang on for a few weeks, I can save his neck." Lonnergan finished his coffee and put on his hat. Rising, he said: "Let me tell you something, Rance. A girl like Nora isn't to be won by showing her your muscles. Maybe Libby Caddo, but not Nora Clay. You'll get a lot farther with a nicely turned phrase about her hair than you will by knocking the tar out of her beaux."

"Jim," Rance said wearily, "I could turn a cow inside out easier than I could turn a nice phrase. As Uncle Ad says . . . 'To some is the gift of a golden tongue, and to some the gift of silence.' I'm great for keeping my mouth shut when I go makin' love."

All the next day Rance thought about what the lawyer had said. He tried to convince himself that what Nora thought about him did not matter, but the need for her was with him always, touching everything he did, and, when he dreamed, it was not of Libby's dark beauty that was his for the taking, but the inaccessible, gentle loveliness that was Nora's. Lonnergan was right. When she was won, it would be by some man who could say in words what it would take Rance years to tell her. And so, he told himself, there was no use heaping any more fuel on that dead blaze. Just at dark Rance Kirby left Skyline Ranch to keep his tryst with John Caddo's daughter.

Darkness filled the roaring gorge of the Smoky, and the air was cool and moist. Shortly after he passed Lookout Point, he heard a night bird's cry, clear and sweet through the murmur of tumbling water. It hit him suddenly, seconds later, that there was something wrong with the sound. It was the call of a mountain quail. Rance Kirby laid the rein across the pony's neck and spurred into the brush. The whistle came again, with no attempt at deception: one sharp blast that ended in a rifle crash and brought several more guns pounding through the echoes.

Rance heard the brush around him crackle as slugs broke through the matted manzanita and buckthorn. He pulled the pony in beneath a rimrock ledge and tried to get a mental map of the situation. The man who had whistled — the nearest gunman — sent another shot upward at him, across fifty feet of blackness. Rance jumped as the lead blasted into the rock behind him. He got a tight hold on the reins and leveled his saddle gun at the base of a scrub oak down the slope.

He fired once, and, as he levered another shot into the chamber of the Burgess, he heard a man grunt and scramble away. He allowed for the movement and put a second shot into the ambuscade. The man cried out, a single gasp of shock.

Now the other guns came in, hammering out a wild death chorus of exploding shells and ricocheting lead. Beneath him the pony trembled. Rance Kirby made out the positions of the bushwhackers, forming a rough right triangle. The longest leg of the triangle was above him. He spurred his horse up the bank, stumbling and sliding, feeling the hungry rake of the thorned buckbrush. If he could break through at this point, he knew an old cow trail far above he could follow to the Falls House.

Directly ahead of him gunflame flared startlingly. He could hear the bullet strike his pony, a loud slap. The animal grunted, mortally hit. Rance threw himself from the saddle as it went down, landing in a dense manzanita.

Again the guns were barking, the rifleman who had downed Rance's pony firing steadily. Two of the gunmen were closer. Rance Kirby knelt there, reloading his gun and trying to ignore the slugs that snapped through the thickets around him and whined off the rocks. He was afraid, and not ashamed of it.

He dared not fire again except as a last resort. They had him, like a badger in a pit. He felt a macabre kinship with Rudy Guss and those others who had pitted themselves against the wolf pack. They, too, had stuck out their chins and announced how tough they were. And they had found that one bullet weighs more than all the bragging in the world.

He heard the man above him begin to move down through the brush. The others were dragging themselves closer, too, but this man was within fifty feet. Rance sat back and waited, the .44-40 covering the outlaw as he crawled nearer. When they came face to face, it would all be a question of who spotted whom first.

Now the gunman heard the horse threshing, and his forward movement stopped. Again he pressed ahead, with greater caution. The others on the downslope were coming up, too, wondering whether their man was dead, or whether they would have the pleasure of finishing him.

The brush in front of Rance Kirby parted, and a shadowed face — the face of a Mexican he didn't recognize — showed in the breech. Rance fired, saw the bullet punch a hole in the man's forehead, saw the blood begin to spill, dark and thick. He sprang up and stood over the man an instant. By the look of him, he was a border-hopper, a stranger to this valley, and that was all Rance needed to know.

The others down the slope were calling tensely in Spanish: *"¿Qué pasa?"*

Rance called back: *"¡Ya 'stá 'ueno! ¡Mire!"*

He heard them coming confidently through the brush, and swiftly, quietly, he turned and went up the hill toward the cow trail. When they found their dead partner instead of the *gringo*, they began to swear and fire indiscriminately. But by that time Rance was high above them, mounting the dead outlaw's pony.

There was one thing about Libby Caddo. If she liked you, she didn't make a secret of it. When Rance reached Hanging Rock, she put her arms around his neck and kissed him, and he could feel her trembling.

"I knew you'd get through, Rance," she said. "I heard the shooting, but I knew all the wolves in the Bend couldn't stop you."

Rance sat down on the ledge that thrust out from the mountain a hundred feet above the confluence of the rivers. "I wish I'd been as sure," he said. "I got two of them. I'm on their list now for sure." He rolled a cigarette. "Did your father know you were going to meet me?"

Libby laughed. "Of course not. But somebody must have known you were coming."

"Nobody knew but Casoose."

Libby said: "You should kill that old Mexican. I don't trust any of them."

The coldness of it startled Rance. "Casoose is all right," he said shortly.

Libby shrugged. "Have it your way. Do you know why I wanted to see you?"

"I thought maybe you wanted to marry me for my money," Rance said. "You'd be the leading candidate for the earliest widow in Three Rivers."

Libby did not smile. She looked down at the pale flood below the falls, her face very serious. Her hair was shining and dark upon her shoulders, and her eyes looked moody in the moonlight.

"Do you know," she said, "I may be running the Ladder Ranch sooner than I thought. The way Dad has been forcing himself, he's going to be dead before his time. The more land he gets, the more he's got to have. He drives himself on, riding too much and sitting up all night to figure and plan. The doctor told him he wouldn't give him over a year at the rate he's failing."

Sympathy for the crippled range king did not come easily to Rance. He had never liked or trusted him. He said: "Maybe he'd be better off if he let men like Clay alone."

"It's his business," Libby said. "But when he goes, it will give me a free hand to do a lot of things I've wanted to." She looked up at him, beginning to smile a little. "Maybe I'll even marry."

Rance smiled. "Rocky ain't such a good-looking man any more," he said.

Libby sniffed. "Rocky Taylor is a stupid fool. He'll never be

178

more than a second-rate ramrod. Dad's hired him, now that he's left your outfit. I don't know why. But Rocky isn't the one I meant."

Rance asked: "Who is it?"

Libby smiled petulantly. "Who else could it be? We're out of the same mold, Rance, you and I. We live for ourselves. We don't care what anybody says or thinks, just so he doesn't get in our way. With the Skyline and the Ladder under one brand, who could ever stop us? We'd own the Big Bend."

Something in her voice, in the hard shine of her eyes, took Rance's breath. She had her father's ambition and drive, and a lot more that made her more desirable — and more dangerous. It was hard for him to catalogue his emotions when he thought about it. Nora Clay had beauty and depth, a quietness that touched something deep within him. Libby set a man on fire, turned his head with foolish thoughts that would make him trouble. Rance guessed he wasn't fool enough to marry a wild-cat.

He said: "I reckon we're alike, all right . . . too much alike. It'd be two catamounts in one barrel."

"Is that what you think?" Libby asked him.

"What else can I think?" Rance said. "I know both of us too well."

Libby's chin was up, proud and angry. She said: "It's Nora Clay."

"Nora wouldn't have me if I were candy-coated. It's nobody. Just common sense."

Libby was silent for a moment. "I suppose I should be angry," she told him then. "I wish I could be. I'm sorry for both of us. You're in love with Nora, and she'll never have you. I could make you happier than you'll ever be with anybody else, Rance, but you've got this idea in your head."

Rance stood up. "Some day you'll thank me," he said.

"You're still the prettiest girl in Three Rivers." He tried to pull her into his arms, but her open hand stung him on the mouth.

"Thanks just the same, Mister Kirby," she said. "I've still got some pride."

Rance stood there, looking down at her shadowed, cynical face and feeling the sting of her hand on his mouth. He realized at that moment how little he knew about women, good or bad. That last remark of hers suddenly meant a lot. He hadn't wanted to hurt her, but he was sure that he had. She would be fine as a casual friend, but she would be dangerous either as a lover or as an enemy, and it was in his mind that she was not far now from being an enemy.

He took her arm. "I'll ride back with you," he said. "No woman ought to be alone at night, out here."

"I'm all right," Libby said. "You'd better run back to your big, empty house and make sure Casoose is all right."

Rance picked her up, struggling, and carried her back to her horse. He was laughing. "You'll do for a wildcat if we ever run short," he told her.

While he held her, he kissed her. All the stiffness went out of Libby, and, when he put her down, he knew she was crying. Rance helped her to her saddle. He felt a rueful sort of closeness to her at that moment, and he put his arm around her.

"Love is no fun, Libby," he said. "Heaven must be a place where you get the one you want."

Libby's voice was choked. "It doesn't happen any place else."

Rance had not volunteered to take Libby Caddo home for purely altruistic reasons. The girl was probably safe enough, for she was capable, and she carried a saddle gun. He had in mind a little talk with John Caddo.

At the river they said good night, and he watched her ford

the shallows. When she was out of sight, he crossed the stream behind her and rode up the grassy swale to the low ridge that surmounted the Ladder headquarters. All was dark below him, except for one lighted window in the big L-shaped ranch house. Rance dismounted and sat on the slope until he saw Libby's light come on and, presently, go out.

Leaving the pony in the shelter of a sandy wash, Rance approached the house, passing the corrals downwind so that the animals would not give warning. Through a pin-point hole in the window shade he could see John Caddo humped over a desk. The rancher had one hand shoved into his thin sandy hair, and he was making figures on a big yellow pad with a pencil.

With his gun Rance jammed a hole through the glass and reached in quickly to let the shade fly up. He kept the gun on the startled rancher. "Sit still and keep your mouth shut," he said. He unfastened the catch, raised the window, and stood, leaning on the sill.

"Have you gone crazy, Kirby?" Caddo demanded. He sat hunched in the swivel-chair, his tawny eyes shining with the lamplight.

"I've been havin' nightmares," Rance told him. "I had one tonight and couldn't sleep, so I rode down to talk to you. I got the idea you were going to try to throw old Webb Clay off the Block B."

"So I am," Caddo said. "I bought the place for taxes. He leaves tomorrow, if you're interested."

"I'm just linking it up with something Job Hatfield told me. You're asking for trouble, John, when you go poking into Smoky River Cañon."

Caddo said irascibly: "I can take care of all the trouble that comes my way. I'm tired of you and your cheap threats."

Rance worked the hammer of the gun back and forth, watching him. "I'm just wondering why you want that little twenty-section strip of Clay's so much. Maybe it's so you can bring Skyline cattle in without any trouble, in case you get any of my beef mixed up with yours. Or maybe it's just for the land. Whatever it is, pardner, you aren't going to have it."

Caddo smiled. "Every day you talk bigger. You haven't made your first brag good, yet."

"That's why I'm making this one. I'm beginning to get tired of drygulching and cow stealing. Clay's one of the few men left that we need around here. I don't have to tell you that you've jobbed him. Lonnergan is smelling around that tax deal of yours. I don't aim to see Clay thrown off till we break up your little game."

"I've given him warning," Caddo said. "I mean to make it stick."

"I didn't come to argue," Rance said. "If Clay goes, you go. I'll see your houses sacked and your feed burned. Those boys of mine are like a bunch of Comanches once they get started."

Caddo lost some of his lofty scorn. Possessions were everything to him, and he knew what might happen if the wild bunch from Poverty Creek were ever organized. He said: "If you touch me, I'll see you hang."

"If I have to burn you out," Rance told him, "I doubt that you'll be alive to do anything about it."

Behind Caddo the office door opened quietly. Caddo, seeing Rance's glance shift, turned to look into the dark hallway. It was impossible for Rance, from his position, to see who stood outside, but Caddo frowned and said impatiently: "Well?"

Whoever stood in the hall did not bandy words. A gun crashed once, rolling gray smoke and pale flame into the room, and John Caddo's long fingers clutched at the chair arms. He gasped, falling against the backrest. He began to breathe in a ghastly, strangling fashion, and with each breath blood bubbled on his lips.

Rance Kirby, through the shock in him, knew one thing. To be caught here might mean hanging. He heard men begin to call out questioningly in the bunkhouse, and the bang of a door thrown open. He ran down the wall and passed around the rear of the house.

As he went past the back porch, a gun bellowed from the doorway, deafening him, throwing him off balance. The bullet whipped through his jumper. Rance fired into the dark opening and kept running. Men seemed to be springing up everywhere, pouring out of the bunkhouse and running to the corral, to the big commissary. Now Rance heard Rocky Taylor's voice, shouting orders. From the house he heard Libby's voice, raised in terror.

He went under the corral bars and worked his way through the excited animals. He unlocked the feed barn and went into the musty, black interior, striking a match after he had closed the door. In the opposite wall he saw the rear door. He slid it back and stepped outside. He began to run, keeping low, heading for the water gap across the dry arroyo where he had left his pony. When he reached it, he was winded, his chest heaving as he crawled under the barbed wire.

The sounds and lights were far behind him then, and he was mounting his pony and loping down the arroyo to where it joined the Blue. The turbulence in him did not have all its roots in sheer excitement. Shadows were marching across his mind — Rocky Taylor's, Webb Clay's — and Libby's. Many men had a reason to kill John Caddo, but these three stood to profit more than others, and he thought that Taylor and Libby might be capable of such a thing any time, and Clay, if he were crowded.

Rance Kirby was wishing for a drink as he rode the dark trail. He was seeing another side of the range war that was about to envelop all the Three Rivers country, and he did not know exactly where it would stop.

Back at the Ladder ranch house Rocky Taylor was a lot more certain than Rance Kirby about who had killed John Caddo. Libby had come from her room when she had first heard the gunshot and the subsequent commotion. She had been in bed and wore a light wrap over her nightgown. She was kneeling beside her father's body, sobbing, when she was startled by Rocky Taylor's voice, coming from the window where Rance had earlier been standing and talking to Caddo.

"This is just where he stood when he fired the shot," Rocky said.

Libby rose and moved quickly toward the broken window, tears streaming down her face. "Who? Who fired that shot, Rocky?"

"Webb Clay. I saw him running away, Libby, and even fired at him. I missed. He had his horse hidden near the water gap across the dry arroyo. You want I should ride to town for Cave Jackson?"

Libby dried her tears on a sleeve, her eyes now flashing with anger. "No," she answered, "we don't need the sheriff. We'll burn those Clays out. Dad gave Webb Clay a deadline. He crossed it tonight. Ladder will pay back Webb Clay, one way or the other."

VII

Rance went down with Casoose Corrales the next morning to the Falls House where he met with his new cowhands. On the way down they searched for the men he had shot the night before. Blood stains were still prominent in the brush, but the bushwhackers had buried their own dead.

Rance said to his crew: "This is a little early for a beef roundup, but we're starting one. It's fifteen miles down the Smoky to the Big River. On the way down we'll work every gully and ridge for cattle. Any strays with no brand, my brand, or a Mexican brand is ours. Anybody that wants to back out has still got time. There'll be a bonus of a hundred dollars for every man that stays with me. But he'll earn it."

Abel Cooney licked the cigarette he had rolled. He asked: "Where do you want the gather kept?"

"At The Slide," Rance told him. "After tomorrow we'll hold them wherever we find a likely spot."

That day they worked the range from the falls downstream a mile. The country was turned all on end, rough, scrub-timbered slopes where a man needed a real mountain pony. They used breast rigs and cruppers to take up the shock of a hard-running steer when it hit the end of the rope, for it meant almost sheer death to have a saddle turn in this kind of country.

At the end of the day Rance looked over the cattle penned in the little box cañon below The Slide. They were fat from eating bluestem and not being worked. If the rest of the drive turned up stuff like this, he had made a good investment.

They moved gathered cattle down the cañon the following day, penning them up in a blind cañon with Al Parsons, a freckled, gangling young 'puncher from the Poverty, riding herd. From that point they worked on down the gorge.

Near sundown Rance called it quits for the day. He had chosen for the campsite that morning a clearing on the bank of a sandy creek. Ike Bradley, the roundup cook, had stew ready when the crew straggled in. He had biscuits as big as horseshoes, browning in the Dutch ovens, and coffee, boiling in a pot like a bucket.

Tired as they were, the boys revived enough to hoorah the

cook as he dished up the grub. It seemed to Rance that there was someone missing, and, when he counted noses, he discovered that Al Parsons had not been relieved. After eating, he said to Abel Cooney: "Casoose and I will stand bob-tail guard on the day bunch. Send a couple of boys up to relieve us at eight o'clock."

Cooney nodded. "I'll come up with Baldy," he told him.

Rance and the Mexican pushed along, trying to make it before dark. It grew dark early on the Smoky, and cold came with it. Al would be glad to head for the campfire and a belly full of chuck. They were not far from the blind cañon when a sound came to them that was alien to the primeval silence. It could have been a rock slide, or it could have been the echo of gunshots pouring down the cañon. Rance and the foreman touched their horses to a lope with one fear.

When they reached the box cañon, they found Al Parsons, lying on the sand at the mouth of the wash. His pony was gone, and Al lay with one cheek pressed against the sand and his hands clutching at it. From far off there was the sound of horses running. Rance turned the 'puncher over. His body was sodden with blood. Bullets had gone into him from a dozen angles, pounding and tearing. The dazed eyes looked at Rance, seeming to know him.

He whispered, his jaw hardly moving: "Lots of 'em, Rance. Masks. They came . . . from the river."

The boy couldn't live, but Rance turned quickly to Casoose. "Take off your shirt," he said. "We'll need yours and mine both to plug him."

Casoose was unbuttoning his shirt when they heard the cattle coming. It was like a distant cannonading, at first, but quite suddenly it rose to a close and terrifying thunder. Blocked by the sharp angles of the cañon, the sound now rolled past the nearest bend with an imminence that brought Rance and the Mexican up straight. Then, without a word, they bent and raised the wounded man by his arms and legs.

The cattle streamed past the bend and rolled toward them. Shaggy heads were up, and long, brush-honed horns clacked like sabers. It was fifty feet to the shelter of the boulders at the side of the cañon.

Rance could see Casoose's lips, moving in prayer. The Mexican had his eyes on the rocks, not even glancing at the herd that filled the whole floor of the cañon. Without the burden of the dying man they would have had some chance. This way they were bucking a game in which they held all deuces.

Rance stopped and heaved Parsons across his shoulder. He yelled at Casoose and made a gesture with his free hand. The Mexican hesitated an instant, then he was racing across the sand into the jumble of boulders.

Rance had all the weight of the dying man now, but he was packing it in such a way that he could run without sidling crab-fashion. His knees wanted to buckle under him, but he kept pounding along through the maddeningly soft sand. The first of the steers streaked past him, one thundering by in front of him so close that he had to stand an instant. Behind him they were plunging from the mouth of the cañon and dispersing through the trees, making for the thickets along the creek.

Suddenly it was over, and Rance was lying on the sand, crouching against a boulder, while the cañon floor shook from the impact of a thousand hoofs. Their ponies had loped away, and a small, chilling fear was in Rance Kirby. They were alone in the wilderness of Smoky River Cañon with only their sidearms and no horses. It was not the kind of odds that made a man overconfident.

The day's gather was gone in sixty seconds. Nothing remained in the dark cañon but the echoes of the crashing passage of the cattle through the brush, the dust of their headlong run.

Then they heard the horsemen. Riding at a high lope, they came arrogantly down the cañon, laughing and swinging ropes, ten men who wore flour sack hoods that were dirty gray blurs in the night.

Rance rubbed his thumb across the sight of his long Colt. He laid Parsons's gun on the sand beside him. "This is Al's party," he said to Casoose.

The Mexican nodded, laying the barrel of his revolver in the notch of the rock.

When the riders were abreast of them, they opened up. In an instant the cañon was filled with rearing horses and yelling men. Two of the outlaws pitched from their saddles. Rance and Casoose emptied their guns into the mob, and Rance reached for the extra six-shooter. Lead was beginning to come their way, whining off the rocks and chunking into the dirt bank behind them.

A man yelled something, and the night riders spurred into the brush. Two ponies ran with them, riderless. Rance and the Mexican reloaded, dug in behind new rocks to meet an attack from another angle, and waited. They let ten minutes go by. The Smoky River gang had melted into the night. Apparently they were making no fetish this time of burying their casualties. The men they had left behind were dead when Rance and Casoose Corrales ventured out. They pulled off the masks, inspecting the dead faces in the deepening gloom.

One of the men was a Mexican with a stringy black mustache and sharp yellow teeth like a gopher's. The other man, an Anglo-American, brought a grunt from Casoose.

"*¡Ai, hombre!* I am cooking food for these man's belly two years. Pinto Roberts. He ponch cows for Guss."

Rance said: "When they're all tallied in, we'll find more than one of his boys was drawing pay from two sides."

While they were inspecting the outlaws, Al Parsons drew his

last breath. They scooped out a shallow grave in the wash and piled rocks on his body to discourage timber wolves until he could be decently buried. Then they started the long hike back to camp.

It was nearly eight o'clock when they limped in on spiked boots that had never been designed for walking. Their ponies had drifted in a few minutes before, and Abel Cooney was organizing a search party when they came into the firelight.

Rance drank a cup of black coffee before he offered any explanation. All the men who were not out on herd duty were sitting on their blankets, watching him. At length he said: "We're starting to earn our bacon and beans, boys. Al was killed tonight. We dropped two of them. I don't look for things to get any quieter from now on. Anybody that doesn't want to leave a widow can move out in the morning."

VIII

The crew was still intact when they started work at dawn. Rance had a fierce pride in these men who had little to gain by sticking it out, and a lot to lose. In Three Rivers they had to drink alone, but put them in a spot like this, where a man's values were suddenly revealed under a strong white light, and they were kings, and a little better. Hooligan Cañon. Some day men would write that after their names the way a man would say: "I was at Gettysburg."

They worked deeper into the cañon, going slowly, proceeding in pairs. From boyhood memories Rance was picking fragments that fitted in with the things he was seeing now . . . a stretch of white water with black roots, jutting through the foam like a forest of stumps . . . a cliff almost covered with Indian pictographs . . . a gorge pocked with wind caves.

He was remembering something else that set his spine to tingling, and in the afternoon he said to Casoose: "I'm going to take a *pasear* down to the river. Keep the boys busy. Better double up the guard in case I'm not back in time."

"No, *compadre*," he said. "Four eyes see twice as much as two. Two guns shoot twice as fast as one. I go along, *sí?*"

Rance smiled. "Where I'm going, two men would crowd the trail."

Casoose raised his hands in despair. "*¡Ojalá qué hombre!* You know what is said . . . where the angels fear to go, there rushes the fool."

"I'm no angel, so I'll rush in."

Rance rode along the cliff, searching for landmarks. The river was about fifty feet wide at this point, filling the floor of the deep and murky gorge. There was no semblance of a trail. All the broken ledges in the cliffs seemed to slant down to meet the water. The cañon turned and twisted, and the wind that came up was cold and moist.

Across the river Rance saw a peak shaped like the horn of a saddle. Memory stirred strongly. He left his horse tied to a juniper and scouted cautiously along the brink. Near the bottom he suddenly saw it. A cave that was like an eyesocket. A narrow trail only ten feet above the water level crawled along the cliff under overhanging ledges, in and out of breaks in the moss-stained wall.

He tried to recall how he had reached the trail from the cliff. The drop from ledge to ledge was too great. The hand-and-foot-holds were all slimy with moisture. Then he remembered the fissure in the cliff, like a great knife slice. He made his way through the brush, watchful.

In about twenty minutes he came out of a creosote thicket

onto a narrow gap in the earth. He was able to lower himself by getting his back against one rough wall and using roots and rocks in the opposite wall as support for his feet. It required fifteen minutes of this punishing labor to reach the bottom, some forty feet below. He was breathless, sodden with sweat, and his back was raw and sore.

Now he stood on the rubbled bottom of the fissure, hearing the wind sough past the mouth of it, some distance ahead and much lower. When he reached the mouth, he stood, looking down at the brown river, seeing the narrow man-made trail just above it, and feeling a shakiness in his legs. There was a loneliness here like that of an empty cathedral. There was only the mutter of the river, a low-voiced warning, and there was the cold dampness of the air to chill a man's skin.

Rance dropped to the trail. He had his gun in hand, and he looked southward, toward the Rio, and then north. There was much burro sign on the trail, old and new. There were marks on the cliff as though pack animals had been scraping along this passage for a century. He started toward the cave.

When he reached it, he hesitated, listening. He heard nothing, and after a moment he went up the smoothly-worn slope to the interior. Standing there, it was like having a scene from the past projected onto his mind. There was the floor, that sloped up to meet the ceiling fifty feet back. There was the legend on the ceiling, written in candle smoke in old Spanish characters — *Pasó por aquí* — followed by a list of names of men dead two centuries. There were the blackened stones of an old campfire.

As a boy Rance had crawled through the low passage that gave into the greater cave beyond. There he had seen men, working among piles of booty, the scene illuminated by a score of lanterns. He went back to the passage now and crawled into the big room. He sat back on his heels for a moment, sniffing the mustiness of stale air. He had his gun firmly against his hip.

Fear went suddenly over him like ice water, as metal rasped against metal a few feet away. Light bored through the blackness from a bull's-eye lantern splashing over him blindingly. A man said in Spanish: "They come looking for gold, and we give them lead."

Rance Kirby flung himself forward on his face, firing as he fell. The outlaw's gun roared, spitting flame and lead. The bullet glanced off Rance's left hip, hurting no more than the blow of a fist. The sounds of the guns was a physical impact against his ears, deafening him. Rance heard no cry from the guard, but the lantern crashed on the floor and sent its white beam upward at the ceiling.

Another cartridge exploded, but Rance Kirby had moved away, and the slug screamed off the stone wall. He fired twice more at the gun flash. The second time left no doubt that he had got his man. The gunman moaned, and a body crumpled on the floor with a soft, boneless sound.

For a long time Rance sat there, shaken by the concussion and the beginnings of trouble in his wounded hip. He had a curious feeling of floating in space. There was nothing of this world for him to grasp except the ray of the lantern. Everything else was silence and blackness, lapping at the shores of the light. He crawled to the lantern. He turned it on the gunman and saw a Mexican in a straw sombrero and a *vaquero's* work clothes. Rance took his gun as a precaution, although the man was breathing in a gasping fashion that could not have been simulated.

The lamplight revealed piles of boxes and rawhide *aparejos* on the floor of the cavern. Here was where luckless Chihuahua freight trains had been detoured for generations. Rance limped about, digging into some of the boxes. He found what he had expected to find — a hodgepodge of merchandise of all descriptions: lamp chimneys, liquors, cheap clothing, cooking utensils, all the miscellany of household goods the villages of Chihuahua had to import from Mexico City or the States. Such articles would have a high ransom or resale value.

Yet Rance knew that Smoky River Cañon had been guarded for more precious booty than this. He was thinking of the silver mines of the Padrones, fifty miles to the southwest. He kept moving about the cave, inspecting heaps of merchandise. The shock of his wound was wearing off, and the pain grew more insistent. He could not place all his weight on his left leg without driving a surge of cold blackness through his head.

Far in the back he found it. Piled like cordwood against the wall was a rick of bar silver. He lifted one of the ingots and read the mint stamp: 1859. Others bore more recent dates. It came to him that for all the lives the treasure had cost, for all the men who had bled and fought to gain it, probably no one had ever profited from it. All these years it had lain here, piling ever higher, but whoever called himself king of Smoky River at any particular time was too busy keeping intruders out to enjoy his wealth.

The lantern seemed to flicker, to gutter out. *Out of oil,* Rance thought vaguely. He was not conscious of dropping the lantern, nor of falling, for the blackness was all in his brain. . . .

Much later he came to, weak and sick. The lantern had gone out. There were some pallid highlights on the walls where a few feeble rays seeped in through the mouth of the cave. Panic laid its cold fingers on Rance Kirby's throat. *To die here like a rat!* he thought. *To die with a mountain of stone between me and the sun.* He got on his hands and knees and groped back toward the entrance.

He was halfway through the passageway when he realized someone else was crawling through from the other side. Rance

193

saw the crawling shape stop.

A man's voice inquired: "Pete?"

Rance tried to make his voice strong, as confident as the gun barrel he shoved against the newcomer's shoulder. He said: "Uhn-uh, Rocky. It's your old friend and bosom companion."

Rocky Taylor flinched. His voice was a gasp. "Well, I'll be damned!"

"You surely will," Rance told him, "if you try to go for your hardware. I'm prospecting. What are you doing?"

Taylor could still grin, his blocky face just visible, still scarred from their recent battle. "You got trumps," he said. "And you come to a good place to prospect. Gettin' back may be the tough part."

"I don't look for much trouble. It's a funny thing, Rocky, but I never credited you with enough savvy to ramrod an outfit like this."

"I don't. Well, not exactly." Taylor sighed. "I suppose now you want to know all about the cañon and who killed Rudy Guss."

"You're a good guesser. I'd also like to know who led the bunch that killed Al Parsons." Rance wished the pounding and burning in his hip would stop. It was hard to dam the waves of pain.

"Johnny Caddo had Rudy killed," Rocky stated. "Didn't know Al was even dead. A couple of Mexes killed Guss for Caddo. He thought he'd move right in here, but you coppered him. Guss was running the shebang before, putting up a big howl about how he never got to stick his nose in here because of all the badmen. But he was the boy."

"I'll believe that," Rance told him, "when I see it written in the family Bible. I want to know who decided to kill Al."

Rocky said sullenly: "Dammit, Kirby, I'm only working for a living myself. I don't know half what goes on. Since Caddo was murdered, I'm taking orders from Libby. She's following pretty well the lines her old man set out. He had the idea that he'd like to slap his brand on all the Smoky River cattle before somebody else did, while the place is still without a boss. Me and some of the Ladder boys came down here to do some art work with a running iron. We were supposed to move the cows down to the Big River. Then we'd try to get them around the Dead Horse Mountains to the Ladder range. I don't know how we were supposed to get them across Webb Clay's spread, but Libby thinks he'll drag his pin pretty soon anyway." He added, as though feeling a weak point in his story: "I knew about this cave from one of the Mex jinglers we had when I worked for Rudy. I just thought I'd see whether there was anything here beside corncobs two hundred years old and a few clay pots."

Suddenly the sickness in Rance Kirby's brain was something he could no longer fight. There was a viciousness in his voice that come from desperation.

"You wouldn't know the truth if you was introduced to it," he said. "Rudy Guss was too old and fumblin' to run this outfit. And you're too narrow between the ears. Somebody's sitting up there with a big gun and a lot of ideas, running the show just like always. Maybe it was Caddo, but if it was, it's not the way you tell it. I'm letting you go, Rocky, but get out of my sight fast. I mean now!"

Taylor may have sensed that Rance was on edge for rash action. It did not take a very smart man to know that a shaking hand and a rising voice meant trouble.

He said: "OK, Kirby. It's your party."

After he had gone, Rance lay still a long time. At last he ventured onto the slippery river trail, walking painfully back toward the slot. He did not know how he would make the climb back up the wall. When he reached it, he rested for fifteen minutes and started back up the steep, narrow incline. At the spot where he had descended, he was surprised to find a rope ladder, hanging from the top. Taylor had probably used it. No doubt it was part of the regular equipment. He did not try to puzzle out whether Rocky had left it hanging down here for a purpose. Very slowly he climbed it.

By the time he reached his pony the sun indicated that it was past three o'clock. Rance dragged himself into the saddle and rode back to the new roundup spot.

For a long minute he sat looking at the deserted clearing, trying to understand what had happened. Cooking gear littered the ground. The stake-and-rope-remuda was uprooted and tangled in the undergrowth. The cook's pack animals, picketed a little way off, were both dead. Ike Bradley lay face down across his cook fire, his clothes burned. He had been shot while he tended his Dutch ovens.

Rance stumbled over to the canvas waterbags, hanging on a tree, and drank greedily, trying to drown the fever out of his head. He heard a sound in the brush. He drew his gun, fumbling it, and then he saw Casoose Corrales, coming toward him.

Casoose looked at him, sadly wagging his head. "They jump us up yonder, in a little park," he said. "They are fourteen, fifteen. We are eight. This park is where the whole gang stays. I want to fight, but somebody says . . . 'They got us, boys. Let's git!' I guess they kill Ike after that."

"Get any of the boys?"

"Abel Cooney, *sí*. He goes down like a sack of grain. I think . . . is dead. No use estopping."

It was not going to be easy to tell Uncle Ad about it, Rance thought. Uncle Ad had told him: "Out of violence cometh bloodshed and grief."

They started back, Casoose riding close to Rance to catch him if he fell. They had gone about four miles when they heard a horse snort somewhere ahead. Casoose drew his saddlegun and rode ahead. When Rance came up with him, he was talking to Abel Cooney.

Cooney looked a little shaken, pale in the lips, but he was not hurt. "They grooved me like a noll on a ridge," he said. "My head feels like a stick o' Atlas gettin' ready to go off. They figgered I was dead, I reckon, and left me." He looked at Rance's bloody pants leg, at his white face. "Cripes, boss . . . what'd you tie into?"

Rance rode past him, letting the Mexican explain.

Afterward, he couldn't have told how he made it to Skyline. Casoose wanted to stop at Falls House, but Rance said grimly: "I'm going up."

"¡Ai, Dios!" the foreman swore. "You lose blood like the estuck pig. You will die on the trail. I, Jesús Corrales, tell you!"

Rance rode past the corrals at Falls House and hit the Skyline trail. He had it in his head, through all the madness of fever and sickness, that he was finished if he did not make it to Skyline Ranch. Up there nobody could whip him. In the big brown fortress he was a giant. Down here he was just another Hooligan Cañon long-looper whom the wolves had cornered and would tear to pieces at their leisure.

Casoose had to drag him from the saddle when they reached the house. Rance remembered reaching the porch, and after that it was all a confused, tumbling stream of nightmarish sights and sounds that carried him on to darkness.

IX

When Rance woke up, it was like being born again. He had no idea where he was, how long he had been out, what day or hour it was. He lay on a bed, staring up at a ceiling of cottonwood branches arranged in a herringbone pattern while these questions drifted lazily and unimportantly through his mind.

The ceiling finally gave him the answer to the first question. Such *vigas* could exist only in his own ranch house. He had the answers to the other matters from Nora Clay.

Nora came in while he was trying to decide whether or not to get up. She stood above him, dressed uncharacteristically for a woman in the range country in Levi's, a light plaid flannel shirt, and a blue silk neckerchief, blonde and unreal, the light from the window making her hair shine. Rance looked at her, feeling the same old yearnings and thinking: *this is the only gold in the world that's worth dying for.*

Nora pulled a goatskin chair up to his bedside. She said to him: "Maybe this will teach you not to play with the neighborhood bad boys." She was smiling.

"You're a good nurse," Rance told her. "Never frighten the patient. Will I die? Or am I already dead?"

"You won't be so rugged for a while. But the doctor tended to your wound. There's no infection."

"How did you get here?" Rance asked her.

"Casoose came after me. He wanted me to suggest someone to nurse you. I thought we might as well have the job done right." She put a pill in his hand and held a glass of water for him. "Now you've got to sleep."

There was a time when Nora rode sidesaddle or in a buggy. Now she rode astride, perhaps because she regarded herself a working rancher right alongside her father. But, however rough the work, occasionally an expression of delicate vulnerability would cross her face, lodged deeply in her blue eyes. Rance loved just looking at her, listening to her.

The next time they talked, he was able to sit up and eat a bowl of beef broth. Nora sat there, watching him. She had something on her mind that traced a frown between her eyes. Finally she said: "What is Libby Caddo to you?"

Rance glanced at her then out of the corner of his eye. "Just a friend," he said. He saw the expression on her face and added: "A pretty good friend."

"You talked about her," Nora told him. "All kinds of wild talk. I didn't know she meant so much to you."

Rance finished his soup and lit a cigarette. "We sorta have to go after what we can get," he said. "How's Rocky?"

"I only saw him briefly earlier today. He rode over to warn us that Libby is convinced Dad killed John Caddo. She is planning to raid us tonight. Dad's ridden to town to tell Cave Jackson and Jim Lonnergan. He intends to fight, and he wants their help." Nora spoke crisply. Suddenly she said, as though it were something she had wanted to tell him for a long time: "Oh, Rance! Do we have to stand off at arm's length and make faces at each other? I want to talk to you . . . seriously."

"All right, Nora. I'm flat on my back and can't help myself."

Nora's eyes were sober. "I have to admit after all this time that I have been wrong," she said. "The way in which we've been living has fallen to pieces. We won't be pushed any more. Not by Libby Caddo any more than by her father. We've been proud, but not smart."

"I know Webb didn't shoot John Caddo," Rance told her.

A shadow crossed Nora's face. "How do *you* know?"

199

"I saw it happen. I was standing outside the living-room window when someone inside the house shot him. It couldn't have been your father."

"You *saw* it happen?" Her blue eyes were bright, about the same rich blue as her neckerchief.

"I was warning him away from doing any harm to the Clays. He turned while we were talking and recognized whoever was standing there. I couldn't see who it was, but Caddo spoke to whoever it was, as if he knew the person and didn't like being interrupted . . . and not by an intruder. After he fell, I ran. I figured Libby and her crew would believe I'd done it if I were seen. I haven't any idea why she thinks Webb shot him. Your father's doing the right thing, though. He's doing just what I'd do. I'd set tight and dare anyone to throw me off. And I'd kill any skunk who tried."

Nora nodded grimly. "I don't think you're as tough as you talk, Rance. But that's what Dad says he going to do. He feels he should have fought back a long time ago." Her gaze became gentle. "You know, Rance, when you aren't trying to show the world how tough you are, you're rather nice. And I didn't really mean what I once said about you owning Skyline before you could court me. I was angry at you, that's all."

Rance grinned, reaching for her hand. "You're not angry at me now, are you?"

She shook her head.

"Do you think I might come courtin' up Blue River sometime?"

Nora smiled as she withdrew her hand and moved toward the door. "Sometime," she told him.

Later that day Uncle Ad Cooney came to visit Rance, bringing a quarter of beef, probably stolen, on a pack horse. As he stood in the doorway Cooney looked like a slightly seedy St.

Peter with his long, dirty, brown beard and whiskey-shot eyes, a chest like a graze bull's and the crusader's light in his eyes.

He said to Rance: "Nothin' wrong with you that a slab o' good red beef won't fix up. I've got the Mex warmin' 'er up a bit. Thought a line or two from the Book might comfort ye."

Uncle Ad opened the Bible and read for a spell. Rather than cheer the sick man, it gave him gooseflesh. When Uncle Ad finally closed the Book he asked: "What you going to do now, Rance?"

Rance said: "I don't know. Go back sometime. Casoose found their headquarters, a little park with cabins where about fifteen of them stay. Next time I'm going to run them out . . . to the last yellow dog."

"Time," said Uncle Ad, "that something got done. Next thing we know they'll be sending a tax collector up Poverty Creek."

After Uncle Ad left, Rance got out of bed and walked up and down the room. His hip gave him a stab every time he took a step. When he walked too fast, his head swam. But after a while he began to find a little steadiness, especially after swallowing some Mexican *aguardiente*. He was back in bed when Nora came to give him medicine at five o'clock.

Nora didn't have much to say. She was grave as she tidied the room up for the night. Clearly she was worried and, notwithstanding Rance's suggestion that she remain all night at Skyline, she felt it was her place to join her father at the Block B. She was certain that Cave Jackson would do what he could, especially with Jim Lonnergan to prod him. After she left, while it was still light, Rance rose and dressed. He buckled on his Colt and, as a concession to his condition, donned a heavy sheepskin jacket. He went out and caught his horse in the corral. Throwing the heavy stock saddle across it taxed his strength, but he got the Tipton laced and rode carefully around behind the barn and down the trail.

He found Abel and the rest of the men at the Falls House. "How'd you boys like to make a little bounty money?" Rance asked them.

Abel frowned. "If you go along, we'll have to carry you back. You look like you'd climbed out of your grave before they could cover you up."

"Exercise is all I need," Rance told him. "I gave Caddo a warning about running Clay out. The same advice goes for Libby. She's got her boys raiding him tonight. So we'll have a little quilting bee while they work."

"What've you got in mind?" Abel wanted to know.

"I've got a pocketful of matches," Rance said. "I'm going to build a little fire to warm my hands by."

They were in the hills above the Ladder ranch when a group of 'punchers loped out of the headquarters on Blue River an hour later. Rance did not waste time after he was sure they were on the way. He did not aim to see old Webb Clay and Nora try to stand off fifteen raiders single-handed. He wasn't at all sure that Cave Jackson could do anything about the Ladder until *after* the raid.

Rance left the men in the barranca and rode boldly into the yard. He scanned the dark ranch house carefully before he called: "Libby!"

There was no answer, but he rode slowly through the sprawl of buildings before he summoned the others. They spread out, some taking the outbuildings. Three men entered the barn to ignite the hay while Rance and Abel went into the house to scatter pitch-pine chips from the wood basket everywhere a blaze could catch. When they left the house, flames were bursting from the great flat-roofed barn. The harness shed was the base of a roaring column of red.

Out in the yard the heat crowded upon them stiflingly. Dust devils eddied and scurried along the ground. Rance ran to let the screaming animals out of the corral. He fired a shot to signal the retreat.

They were gone from the ranch ten minutes after they had struck it. Riding hard, they crossed the Blue and took the trail into the timber. Hooligan Cañon had made a boast, and the square-jawed men from Poverty Creek had kept it.

Rance was totally exhausted by the time they reached the Falls House. His hip was a steady, pulsing pain. Days of inactivity had left him soft, and they had ridden hard tonight. Before starting up to Skyline Ranch, he had two cups of coffee with the men in the bunkhouse. Around midnight he left.

He had not quite arrived at the ranch house when he heard the strike of shod hoofs on the trail below him. Rance jerked his Colt from his holster, reined into the shadow of a hackberry, and dismounted. He held his horse's nose as the rider jogged past him. He started, then he called: "Bringing the war to Skyline, Libby?"

Libby Caddo reined in sharply, searching the brush. Rance went out to meet her, but he kept his gun at the ready. It appalled him to think of firing at a woman, even if only to frighten her. Yet, if this girl had enough of her father's twisted mind, he might have to do it.

Libby's features were drawn and appeared bloodless in the moonlight. Her hat was off and hung down her back by the string, letting her black hair fall loosely on her shoulders. There were shadows, as from smoke smudges, on her pale cheeks. Suddenly she reached out to him, crying his name, no longer the hoyden, but a woman desperate and hurt.

"Rance! Why did it have to happen? Why did you do it?"

He holstered his gun and lifted her from the saddle, feeling her slim body trembling as he held her against him, and yet part of him was still vigilant. "I tried to convince your dad I meant it," he said. "I'm sorry it had to be like this, Libby. But Webb Clay deserves a better deal than you were going to give him."

Libby looked up at him, her body arching back in torment and anger. "How can you defend him? He killed my father! Rocky saw him do it."

"If Rocky told you that, he lied."

"Oh, I don't know what to think!" she exclaimed, pulling sharply away from him. "I thought Rocky loved me. He and his men rode with us tonight. Then, when the sheriff's posse rode in, just after we'd fired the barn, Rocky lit out and took his men with him. The Ladder riders were little better. They're afraid Cave Jackson will arrest them. When they saw what had been done to Ladder, they rode out, too! I'm alone now, Rance. I have no one else I can turn to. Dad saw Clay as a weak and fumbling man who could never amount to anything in this country. He didn't believe there was any reason Webb Clay shouldn't make way for an iron like ours. I believed Webb Clay killed Dad. That's mostly why I did it. You can't see that, can you? Sometimes you reason like a Sunday school teacher."

"And sometimes," Rance told her, "you reason like your father. You sent Rocky to run all the Smoky River cattle out before I could tally them. And I don't know but that he was leading the crew that killed Al Parsons and Ike Bradley."

Libby said soberly: "No, Rance. I sent Rocky to cut out any of my cattle. That's all. If he's tied up with the others, I didn't know it."

Rance shrugged. "Well, it doesn't matter now. The deal's finished, and we've got to stand pat on our cards. We'll have to play 'em out the way we see best. Maybe, when Webb Clay learns what's happened to your place, he'll not press you, if you don't press him on the taxes. Let Cave Jackson find out who really murdered your father. That's his job. You should have gone to him straight off when it happened."

Rance knew from Nora that Rocky had warned the Clays about Libby's plan for the raid. He didn't tell her that. He still wasn't certain why Libby had come to Skyline, or what she wanted.

Libby let Rance turn the stirrup for her, raising her foot. When he started to help her into the saddle, he saw that she was crying. She turned then and clung to him for a moment, her face pressed against his shoulder.

"Oh, Rance," she said, pulling up her head. "We could have had everything, but now we'll have nothing, not even each other. They're devils, that Smoky River bunch. Too tough and too smart for us. Can't you see what's happened? They've got us . . . the biggest ranchers in the Bend . . . fighting each other! And they'll be the ones to take what's left. I'm . . . I'm afraid, Rance."

Rance Kirby regretted now, what he had done this night. It seemed, more than ever, that Uncle Ad was right — the Bible was right — and from violence came only bloodshed and grief. Libby had given words to the same fear that lurked in his own heart. From now on they mustn't continue fighting each other as well as the cañon men.

Rance said: "Libby, I want you to stay at Skyline tonight. We both need sleep, and I want to work out something for the future with you before this goes any further."

He expected her to demur, even though she no longer had a place of her own at which to sleep. After all, he couldn't very well ask Nora Clay to come over and play the rôle of chaperon. But Libby surprised him. She accepted his offer without protest, and thanked him for extending it.

Up at the ranch house Rance showed Libby the spare bedroom, the very one he had occupied the night Rudy Guss had been murdered. Then he returned to the parlor. There was a chill in him that only a roaring fire and a long drink could drive out. He poked up the coals in the big stone fireplace and laid an ironwood log in the grate. There was magic in this combination of warmth within and without. Rance was asleep before he had finished the drink.

He might have slept an hour. When he awoke, it was to find himself on his feet before the fire, trembling. The house still echoed to the explosion that had blasted him from his sleep. His first thought was of the porch, for the sound had been exactly like the one that had preceded the death of one of Rudy Guss's murderers. When he looked out the window, he could see a rider dismounting. He reached for his gun and ran to the door. He met Casoose as the latter entered, his Forty-Five in his hand.

"¿Qué pasa?" the Mexican demanded.

It was then that Rance realized for the first time the significance of the blast. He felt physically sick. "Casoose, what are you doing here?"

"Jim Lonnergan was with the sheriff's posse tonight that interrupted Libby and her men at the Block B. He rode up to the Falls House to see you, to tell you that only the barn is gone. The house is safe. The sheriff and the posse were with him. They're putting up there for the night. I came here to tell you. None of them knows what happened at Ladder yet. When I rode in just now, I saw a man. It was difficult to be sure in the dark, but it looked like Rocky Taylor. After all these years I know how he sits a horse. He was riding away, fast. He must have been nearby, watching or something. Did he take a shot at you?"

"I'm all right, Casoose. I want you to go down to the old wine cellar for me."

"It's locked," Casoose objected.

"I think it's just been unlocked. Take a lamp. I'd rather not go down myself."

There was no eagerness in the foreman's manner, but he took a lamp and went cautiously down the stone steps. When he came back, five minutes later, he was pale and shocked. He put the lamp back in the bracket and drank a great gulp from the whiskey bottle on the table. Then he sat down, shook his head sadly, and said: "¡Pobrecita! Through the heart."

Rance said: "Libby?"

Casoose nodded. "How did she get in here?"

Rance helped himself to the whiskey. "I invited her up," he said. "This is Rudy Guss's party. He left a cocked gun fixed so that when the door of the strong room was opened, if anybody ever got his keys, he'd be killed. Guss would know how to discharge the thing into the concrete door before opening it. Libby was too ambitious for her own good. She was after the thirty thousand dollars I paid for the ranch, I suppose. All I'm wondering is where she got the keys . . . but I think I already know."

He went outside and stood for a long while on the porch, staring down into the dark, whispering gorge that had cost five lives since he took over the Skyline Ranch. He thought of the dark-haired, lovely girl, lying in the cellar, and suddenly he was sick to death of the sight and smell of blood, of the greed that made this valley a charnel house. He had had his fill of treachery and of men who came out at night, like prairie wolves.

He said to the Mexican when he went in: "I'm going down the Smoky again tomorrow. I'm going to take every man I can round up, including the sheriff and his posse, if they're willing to come, and pry those gun wolves loose with their own weapons. This time I'm not coming back until the job is done. And

I'm going to drag out the kingpin at the end of a rope."

Casoose replied gravely: "Sí," not questioning him, as though he understood that this was a holy duty they had before them. He took a blanket from the couch and went downstairs to cover the girl's body.

They rode out before dawn. Rance met with the sheriff and his posse at the Falls House and, having secured their agreement to join in the hunt, he rode up the Poverty. He told Uncle Ad what he had in mind.

"I'm hiring all the guns I can," he said to the patriarch of Poverty Creek. "And I'm offering more than gun wages for this job. I'll have more range than any man needs when I get that gang cleaned out. I aim to lease Smoky River land to every man in Hooligan Cañon that wants it."

"I been here since the cañon was a gully," Cooney said. "I'm satisfied with my lot. Most of the boys jest ain't ranchers. Why stir 'em up?"

"They've never had a chance," Rance told him. "Now they're going to get it, but they'll have to fight for it. I don't reckon you'd let Cain go for a few days?"

Uncle Ad's eyes were stern. "No. Abel's all I can spare. I don't rightly approve of this, Rance. It's ag'in' the Word."

"I'm sorry, Uncle Ad. I don't like it, either. But I've got to do it."

Rance enlisted five more ranchers. He watched their eyes when they heard his offer of land, and the way they shone was all the proof he wanted of their willingness to work this range if they ever got it.

He was surprised to find Webb Clay at the Falls House when they rode in. The peppery little Yankee sat on a corral bar, smoking his corncob pipe. He said to Rance, fingering his wispy goatee: "Listen. When I get on the butt, I don't need anybody to show me how to fight. And one more thing, Rance. I don't need a nursemaid, either."

"That's fine," Rance said. "Why tell me about it?"

Clay snorted. "I went over this morning to tell Libby Caddo I'd put a bullet through any Ladder 'puncher that crossed my land again. Damn me if she hadn't been burned out. Thanks for your interest in me, Rance, but I'll do my own fighting from here on out."

Rance grinned. "Thought you didn't believe in it."

"I don't know what I believe in," Clay flared, "but I don't believe in getting pushed around any more."

Cave Jackson greeted Rance warmly, pleased at last to be putting an end to the killing and rustling. Jim Lonnergan gravely shook Rance's hand. It was incredible to see the lawyer here, but now everything was different — Webb Clay was even here — so perhaps it made sense. Rance's men were sworn in as deputies by the sheriff and then they joined the members of the posse at the corral, saddling their ponies, and getting ready for the ride. Each man carried a saddlegun that he checked before shoving it into the boot. Abel Cooney wore two Forty-Fives. There would be eighteen men to throw lead back at the Smoky River gang when they clashed.

Webb Clay's horse was still saddled from his ride here. He'd been sworn in, too. He sat his saddle alongside Rance. "It's good to be a part of this," he said.

Rance told him: "When this is over, an honest man won't have to go around apologizing in Three Rivers."

"All I hope," said Clay, "is that I run into Job Hatfield."

"Maybe you will." Rance said.

It was noon when they started, and they pushed the ponies briskly to reach the cañon hide-out before dark. Cave Jackson put a scout on the ridge to forestall an ambush, and he kept the men from bunching, so that in event of a surprise they would not be shattered by one crashing salvo. They rode silently down the gorge.

Long before dusk they reached the spot where the cook had been murdered. By now every man rode with his rifle across the swell of his saddle. Casoose took the lead, for neither Rance nor the sheriff had been with the crew when they had blundered into the outlaw hide-out before.

A few hundred yards below the meadow they dismounted and filtered through the thick stand of scrubby piñons. Webb Clay was beside Rance when they had their first glimpse of the park. The cabins stood near the trees, a string of peeled pole corrals behind them. Clay said: "*Pshaw!* Corral's empty. Likely nobody home."

Cave Jackson aimed a shot at the door of the main cabin. The slug struck white splinters from the plank. There was a long, trembling silence. Then Jackson gave the command for a fusillade. Bullets tore through the unglazed windows and chopped at the doors. They heard the racket of breaking china and clattering pots and pans. One of the doors swung inward under the pound of the lead.

Finally the shooting ended, and the sheriff went gingerly from the trees, approaching the cabins from the west. But the camp was deserted.

They held a pow-wow back in the trees. Abel Cooney drew nervously on a crooked cigarette. "Maybeso, they're acrost the border, raidin'," he said.

"If they are," Rance said, "they'll find a rousin' welcome when they try to get back into the cañon. There's another possibility, though. Maybe our raid the other day threw a scare into 'em. Down in the gorge there's a cave full of all kinds of truck, including bar silver. If they're afraid of being run out, they'd probably try to freight out all they can carry first. Let's have a look."

The sheriff agreed, and once more the men set out. Rance suspected that something was doing in the cañon by the fact that the ladder was still down. One by one the men descended, following Rance who led the way to the outlet above the river. His hip was bothering him greatly, and he walked with a painful limp. Sheriff Jackson posted Jim Lonnergan as a guard to prevent anyone approaching from the south. The rest started toward the cave.

Rance heard suddenly a sound that rang in his brain like a gunshot. The stamp of a shod hoof! Around the bend he glimpsed a line of pack animals stringing from the cave, already loaded but waiting patiently for the 'skinners to start them. To the men behind him, Jackson, Cooney, Webb Clay, and Casoose, Rance said in a low voice: "They're in the cave. Pass the word down. We've got 'em bottled up."

He went ahead, faster, on the inside of the line of pack animals. When the blow came, some sharpened sense gave Rance warning, and he twisted in time partially to evade the downswing of Abel Cooney's gun barrel. He felt the weight of it grind against his collar bone, and he sagged to his knees. Cooney ran past him, yelling.

"Rocky! It's the payoff!"

Rance heard Cave Jackson swearing, demanding to know what was up. He stumbled to his knees and ran ahead. When Abel Cooney turned and slammed a shot at him, he fired without slackening his pace and saw Cooney stumble forward with hands over his face.

The burros stampeded, some of them plunging into the river and the others racing past the Hooligan Cañon men. The 'punchers took a pummeling as the loaded *aparejos* buffeted them, but they had their backs to the cliff and were able to stay on the trail. From the cave came sounds of spurred boots pounding across the rocky floor, of men shouting and preparing for action.

Rance threw himself flat as he gained the cavern, firing upward at the three men who had come from the passage to the larger room. Behind him, Sheriff Jackson, Casoose, and Webb Clay took up prone positions to pour their fire into the cave. Two of the men had been carrying bar silver. They dropped the ingots and fumbled off their shots. Rance saw them falter, rocked by the force of whining Forty-Five lead. He jacked another into his Colt, waiting for the next man, and that man, firing from the gloom of the passageway, was Rocky Taylor.

Casoose Corrales's old buffalo gun roared before Rance could get off a shot. The slug, as big as a man's finger, struck the ex-ramrod in the head. Taylor lay, moving spasmodically, blocking the passage.

There were sounds of shouting from inside the cavern, the high-pitched voices of men in panic. Presently they quieted, but no more men attempted to escape. In the interval of quiet the sheriff called out:

"All right, boys. This is Cave Jackson. It's all over. Come out with your hands high or we'll send back for dynamite and do it right."

There was no choice. The outlaws crawled out of the cave like cowed dogs. They were a motley group of border riffraff, Mexicans and half-breeds, and the only familiar faces in the group were the dead faces of Rocky Taylor and those of three other former Skyline punchers. Webb Clay appeared disappointed.

"So Rocky was their boss," he said.

"Rocky was only a lieutenant," Rance said. "The big man wouldn't risk his life in a brawl like this. He was smart enough that he didn't have to." He turned away. "Help me load Abel on a pack animal. I've got to take him back to Uncle Ad." Then his hip gave out on him, and he collapsed.

They reached the Falls House around midnight. Sheriff Jackson and the posse had ridden on to town with the men of the Smoky River bunch who had surrendered as their prisoners. The sheriff had left two men guarding the loot until it could be brought back to town. Jim Lonnergan had gone on with the posse.

Lamps were burning inside the main building. Nora was there on the porch, waiting, still dressed in Levi's, this time with a light blue denim shirt and a yellow silk neckerchief. Webb Clay helped Rance down from the saddle while Casoose saw to Abel's body, and the others tended to the horses.

Nora saw her father helping Rance. She rushed down the two steps and over to the two men.

Rance said: "It was a good fight, Nora, but you were right. I'm not as tough as I thought I was."

"You did just fine, Rance," Webb assured him.

Nora got on Rance's left side to help him.

"I didn't mean I was so weak I need two people to help me," Rance said to Nora, but he put his arm around her just the same.

They lowered Rance onto one of the bunks. Nora's peaked sombrero was fastened by a string. She pushed it back now off her head, and her light blonde hair gleamed in the lamplight as it cascaded around her shoulders.

"I have coffee brewing," she said.

"Pour it out for the men," Rance told her, glancing at the exquisite roundness and proud carriage of her figure as she moved toward the stove. "Just seeing a woman as beautiful as you are should be enough. But if it isn't . . . if one of them should pat your backside . . . just ignore it. They've earned it."

Nora, blushing now, turned to look at her father. Far from being offended, he was smiling. He said: "It's late. Since Nora's here, do you mind if we put up with you till morning, Rance?"

"There's plenty of room. Glad to have you," Rance said. He was smiling, too.

"Is somebody going to tell me what happened?" Nora demanded.

"Let Webb do it," Rance sighed. "Once through it was enough for me today."

They slept until dawn. They all had breakfast, prepared by Casoose and Nora together. Rance saddled Nora's horse for her. They held hands briefly, and Nora caressed Rance's cheek before she mounted. She and her father rode out toward the Block B. Rance, over Casoose's protests, felt rested enough to ride up Poverty Creek. Casoose tied Abel's body, now wrapped in a blanket, onto the back of a burro.

Uncle Ad was reading the Bible on the kitchen table when Rance rode up. The old man looked at Rance as he stood in the doorway. He said shortly: "Somethin's wrong."

"They got Abel," Rance said. "We cleaned 'em out. I'm sorry, Uncle Ad. If there's anything. . . ."

The rusty-bearded cowman pressed his fist against his forehead, his head bowed. "Nothin', Rance," he said, his voice muffled. "Jest leave him." But as he turned away, Uncle Ad asked: "Did you find out who's the kingpin this time?"

Rance looked into the old man's eyes. "No. Rocky Taylor was bossing them, but I don't think he was the kingpin. He killed Caddo, I'm pretty sure, hoping to win Libby and the ranch. He wouldn't have bothered if he was already the big boy."

Rance stood there awkwardly while Cooney got a pickaxe and shovel. Cooney led the burro bearing Abel's body up to the grave plot among the trees. Rance went carefully up the slope behind him.

He stood where he could read the two headboards that leaned dejectedly in the mottled shade. For days, ever since his first visit up here, Rance Kirby had been troubled by something he had seen, without quite knowing what the disturbing factor was. Now he knew. There were too many graves.

One of the headboards said:

Sacred to the memory of Mary Cooney
Rest in Peace

The other said:

Sacred to the memory of Cain Cooney
son of Mary and Adam Cooney
June 15, 1887

June fifteenth was the day Rudy Guss had been murdered.

Suddenly Uncle Ad saw him. He straightened slowly, leaning on the shovel. He said: "Well Rance?"

"I didn't know Cain was dead."

Cooney's stern features did not alter. "He was killed two weeks ago. Fell off a horse."

Rance shook his head. "No, Uncle Ad. Rudy Guss's gun trap killed him. You and he and Abel broke in, figuring to get all the treasure he'd been storing for years, money you'd paid the old miser to leave you alone, and money he'd made off his cattle. When you failed, you had Rocky give Libby the keys you'd stolen, figuring to let her take the risk, if there was any. She hated me enough and was ambitious enough to do it. But you didn't have to kill Guss to get Smoky River, because it was already yours. It's been yours for fifteen years, hasn't it? It took a tough, smart man like you to hold it."

Uncle Ad did not move.

Rance Kirby said: "Don't make me do it, Uncle Ad. Take your gun out slow and drop it."

Cooney's shovel abruptly moved, throwing dirt in Rance's face. Rance ducked, going to his knees, his hat knocked off. Cooney had his big Forty-Five out, and his face, behind the cocked hammer, was like something out of the inferno — the eyes blazing and the bearded mouth open, twisted as if in profanity.

Rance shot him in the breast before his hammer dropped. He shot him again, when he stood swaying there, still trying to get off his shot.

Uncle Ad slowly went down, no longer the kingpin of Smoky River.

Rance Kirby rode away. He put out of his mind the thoughts that tried to crowd it — of bloodshed and treachery. All Rance Kirby wanted was to be a cowman among cattlemen. He didn't want to have to apologize to anybody for being from Hooligan Cañon, but on the other hand he didn't want small men doffing their hats when he came down the walk.

Now that he had established his right to Skyline Ranch, he found he didn't ever want to set foot in the grim, massive fortress again. He would build another place down in the valley, where the sound of the falls was a lullaby at night, and the grass was green under friendly trees. The kind of a place a man could bring a girl like Nora to with pride.

The End

BACK TO MALACHI

ROBERT J. CONLEY
THREE-TIME SPUR
AWARD-WINNER

Charlie Black is a young half-breed caught between two worlds. He is drawn to the promise of the white man's wealth, but torn by his proud heritage as a Cherokee. Charlie's pretty young fiancée yearns for the respectability of a Christian marriage and baptized children. But Charlie can't forsake his two childhood friends, Mose and Henry Pathkiller, who live in the hills with an old full-blooded Indian named Malachi. When Mose runs afoul of the law, Charlie has to choose between the ways of his fiancée and those of his friends and forefathers. He has to choose between surrender and bloodshed.

___4277-0 $3.99 US/$4.99 CAN

INCIDENT at BUFFALO CROSSING

ROBERT J. CONLEY

The Sacred Hill. It rose above the land, drawing men to it like a beacon. But the men who came each had their own dreams. There is Zeno Bond, the settler who dreams of land and empire. There is Mat McDonald, captain of the steamship *John Hart*, heading the looming war between the Spanish and the Americans. And there is Walker, the Cherokee warrior called by a vision he cannot deny—a vision of life, death...and destiny.

___4396-3 $4.50 US/$5.50 CAN

THE ACTOR

ROBERT J. CONLEY

Bluford Steele had always been an outsider until he found his calling as an actor. Instead of being just another half-breed Cherokee with a white man's education, he can be whomever he chooses. But when the traveling acting troupe he is with arrives in the wild, lawless town of West Riddle, the man who rules the town with an iron fist forces them to perform. Then he steals all the proceeds. Steele is determined to get the money back, even if it means playing the most dangerous role of his life—a cold-blooded gunslinger ready to face down any man who gets in his way.

___4498-6 $4.50 US/$5.50 CAN

Dorchester Publishing Co., Inc.
P.O. Box 6640
Wayne, PA 19087-8640

Please add $1.75 for shipping and handling for the first book and $.50 for each book thereafter. NY, NYC, and PA residents, please add appropriate sales tax. No cash, stamps, or C.O.D.s. All orders shipped within 6 weeks via postal service book rate. Canadian orders require $2.00 extra postage and must be paid in U.S. dollars through a U.S. banking facility.

Name_____

Address_____

City_____State_____Zip_____

I have enclosed $_____ in payment for the checked book(s).

Payment <u>must</u> accompany all orders. ❑ Please send a free catalog.

CHECK OUT OUR WEBSITE! www.dorchesterpub.com

MOVING ON
JANE CANDIA COLEMAN

Jane Candia Coleman is a magical storyteller who spins brilliant tales of human survival, hope, and courage on the American frontier, and nowhere is her marvelous talent more in evidence than in this acclaimed collection of her finest work. From a haunting story of the night Billy the Kid died, to a dramatic account of a breathtaking horse race, including two stories that won the prestigious Spur Award, here is a collection that reveals the passion and fortitude of its characters, and also the power of a wonderful writer.

___4545-1 $4.99 US/$5.99 CAN

Dorchester Publishing Co., Inc.
P.O. Box 6640
Wayne, PA 19087-8640

Please add $1.75 for shipping and handling for the first book and $.50 for each book thereafter. NY, NYC, and PA residents, please add appropriate sales tax. No cash, stamps, or C.O.D.s. All orders shipped within 6 weeks via postal service book rate. Canadian orders require $2.00 extra postage and must be paid in U.S. dollars through a U.S. banking facility.

Name_____
Address_____
City_____State_____Zip_____
I have enclosed $_____ in payment for the checked book(s).
Payment <u>must</u> accompany all orders. ❑ Please send a free catalog.
    CHECK OUT OUR WEBSITE! www.dorchesterpub.com

MAX BRAND

THE ABANDONED OUTLAW

No writer captures the American West better than Max Brand. And nowhere is Brand's talent more evident than in these three classic short novels, all restored to their original length, and collected in paperback for the first time. In "The Gold King Turns His Back," young Miriam Standard is more than capable of running her father's ranch, but finds she has much to learn about the Westerners' meaning of honor. In "The Three Crosses," an ominous prediction leads a cowpuncher to a showdown with a notorious gunfighter. And the title novel finds a young woman caught in the middle of a lifelong rivalry between two men, one of whom is an outlaw. Experience the West as only Max Brand could write it!

___4465-X $4.50 US/$5.50 CAN

Barjack

ROBERT J. CONLEY

Barjack isn't a big man. But he is ornery. When he comes to the town of Asininity he doesn't plan on staying long. But that is before he runs into a bit of trouble in the saloon. When the fighting is over and Barjack is the only one still standing, the head of the town council offers him the job of town marshal. To Barjack it is just another job, as good as any other. Trouble is, it is a job that makes him enemies—bad enemies like the Bensons. A while back Barjack rounded up the five Benson brothers for murder and rustling. One brother was hanged, the others sent to the pen. And now the surviving brothers are out and coming back to town with one purpose in mind . . . to make Barjack pay.

___4687-3 $4.50 US/$5.50 CAN

BRANDISH

DOUGLAS HIRT

FIRST TIME IN PAPERBACK!

Captain Ethan Brandish has finally given up his command of Fort Lowell, deep in Apache territory. But the vicious Apache leader, Yellow Shirt, has another fate in store for him. He and a group of renegade warriors attack a stage station and ride off just before Brandish arrives. But the Apaches are still out there—watching and waiting—and Brandish must risk his own life to save the few wounded survivors.

___4323-8 $4.50 US/$5.50 CAN